$\mathcal{W}$HERE I $\mathcal{B}$ELONG

Books by Rachel Ann Nunes

Ariana: The Making of a Queen
Ariana: A Gift Most Precious
Ariana: A New Beginning
Ariana: A Glimpse of Eternity

Love to the Highest Bidder
Framed for Love
Love on the Run

A Greater Love
To Love and to Promise
Tomorrow and Always
This Very Moment

This Time Forever
Bridge to Forever
Ties That Bind
Twice in a Lifetime

A Heartbeat Away
Where I Belong
Daughter of a King (picture book)

WHERE I BELONG

RACHEL ANN NUNES

BONNEVILLE BOOKS ™
Springville, Utah

ISBN: 1-55517-715-8
e.1

Published by Bonneville Books
Imprint of Cedar Fort Inc.
www.cedarfort.com

Distributed by:

Cover design by Nicole Cunningham
Cover design © 2003 by Lyle Mortimer

Printed in the United States of America
10 9 8 7 6 5 4 3 2 1

Printed on acid-free paper

Library of Congress Cataloging-in-Publication Data

Nunes, Rachel Ann, 1966-
 Where I belong / Rachel Ann Nunes.
        p. cm.
 ISBN 1-55517-715-8 (acid-free paper)
1. Young women--Fiction. 2. Women painters--Fiction. I. Title.

PS3564.U468W48 2003
813'.54--dc21
                            2003014677

Dedication

For my daughters.
Being your mother is one
of the greatest joys of my life,
one I wouldn't trade
for any worldly success.

Prologue

Sixteen-year-old Tanner Wolfe was shooting baskets on the new court they had laid on the side yard when a huge moving van lumbered up the driveway at the house next door. The court sat near the property line where the cedar fence began, so he had a clear view of the neighbors' front drive. He glanced once and then peered with interest out of the corner of his eyes as he prepared to shoot, curious to see who would emerge from the moving van and the large twelve-seater passenger van that followed it.

A man climbed from the driver's seat of the moving van, came around the front, and opened the other door. A little boy jumped into his arms. At the same time a stream of children began emerging from the passenger van. A tired-looking woman followed them up the drive. Then an older girl came from the moving van, slipping gracefully down to the cement.

Tanner faltered and missed the basket. It wasn't that she was the most beautiful girl he had laid eyes on—he was really too far away to see her features clearly—but her long hair and her graceful movements made him want to stare.

As he dove for his lost ball, he heard laughter coming from the girl. Had she noticed his fumble?

Face flaming, Tanner shot again and made the basket. He cast a triumphant look toward the girl, but she was already walking away, hefting a small child in her arms. Her waist-long, light brown hair fanned out behind her like a curtain separating them.

Tanner's smile died and the ball fell from his hands. *Bump, bump, bump, bump*—it came to a slow stop.

The children and parents were all quickly disappearing into the house. Tanner wasn't sure, but there seemed like at least a dozen small faces.

"Tan?"

He turned in the direction of his dad's voice. Damon Wolfe was coming across the grass toward him. His yellow-blonde hair stood up slightly on his head, but his short moustache was combed neatly over a generous mouth.

"I was watching you from the window. Great shot! But what's wrong? Why'd you stop?"

Tanner shrugged. "Nothing. Just some people next door. Looks like they're moving in."

Damon's attention shifted. "Oh good. I was glad to hear they finally sold that house. I miss having neighbors. Do they look nice?"

"Noisy," Tanner said. "They've got about a hundred kids."

Damon's amber eyes gleamed with amusement. "Nope. Only eight from what I heard. Come on, let's go meet them. I'm sure they'll need some help unloading."

Tanner gave a half-hearted groan.

"Come on, son. You know it's a privilege to help our fellow man."

"Okay, Dad." Tanner gave him an appropriate smile and walked a little faster. Truth be told, he was curious about the new neighbors—or at least about the girl.

Damon hesitated. "Oh, wait a minute. Just let me run inside and tell Kelle so she can call a few more people over. From the looks of that van, we're going to need help."

As he waited in the drive for his dad to talk to his stepmom, Tanner wondered why the new neighbors didn't have a moving company to help them. While their house definitely did not have the fifteen thousand square feet the Wolfe's Victorian mansion claimed, it certainly wasn't small. "Must be because they have so many kids," Tanner said aloud, surveying the square, red-bricked house. "Too busy paying for braces to pay movers."

His eyes caught a movement inside on the second floor, and he turned away quickly so he wouldn't be caught staring.

"Okay, Tan, I'm ready."

Tanner rolled his eyes in irritation at his dad's nickname for him. Damon shortened nearly everyone's name. Tanner's little sister Isabelle had been Belle since her birth. His mother, Charlotte, had been Char during her short lifetime. His stepmother, Mickelle, was now Kelle. His stepbrothers, Bryan and Jeremy, were Bry and Jer, and his sister Jennie Anne had become Jenna on the day Damon and Mickelle had announced their intent to adopt her. Nobody else in the family used the nicknames; in fact, they were rather annoyed by them, but his father persisted. Tanner was long accustomed to going through life being called something people did to their skin.

They moved down their own tree-lined driveway to the sidewalk and then over to the neighbors'. Tanner felt nervous, though he didn't know exactly why. It couldn't be because of the girl. He was dating Amanda Huntington, one of the best-looking girls in school. He wasn't looking for anyone else.

They were almost to the double front doors of the house when a man emerged from the garage.

"Hello!" Damon called, turning in his direction and holding out his hand. "We're your new neighbors. I'm Damon Wolfe and this is my son, Tan. We came over to see if we can give you a hand."

"Sure. Gladly." The man grabbed Damon's hand enthusiastically. "I'm Conrad Samis. Nice to meet you." Conrad was as tall as Damon and about the same build, but there the similarity ended. Though he spent many hours in an office, Damon's blonde looks were rugged. His face was angular and his nose slightly hooked. Tanner thought his dad looked tough, and he hoped he resembled him at least a little. Their new neighbor had darker hair, a clean-shaven face, more rounded facial features, and looked rather soft around the waist; his grip was strong as he pumped Tanner's hand up and down, sincerely thanking them for their help.

Damon waved his arms above his head. "I'm signaling my wife," he explained as they stared at him. "She wanted to be sure you needed help before she rounded up more volunteers."

"The more the merrier," Conrad said. "After buying a house that's finally large enough to fit us all comfortably, we thought we'd save money and do the moving ourselves."

"Well, show us where to start."

"Right this way."

Tanner followed the men, keeping a watch out for the girl. He had taken in five large boxes before he found a box that led him to her. She was in the kitchen making sandwiches for a row of small, eager faces. Her mother was there, too, cleaning out the refrigerator. He caught a vague impression of a slight, pretty woman with short blonde hair before his attention returned to the girl.

"Hi," he said to her, immediately wanting to kick himself at the lack of originality. He set down the box in his arms. Across the front the word *kitchen* was scribbled in big letters.

"Hi," she said. Her smile filled her whole face, transforming her features from ordinary to incredible. Tanner suddenly felt weak in the knees. He didn't think he'd ever seen anyone with hazel eyes as beautiful as hers. Not that he was interested. She had way too many freckles for his taste.

Her dad came in from the garage. "This is Tan," he told the girl and her mother. "One of our new neighbors."

"Hi, Tan," they said together.

"Uh, actually, it's Tanner. Dad has a thing with nicknames."

Conrad nodded. "Oh, so that's why he keeps calling me Con."

"Finally, a nickname worse than Tan," Tanner said. They all laughed at that.

"Better beware, Karalee," Conrad said to his wife. "He'll be calling you Kara."

She shrugged. "Everyone already does, except you."

Conrad's booming laugh filled the kitchen. The girl shook her head and spooned tuna onto another piece of bread.

"How old are you anyway?" Conrad asked Tanner.

"Sixteen. I'll be seventeen in November."

"Ah, good. Heather's sixteen, too. You can show her around when school starts."

"Sure."

The girl looked up and smiled again but didn't say anything, so Tanner had no choice but to return to the moving van for another box. His step-brother, Bryan, had come to help. Though he was three years younger than Tanner, he was solid and could carry a large load. Tanner searched until he found another box marked *kitchen* and then carried it inside. But Heather had disappeared again.

"Want a sandwich?" asked Karalee Samis.

He shook his head. "No, thanks."

More cars began arriving, and soon it seemed the whole elders quorum had come to help. Box after box found a place in the house, which wasn't nearly as large inside as Tanner had assumed. When at last they finished, Tanner was breathing hard and wiping sweat from his brow. He wondered if anyone had noticed how hard he'd worked—not that he wanted anyone in particular to notice.

His stepmother, Mickelle, had arrived and was busily helping unpack boxes in the kitchen. Tanner heard her invite the Samises to dinner.

Heather still had not reappeared, but he could hear the *thump, thump, thump* of a basketball outside. He went to investigate. To his surprise, Heather was shooting at the basket hooked to the Samis's garage. She paused, aimed, and sent the ball arcing toward the basket with more grace than he ever hoped to achieve.

"Nice!" he said as the ball slipped through the net.

She reddened slightly, retrieved the ball, and sent it his way. "One-on-one?" she asked.

He nodded and went for the basket.

As he dribbled, she managed to steal the ball away and made a basket. She sent a satisfied smirk his way.

Enough of being nice, he thought. He couldn't let a girl beat him—no matter how cute she was.

When they finally dropped to the grass edging the drive, too exhausted to move, the score was tied. Tanner had never been a star at basketball, but he had always held his own. He had to admit—if only to himself—that she just might be better at the game.

With the bottom of his T-shirt, he wiped the sweat dripping down his forehead. "So, you want to go get some ice cream?"

"Sure. I just need to let my mom know where I'll be."

They went to his house for his restored blue Volkswagen Bug. "Cool," she said. "This car's a classic."

"Yep." He opened the door for her, but she was looking around at the garage, obviously noting the large size, as well as the Lexus and the Mercedes. For the first time, Tanner wondered if his father's all-too-apparent wealth would be a plus or a minus in his relationship with Heather.

In the end, it didn't weigh in at all. Tanner and Heather became friends—best friends. Since one of Tanner's two best friends had recently moved, and the other was seriously dating a girl, he needed another friend. Being new, so did she. Romance rarely, if ever, entered their thoughts.

Years later after they had both finished college, Tanner would wonder if that basketball game on the day they met had something to do with their being only friends. If he had played better, would she have looked at him differently? What if they had not played at all? What if he had told her in the

Bug when they went to get ice cream that she had the most beautiful eyes he had ever seen?

He would never know.

But what developed between them was better than romance—at least at their age. From that day on, they were almost inseparable. They played tennis and basketball together, swam together, and hung out at school dances together. They also dreamed together—him of graduating from college and becoming an executive in his father's software company, and her of painting great masterpieces.

He helped her through her math and science classes, which she had no interest in since she was planning to major in art. She helped him with any projects that involved imagination. She went to the junior prom with a boy named Jason Pruitt, and he went with Amanda Huntington.

Their friendship was precious to Tanner. Though eventually he and Amanda stopped dating, Heather remained his constant friend. Their last year in high school found them both without a date for the senior prom so they decided to go together. Again, Tanner would later wonder if the magic of that night might have changed their future, perhaps pushing their friendship onto another road. But that night her mother went into labor with baby number nine. Heather and Tanner missed the dance to be at the hospital.

After high school, there was college. Since Tanner had finished so many AP courses in high school, he started at Brigham Young University as a sophomore. Though he continued to live at home, school was rigorous, and he had less time to spend with Heather. When they did find the opportunity to be together, he usually helped her with her classes at Utah Valley State College. She struggled with many of her courses, not because she didn't understand the material, but because she had no desire for anything but her art.

When he went on his mission to Japan, they continued to encourage each other with letters. While he was gone, her mother had baby number ten. Heather received her own mission call to Italy before he came home, and she left for the Missionary Training Center two months after his return. Her youngest sister was only a year old.

Tanner moved to an apartment in Provo and immersed himself in his studies at BYU. After another year, he graduated and went to work full time for his father's company. He bought a condo in Orem six months later. When

Heather returned from her mission, he was in Japan on business. That month, her mother had a miscarriage.

Upon arriving home, Heather immediately signed up for college again, this time at BYU. She didn't need Tanner's help now, since her classes were mostly art. She thrived. She spent half of Christmas vacation in Boston with a group of art students, soaking up culture. He was happy for her opportunity. Her excitement about her work showed in her face, making her radiate a beauty that Tanner had never noticed before.

On Christmas Day, he went to her house to give her a soft purple sweater he had purchased in Japan. His heart leapt in his chest when he saw her. He couldn't take his eyes from her face, and he realized immediately that something inside him had changed. Had she always been this beautiful? Had he been too blind to notice?

As she told him about her Boston experience, the regrets and questions began. Why hadn't he told her how beautiful her eyes were when they had first met? Or how happy he was when he was with her? Why had he never tried to kiss her? He wanted to kiss her that day—badly. But he didn't. They were just friends—how could he change the rules now?

Heather graduated in April. A few days later, Tanner left for a two-week business trip to Japan.

For the first time, Japan didn't hold any pleasure for him. Tanner thought only of Heather and how he would rather be with her. He knew he loved her. He finally understood that friendship had to be the base of a successful romantic relationship. Love didn't mean beauty—although she was beautiful to him—and love wasn't merely physical attraction. Love was also friendship, respect, trust, and perhaps most importantly, a spiritual connection.

He vowed to confess his feelings when he returned home. No more wasted time. Maybe now his friendship with the girl next door would become the relationship he had always dreamed of sharing with the woman he loved.

Chapter One

Heather sat on her bed clutching a shirt that belonged to the pile of dirty clothes she needed to wash before leaving. Her eyes stung with unbidden tears. She had told everybody of her decision, everybody except Tanner. For some reason she dreaded telling him.

She forced a laugh. What was she thinking? Tanner was her best friend; he would be happy to hear that her dreams were coming true. He knew how much it meant for her to paint. Of course, this time her news was different from anything she had shared with him before. This time she was leaving Utah for good.

Her room was oddly quiet. Ten years separated Heather from Kathryn, the next girl in the family, so Heather had always enjoyed a room alone. Yet she could usually hear noise coming from the rest of the house—noise that had often made it difficult for her to concentrate even in the privacy of her own room. With ten children in their family, something was always happening. Today the silence seemed to signal that fate agreed with her plans to leave everything and everyone behind.

Sighing, she returned to the sorting job at hand. One pile to pass on to her younger sisters, one smaller pile to become rags, another pile to take with her. She removed the battered suitcases from the top shelf in her closet. They still held stickers from her trip to Boston last winter, but packing them now reminded her more of leaving for her mission.

She closed her eyes tightly as the memories of her time in Italy rushed back. She had loved being in a country that had inspired so many famous painters, but what she most remembered was the Spirit. She had known then without a doubt that she was following the right path by holding to the gospel and to the Church.

Why couldn't she get that feeling back now?

Part of the problem was her own attitude. She just didn't seem to see things the way most members of the church saw them. Everything was either very black or very white to them. Modest clothing, short hair for men, best dress to church. No smoking, drinking, or drugs. No extra earrings or tattoos. Home teaching faithfully done—never mind that it was on the last day of the month. And if someone dared to flout even the smallest part of this checklist, they simply didn't make the grade.

But Heather had learned that compliance to "the list" was often an outward show for some members. In her college and mission experiences, she had met people to whom she could trust her life, and yet they were shunned because of their outward appearances. She had also met some members who appeared to be pious, but were dishonest in their hearts and in their daily lives. How many returned missionaries had she dated who tried to make inappropriate advances and then blamed their lack of self control on her supposed beauty? How many of her artist friends had been swindled by "upright" moral businessmen who stole their work in return for peanuts?

Yes, *people* were flawed, not the gospel—she believed that with all her heart. And yet, how could so much of the so-called Mormon culture leave her feeling this disoriented? What she needed was time away. Time to find whatever it was she was seeking.

A loud thump sounded in the next room, which had been used by the three boys between her and Kathryn until Jacob went on his mission the previous year. Now only Kevin and Aaron shared the space. Each of the other children also roomed with another sibling: Kathryn and Alison, Brett and Evan, Mindy and little Jane. Jacob would be home soon from the Philippines, and Heather knew the family would be glad to have her room. She would have moved out and rented an apartment with friends before now if all her money hadn't gone for tuition—and if the light from the large windows hadn't made this room so perfect for painting.

A door slammed and she heard footsteps in the hall. "You're such a jerk!" someone screamed.

"Not me. You're the one who cheated!"

"Oh, yeah?"

Another argument among her siblings. They didn't fight more than any other family, but with so many children there was always one disturbance or another. One thing for sure, she couldn't paint here anymore. Boston was calling for more reasons than one.

The voices faded as the boys moved down the stairs, likely looking for a referee. Her poor mother would have to deal with them. Heather smiled grudgingly. Resolving arguments was something her mother was good at. No doubt both boys would be out cleaning the garage together in record time. At least it was a nice day for it.

Heather glanced out her window at the Wolfe house next door. May flowers were already in full bloom in the many flowerbeds, and rosebuds covered the white-painted wooden railings on the porch that wrapped around one of the turrets. Tall birch and lofty walnut trees lined the drive and were also scattered appealingly around the yard. She loved the Wolfe house. The turrets on the Victorian mansion brought to her mind an ancient castle, and more than once she had felt a desire to paint it, but she had always needed to finish some other project first for school.

Urgently, she grabbed her camera from her dresser and snapped a dozen photographs in quick succession. Then—as if appearing of its own volition—her large sketch book was in hand, her pencil darting over the page. Later the developed photographs would help her get the colors just right, but for now she would draw the feeling of the house. Because her own house was set at a slight angle, and the birch and walnut trees were spaced widely apart, she had a wonderful view of the Wolfe house—one she never wanted to forget. That house, and especially Tanner, had meant so much to her over the years. Of course, since purchasing his condo in Orem, he technically no longer lived there.

Before she left, she still had to face Tanner, who was due home from a business trip in Japan tonight. She had considered scheduling her flight so that she would be gone before he returned, but felt she owed him a goodbye. Without him, the past seven years here would have been bleak. He had taken the place of the sister she should have had closer in age, something her brothers had never been able to do, and filled the role of best friend and confidant. He had helped her locate reality when she longed only to be in the clouds. She would miss him more than anyone else, even two-year-old Jane. But now was the time for her to leave—before there were no more choices left.

છ

Tanner knew the ring was just right. The thick band was made of woven white and yellow gold, with one-of-a-kind etchings done by a skillful Japanese artist. Heather would appreciate the intricate design, even if her eyebrows raised at the large diamond he'd made the jeweler put into the piece. He couldn't completely escape his culture; men in America offered diamonds to their future brides, and Heather would have the best.

With a last peek at the ring, Tanner slipped it into its box and raised the back of his seat in preparation for landing at the Salt Lake City airport. He couldn't wait to see Heather tonight; he was finally going to tell her how he felt. Since his awakening in December, he had let five long months go by—painful months for him.

Heather had apparently been oblivious to his inner turmoil, which said a lot because she had always before sensed how he felt. He decided that her intense school schedule had put a wedge between them, and let it ride. Now that they were both graduated, it was time to go on with their lives. They could have a home, a family. Heather would be a wonderful mother—just as she was a wonderful older sister to her many siblings. He would work, she would paint. They would love and laugh and grow old together.

He shook his head at his own sentimentality. He still honestly didn't know what response Heather would give to his proposal, but hoped that in the past few months since Christmas she had also experienced some of these same feelings toward him. Though her last semester had been busy, he distinctly remembered a special night of dinner and dancing. Holding her in his arms, he had been completely happy.

He would have spoken that night—the feeling had been right—but some of her artist friends had arrived partway through the evening and invited themselves to their table. Tanner hadn't minded because Heather seemed so content, and he honestly enjoyed the company of her friends. They were talented and dedicated to their work, if not very good at money matters or contracts, which were his forte.

Tonight there would be just the two of them, with no distractions. Her e-mail had said that she would go to dinner with him, and this time he had taken steps to assure they remained alone.

The drive from the airport to Alpine seemed longer than usual, though the traffic was light, even for a Tuesday. As he finally turned in at his parents' drive, he couldn't keep from glancing between the trees at Heather's house. Was she there waiting for him? He wished he could go there first, but he had promised his dad and Mickelle that he'd stop by after his trip.

As he pulled up to the house, his little sister Belle came running from the front door, her long, dark brown hair streaming behind. "Tanner! Tanner!" she screamed.

He was obliged to forego the garage and stop the car. "Hi, Belle!"

She launched herself at him. "I'm so glad you're home. I've missed you!"

He hugged her. "You, too. You look great!"

Her slightly rounded face dimpled. "You always say that."

"That's because you're always pretty." And she was. Only marginally slender, she was soft and beautiful. Every time she smiled, an adorable dimple appeared in each perfectly-formed cheek. Her brown hair curled gently halfway down her back, and her brown eyes, with a hint of their father's amber, were the talk of the eighth grade.

"Is anyone else home?"

"Well, Dad and Mom are, and Jennie Anne. But Jeremy's somewhere playing basketball, as usual, and I think even you'd remember that Bryan's still in Paraguay. Like duh!" She giggled as he tickled her. "Okay, stop. I was just kidding—I know you know he's in Paraguay. Stop!" She broke away from him and ran into the house.

Tanner glanced over his shoulder once more at Heather's. There was no movement around the house, though he couldn't see their backyard. Sighing, he followed his little sister inside.

His stepmother, Mickelle, greeted him profusely in the kitchen, and Tanner felt a rush of love for the woman who had been his mother since he was fifteen. He didn't call her "Mom" as Belle did—Belle had only been three when their mother had died, and she didn't remember her—but he loved Mickelle as much as he had loved his own mother. She had been very good to him and Belle, and to their adopted sister Jennie Anne, giving them the same care and love she gave her own two sons.

"I'm so glad you're home," she said, her gray-blue eyes sparkling. "Thanks for dropping in." Seeing her pleasure, Tanner was glad he had.

"Well, I'm taking Heather out to dinner tonight," he said. "So I had to come here anyway."

"Heather," Mickelle mused, tucking her straight, honey-blonde hair behind her ear. "I really like that girl. I miss having her around so much. I miss having both of you around." She shrugged. "Well, I guess you can't stop growing up just for me. But you might think about arranging me some grand-children before long."

Tanner laughed half-heartedly. Mickelle didn't realize how close she'd come to his real feelings by mentioning Heather and grandchildren in practically the same breath. He felt an urge to confide in her, but bit his tongue. There would be plenty of time tonight—especially if Heather returned his love.

"Oh, I thought I heard your voice." Damon Wolfe entered the kitchen. "Hi, son." He gave Tanner a bear hug. "So how'd it go?"

"Great. The sales people have added a new hospital chain, and I was able to find a really great new manager for the branch. I think it might cut down on my trips there."

"It's about time."

"Good employees are hard to find—you know that."

Damon nodded. "Yep. That's why I hired you."

Tanner looked behind his father to where his sister Jennie Anne had appeared silently. The fourteen-year-old was as thin and freckled as ever. She pushed back her mass of dark brown hair that refused to hold even the slightest curl, and smiled shyly at him. When she smiled, her sharp features became softened, and her brown eyes—by far her best feature—seemed to grow two sizes. "Hi, Jennie Anne," Tanner said. He had never been as close to his adopted sister as he was with Belle—probably because he'd been so old before she'd joined their family, but there was a deep fondness between them. He gave her a hug and was rewarded with another shy smile.

"Well, dinner's about ready," Mickelle said, shutting the oven door. "Are you sure you won't stay, Tanner? There's plenty. You could invite Heather. It would be nice to see her."

"Thanks, but not tonight. Heather and I have other plans." Tanner was relieved when they didn't press. "I'd like to quickly use the shower first," he added. "I didn't stop at home. I have a change of clothes in my suitcase."

"You go right ahead."

Tanner retrieved his suitcase from the car and carried it into the house. He showered and dressed before quickly combing his dark brown hair. When he left the house, his family was just sitting down to dinner.

Damon's amber eyes twinkled. "Say hello to Heather for me," he called as Tanner headed for the door. "And give her a kiss for me, too."

Tanner stopped walking in mid-step. Had his dad figured out his real feelings for Heather?

"Oh, Daddy, you know they're just friends," Belle said with her bubbling laugh. "He's like a brother to Heather."

"I know, I know. I was just kidding." Damon picked up his fork. "Now, is anyone going to pray, or am I going to starve to death?"

Tanner took a deep breath and started walking again. Daring one last glance over his shoulder, he saw his stepmother looking after him thoughtfully.

CR

Heather greeted Tanner at the front door with a wide smile, and he felt a ripple of excitement at seeing her. When had her odd freckles faded, giving her complexion that smooth, finished look? When had her straight, light brown hair gained so many highlights? When had each soft line of her face become so precious to him?

"Hi," he said, grinning like a schoolboy.

"Hi." She glanced over her shoulder. "Mom! Tanner's here. I'm leaving!" Before she finished speaking, her mother had appeared in the entryway behind her.

"Tanner, how glad I am to see you." Karalee held out a hand, which she had been drying with a dishcloth.

Tanner tore his gaze from Heather's face. "Nice to see you, Sister Samis."

"You have fun. But don't get her back too late. She has a lot to do in the morning before—"

"Don't worry, Mom," Heather interrupted. "It's only dinner. I'll be back in a few hours."

Tanner certainly had no plans to get her back that soon, but he nodded anyway.

"Goodbye then." Karalee shut the door behind them as they left.

Heather gave a soft laugh. "You did the right thing moving out when you did. As long as you live in their house, parents will treat you like a child."

"Mine still treat me like a child," he told her. "And besides, you never would have found an apartment with good light like you have in your room. Not to mention that you would have to work more and paint less to pay for it. And I know you don't love your job at the print shop that much."

"You're right. It has been good here." There was a wistfulness in her voice that made Tanner look at her closely, but she smiled and headed for his car.

He opened the door to his new model VW Bug. His family teased him mercilessly about his choice—their favorites leaned more toward brands like Lexus and Mercedes—but he enjoyed the Blue Bug, as he called it. In fact, he had a special fondness for all VW Bugs. He still kept the classic one he had rebuilt as a youth and had used throughout high school and college.

"You haven't been home yet?" Heather asked, spying his suitcase in the backseat.

"Nope. Stopped at my parents' to change, though." Then he added with a smile, "And to shower."

"Whew! Thank heaven for that!" They laughed together.

Their laughter didn't last long. Usually, they were bursting with things to say, but today the conversation lagged almost from the beginning. Tanner wondered if it was just him, or if Heather was acting strangely. Her eyes didn't quite seem to meet his when she spoke.

As he pulled onto Orem's State Street, she asked, "So where are we going?"

"It's a surprise. In fact, you have to put on this." He tossed her a blindfold.

"You've got to be kidding!" But she slipped it on.

He glanced at her and saw a slender hand steal up, one finger hooking a piece of hair near the nape of her neck and pulling it forward. She twisted the lock between her thumb and forefinger—a sure sign that she had something on her mind.

"Is something wrong?" he asked.

"No. Uh . . . I do have a . . . Never mind—it can wait. Where are we going?"

"You'll see." He had thought about taking her to his condo, but at the last minute had decided to use the company building instead. As planned, his assistant, Juliet, should have everything organized, including the meal she had ordered from a local restaurant—probably from Village Inn where her younger brother was the manager.

They passed Juliet as they entered the building. Heather, of course, couldn't see her with the blindfold. Tanner nodded silently at Juliet, and she gave him the thumbs-up sign. Tanner liked the way Heather clung to him, trusting him not to let her bump into anything, instead of holding out her hands to feel her way.

"We're almost there," he said. He put an arm around her, appreciating how the six-inch difference in their heights seemed to be the perfect amount for a great fit.

"Okay, wait a minute." He opened the conference room door and helped her through. Juliet had outdone herself with preparations, as he expected she might do. Tasteful decorations in gold and silver covered the candle-lit room. One end of the long table was laid out with nice china, excepting the plates, which had been placed in an electric warmer on the far end. A green salad and cups of chocolate mousse were on ice. Each detail had been accounted for, from the sparkling white grape juice in the wine glasses to the fresh warm rolls and real butter.

"Smells delicious!" Heather said. She lowered her voice. "Are other people here? I don't want everyone looking at me."

"It's just us," he assured her, reaching up to pull off the blindfold.

"Oh!" Heather stared at the room. "How wonderful! What's it all for?"

"For us. We're going to have dinner here." *Undisturbed,* he added silently.

Heather regarded him a moment without speaking, her brow furrowed. She was obviously wondering why he had gone to such lengths. Unprepared to answer that question yet, he pulled out one of the plush, black leather executive chairs and gestured for her to sit.

"Is it my birthday?" she asked suddenly, her eyes seeming even larger and more beautiful in the candlelight. "Or yours? I mean, I know I tend to forget things like that, but I'm pretty sure your birthday is in the same month as Thanksgiving, and I vaguely—only vaguely, mind you—remember something about being born in January. Although I could be confusing that with one of my siblings, so I would completely understand if *you* got the month mixed up. If you want, I could take my pick of their birthdays and trade."

He grinned. "I didn't mix up your birthday. I'm the one who reminds *you* every year that you're even having a birthday."

"Then what?"

He sighed inwardly. Heather knew him too well to let this go, and she never backed down. But he wasn't ready yet to make his proposal. He wanted to talk about casual things first, to break down any barriers his two weeks away had created. He wanted time to let the soft music set the mood, to recall memories with her that would remind her how much they'd meant to each other over the years.

"Well, there's been a lot of changes in life recently," he hedged. Turning away from her, he flipped on the stereo and then retrieved their plates from the warmer. He set one in front of her, and the other at the head of table where he was to sit.

"Hmm, let's see, I did graduate and then . . ." Abruptly she looked up, her face flushing. "Someone told you! Oh, I was saving it to tell you in person—really, I was. Though for some reason I was nervous about it." She laughed self-consciously. To his surprise, she jumped out of her seat and hugged him fervently.

For a moment, he just stood there. Then at last his arms encircled her body.

"You really are the best friend ever! Here I was worried about how I was going to tell you about the grant and moving to Boston, and you plan this lovely dinner to celebrate. I knew you'd be happy for me—it's a once-in-a-lifetime chance!"

Tanner breathed in the lilac scent of her hair. *What is she talking about?* The heavy pit in his stomach told him that something had gone dreadfully wrong.

Chapter Two

Heather brushed Tanner's cheek with a light kiss as she drew away and settled again at the table. "Truthfully, I'm glad they told you," she said, picking up her fork and testing the tenderness of the chicken breast. "You were the hardest to tell about leaving Utah—I'm going to miss you more than anyone."

"Why don't you tell me all about it while we eat?" Tanner finally recovered enough to say.

"Good idea. I'm famished."

When they had begun their meal, Heather spoke, "You know how I've been searching for just the right job and haven't been able to find it."

"I thought you were going to paint."

"Well, yeah, but I want to make a living, too."

He nearly told her she didn't need to make a living, that she could paint all day if she wanted, and he'd take care of the rest. "What about working in a gallery here?"

She speared a green bean. "No go. Everyone I talked to either paid too little, or wanted other qualifications. I would have to go into computer design to really support myself."

"Are your parents hinting about kicking you out?"

Her fork went still. "No, but I need to get out of there. In fact, I need to get out of Utah altogether. So when my professor told Lorin and me—you know my girlfriend Lorin—that we had the opportunity to work in Boston at a gallery and paint at the same time, well, it was just too good to be true. Think about it! I'll have six months to prove myself, and the grant is extendable after that. For basically as long as Mr. Oldham—he's the benefactor—likes my progress."

With difficulty, Tanner swallowed the bit of chicken in his mouth. He didn't know what to pursue first—the fact that she wanted to "get out of Utah," or more information about the grant she and her friend had received. He opted for the latter. "Tell me about this grant." Under the table he lifted the front part of his foot, balancing on his heel, and moved it up and down nervously. It was a habit Heather had tried to get him to break over the years, without success.

"I thought you knew."

"Not the details."

"Oh." She moved her fork toward another green bean. "Well, it's like this. Mr. Oldham is a rich old guy in Boston who owns an art gallery, and he arranged a grant program for promising artists. He gives us room and board, art direction by Tomás Valencia—he's a renowned artist—painting supplies, and a thousand dollars a month spending allowance. As part of the deal, we have to work two hours a day in his gallery, but then we'll have the rest of the day to paint. Each artist was recommended by a university professor."

"Does this have something to do with your trip to Boston last Christmas?"

"It has everything to do with it. All the recommended artists were invited to Boston last December. We students weren't told about the grants, because Mr. Oldham didn't want us politicking for the positions during our visit. We just thought we'd been invited to see some really great paintings and historic buildings, when actually he was choosing from the candidates. We found out about the grants just before graduation. It's amazing that he chose both Lorin and me. Can you believe it? Out of five total, two of us are from BYU."

"Shouldn't there have been more notice? You only graduated a few weeks ago. If you found out just before that—well, it seems kind of fast."

She slipped the green bean into her mouth and chewed silently before speaking. "Well, I think the old guy wanted to see if we were willing to pull up and leave on short notice. Sort of a dedication test. But we had three weeks to decide. That was plenty. No one turned it down, believe me."

"Why didn't you tell me before?" He tried not to feel hurt that she hadn't shared the information with him.

"I wasn't sure I was going to accept. I mean, my family's here—my culture, my upbringing. Besides, you were leaving for Japan, and I didn't want to worry you."

"It sounds like a good opportunity." The words seemed to come without his permission and at stark contrast to what his heart was feeling.

"I know, but still . . ." Heather set her fork on the table. "It's hard to leave

Utah, but if I don't take this chance, I may never know what I missed."

"You'll miss something by going, too. Choices always mean something is left undone."

"I know that." Her hazel eyes held his, begging him to understand. She had never appeared more beautiful and alive.

"For instance," he continued, "I thought you were considering going for a master's degree."

"I was—once. But now this is the right decision for *me*. I need to find myself. I know that doesn't make much sense to you, Tanner. You've always known what you want. But me . . ." She trailed off, staring at her plate.

"You might be able to find yourself here, if you give it some time."

She shook her head, looking up again. "I don't know that I belong here. I don't seem to feel like everyone else."

"What do you mean?"

"I mean the whole Mormon culture. If you complete a certain checklist, you're okay, accepted. If not, you're a sinner. It's all so black and white. But I see many shades of gray. So many people put on one face at church and another face for the business world. As I sit here, I can think of fifteen—no sixteen—artists who've been ripped off by Mormon businessmen who worship at the same church I do. Maybe it's horrible for me to say, but sometimes it seems my friends need to be doubly sure of a contract if the producer is Mormon. Their contracts take advantage of how trusting we are and makes it impossible for artists to earn a living. More and more artists are turning to other sources to survive. I just . . ." She frowned, and her hand slipped up to twirl a lock of hair. "I just don't know if I want to be a part of a culture that condemns people for not wearing certain clothes or for not acting a certain way, while at the same time applauding those who hide their much larger flaws under a suit and pious attitude."

Tanner reached over and took her hand. "We've had this discussion before, you know. People aren't perfect, and just because a few members of the Church aren't what we think they should be, that doesn't mean the gospel's not true."

"I *know* the gospel is true." Yet the emphatic way she said it told him that she wasn't as sure as she wanted him to believe. "That's not the problem. It's the Mormon culture I worry about. Take church meetings for instance. Men must wear white shirts and ties and dress pants—the uniform of the priesthood. If you show up in jeans, people would stare you right out of the chapel. Even if you wear a blue dress shirt, you stand out. In Italy we didn't care so much what members wore as long as they showed up."

"Well, that's a cultural difference. Members here have understood since they were children that one of the ways they show respect to God is to attend church in their best clothing. Choosing something else just because it feels more comfortable isn't an option because they know it's not really appropriate; yet if that something else was their only set of clothes, it would be acceptable."

"To Heavenly Father, you mean." Heather rested her elbows on the table and let her head drop into her hands, fingers pushing into her hair. "Because people here would stare and come to their own conclusions, just as they do when they see people with no children, or only a few. Never mind the revelation they may have received, or how much heartache they may have gone through trying to conceive."

"That goes right back to the beginning of our argument," he said. "People who judge others do so because they're human, not because they're Mormons. I think you'll find a similar judgment everywhere you go—among people of any religion." A strand of her hair was dangerously close to falling into her salad; he carefully moved it away and she smiled her thanks.

"I guess that's where I'm not so sure," she said. "I sometimes wonder if being members of the 'true Church' doesn't sometimes make people think they have the right to judge."

Tanner grimaced. "I'm sure there are some people who do feel that way, but not the majority. I believe that in general the Mormon culture is positive. For instance, what better place could you raise children than in Utah? And if a faithful member needs help, they get it—from money to pay their mortgage to help moving."

"Yes, we're good at that, I'll agree. Remember, my Mom's had ten children, and I've seen a lot of dinners from very kind members over the years. The Church has great resources and is able to give a lot of support. But in the end that only covers physical needs. What about true love and caring? Emotional support? Receiving dinners—or taking one to someone—has never given me that feeling."

Tanner took a drink of his sparkling grape juice to buy time to consider her words. "I'm not sure I understand," he said at last. "I think the Church gives great emotional support. I've always had someone there when I've needed them—teachers, guest speakers, counselors, the bishop. I believe the Church helps people to reach their full potential in every way."

Heather had begun eating again, but now she stopped. "I don't believe that. At least I don't see it."

"Oh?" He felt they were finally getting down to the real root of her trouble; the rest had just been excuses to leave Utah.

"I'm not talking spiritually here, Tanner. I believe the teachings of the gospel outline spiritual progression very well, but the problem is finding time to obtain the spiritualness. With all the hours spent serving in callings, and with all the necessary requirements of that checklist, people scarcely have time to read their scriptures. Or to become really great at something they're good at."

He opened his mouth to speak, but she rushed on. "Really, my feeling this way is your fault, Tanner. You helped me see that a rounded education is important when all I wanted was to study art. I appreciate that—more than you know. I've seen and understood social, economical, and political events that I would never have imagined had I not finished my education. I've also seen what people can do when they really reach for their potential. Take you, for instance." She pointed at him with her fork. "You graduated early, went to work with your dad, and now practically run an entire arm of the business."

"Well, I am the man's son."

"No, you deserve it. I've seen you with the employees. They respect you, the way you get things done. You love the work and you're good at it."

Tanner was beginning to feel uncomfortable. He did work hard to do a good job, but that didn't mean he deserved a medal—or her praise.

"Still you could do better," she added. "Think about it. If you didn't spend all that time studying to fulfill your calling or being a good home teacher, couldn't you accomplish more at work? Or conversely, couldn't you become closer to your Savior?"

"But working more isn't important to me," he countered. "And I feel closer to the Savior when I'm serving. Besides, I can't work every minute. I need a rounded life."

She frowned and blinked rapidly, fighting tears. "If you don't feel it, then maybe it's just certain fields that suffer—like art. If a male artist can't support his family with his painting, he has to get another job, or his wife must work—and remember that's a big no-no here. How then can he rise to the top and become the artist he could be?"

At last Tanner understood where she was coming from. "He does it slowly, and the Lord will help him."

"But he won't be able to accomplish all that he could if he had time to focus."

"Why not? I once heard a writer say that he believed he only had to do three or four drafts of a novel instead of ten because the Lord knew what a busy life he led and stepped in to fill the gap."

Tears had appeared as small beads on her eyelashes. She took a deep breath. "I know the Lord helps, Tanner, but some things take precedence— like families and callings—until we cannot rise to the top, but remain mediocre. Or maybe we don't do anything at all."

There was a plea in her voice, one Tanner didn't understand. "Heather," he said gently, "what's this all about?" It had to be more personal than she was allowing.

Her face became bleak. "My mother's pregnant again—a few months along. She's not really announcing it yet."

He smiled. "Well, that's great, isn't it? She loves children."

"Yes, she does," came the quiet response. Heather was again staring at her plate, her tears suddenly dry.

"Aren't you happy about it? Is there something wrong with your mom— or the baby?"

"No. Nothing's wrong. Except that last January my mother pulled out her art supplies from the attic." She looked up and smiled, catching him off guard. "She was painting a picture of Mindy and Jane playing in the sandbox. It was really good, despite the fact that she hasn't had much practice over the years. Most people don't even know she paints—tell me, have you ever seen her at it? No, you only know because I told you."

Tanner relaxed in his chair. "But that's great she's painting again. How's it coming?"

"It's not." Heather's brow furrowed and she stared in the air at something only she could see. "She put it away again when she became sick. The smell of paints—she can't take it when she's pregnant. Besides, the children needed her, she said. Don't you see, Tanner? She always puts it away. There's *always* a new baby or a new calling that comes first. I don't know how my mom can possibly reach her potential now—at least not with painting."

"How do you know that's what she wants?" Tanner asked. "Maybe she doesn't feel about it the way you do."

Heather met his gaze. "I've seen the eagerness when she takes her supplies out, when she paints, and I recognize the sadness and reluctance when she stops. I've seen it so many times over the years, only it's just been since my mission that I began to understand it all. That's what made me look in her high school yearbook. You should see what all the kids wrote about her becoming a famous artist. Even her art teacher gave her more encouragement than I ever got from a teacher. I think she once wanted to paint as badly as I do, but then she met my dad and had me. End of story. Now when she's at an age that she might finally have the time, she has to put it all away again."

"There won't always be another baby," he said. "Nature will take care of that. Your mother's what, maybe forty?"

"Forty-four."

"See. The clock's ticking. And besides, your parents must have wanted another child."

"I'm sure they do."

"Eventually their children will be grown."

"Then it will be something else on the checklist." Heather leaned forward and grabbed his hands. "Don't you see, Tanner? She gave up what she could be for her kids, my dad, the Church."

He turned his hands so that he held her delicate ones in his. "It's not only a one-way trip. She gained a lot on the way. Who's to say what was the better role? Who's to say she would have been happier?"

"That's just it," Heather said, pulling away. "She'll never know. But one thing is sure, she won't ever have time to develop her talent to what it could have been."

Now he was finally understanding. "But you are not your mother, Heather. And when you get married, you don't need to have ten children. Hardly anyone does that now anyway."

"But should my mother have had to give up her art for even one or two? How many years must she lose to be a good Mormon?" Tears filled Heather's eyes.

Tanner didn't know how to answer. He had no idea how much sacrifice went into raising children; he only knew it had to be worth it—and he desperately wanted Heather to feel the same way. "Your mother made her own choices."

"I know, and I must make mine. That's why I have to go to Boston. I have to know what's out there before I can decide what I want to do with the rest of my life. I know that's something you may not understand; maybe we're too different for you to ever understand fully, but I like to think that you can, just a little. You know me so well."

Tanner's jaw tightened in frustration. "I do know you, and I suspect that there's more to this than a disenchantment with Mormon culture—Utah Mormon culture at that—and with the choices your mother has made. Right?"

She nodded once, slowly. "Maybe."

Her admission was like a blow. He was so sure of his beliefs that it hurt to think the woman he loved might not share them to the same extent. "There are other ways besides leaving to strengthen or find a testimony," he made himself say.

"This is what I need to do."

"Okay then, I support you." He purposely made his voice matter-of-fact, as though his heart wasn't being ripped apart.

There was a silence between them. He could see the sadness in her face, but didn't know how to make it leave. Taking her in his arms and proposing certainly wouldn't do that, not with everything she'd said. The ring box sat in his pocket, heavy and mocking. How different this night was turning out from what he'd hoped. If Heather hadn't appeared so fragile, he thought he might let his resentment show enough to let her know how hurt he really was that he had been completely excluded from her decision.

She picked up her fork, and so did he. The meal went on. After a few moments of awkwardness, they began to talk more casually about his work and their families. Inside, Tanner's heart felt like lead.

When at last dinner was over—a torturously long time for him, and yet at the same time much too brief—he took her hand and led her to the Blue Bug. She was silent on the way home, and Tanner hurt too much to make small talk. He felt as though he had already lost her.

When they arrived at her place, he walked her to the door. The sun had set, but there was still plenty of light reflecting over the blue sky. Tanner could hear the voices of Heather's many siblings coming from an open window.

"I guess this is goodbye," he said softly.

"Well, I was going to ask you if you could drive me to the airport tomorrow afternoon. Mom's sick, and Dad's got a meeting right at that time, so we're doing breakfast together instead of having him take me. I could have Lorin pick me up, but I'm not sure who's taking her, or if they'd have room with all the lug—"

He raised a fingers to her lips, interrupting the sudden flow of words, then pulled it quickly away. "Of course I'll take you. Be glad to." No matter how it hurt to see her go, he wouldn't deny himself the opportunity. "What time does your flight leave?"

Her mouth twisted in a half smile that hinted at tears. "One-thirty. And thanks. You know, I'm going to miss you—you're my best friend."

"And you're mine." Tanner put his hands in his pockets, mostly to stop himself from giving her a hug. He didn't know if he could take that closeness tonight. She was no longer just a friend, no matter what her feelings were toward him.

"I'll e-mail," she promised. "I'm taking my laptop."

"The laptop—that's a relief," he said lightly. "I don't know if I could read your handwriting if you sent me a letter."

She gave a low laugh. They both knew that his handwriting was the problem, not hers. "Goodnight."

Still facing him, she reached for the doorknob. Panic welled up inside Tanner. Unable to let her go without something more, he leaned toward her and brushed a soft kiss over her lips. He caught a brief glimpse of her beautiful hazel eyes widening before he turned and sprinted back to the Bug. As he drove away, she was still standing on the porch.

ଔ

Heather watched Tanner back out of her driveway. She half-expected him to pull in next door as he had always done when they were much younger, but he turned down the street, likely heading to his condo in Orem. She felt odd inside, and couldn't name the emotion. Her hand went to her lips. *What was that for, anyway?* Tanner had never kissed her in all the years she had known him, except on the cheek when he had come home from his mission.

Shaking her head, she went into the house. The entryway was deceptively calm, but as she went through to the kitchen, she was hit by a wave of busyness. Children sat at the table and counters, finishing up homework. The sound of the piano rang from the adjoining family room, and two of the smaller children, Evan and Mindy, were play sword fighting in front of the darkened TV.

"Will you be quiet?" yelled Kathryn. "I can't concentrate on my algebra when you're making so much noise."

"Kids," their mother broke in with a firm voice, "it's time to get ready for bed. Take Jane and go upstairs to put your pajamas on. Don't forget to brush your teeth. No, not Jane's. I'll help her later, or Dad will. Go on—hurry. We're having prayer soon."

"I'll help her." Heather went upstairs with the younger kids. She couldn't help Kathryn with her math—she had barely survived it herself—but she could help her siblings dress for bed and read them a story. It would be the last time for a long while that she would be around to do it.

When the younger children were ready, they met the others in what they called the prayer room. It wasn't really a room, but a wide hallway on the second floor that overlooked the living room. Everyone knelt down. It was Mindy's turn to pray, and as she did, Heather surveyed the beloved faces. A lump grew in her throat. Though she had been so anxious to get away and be on her own, she felt strangely reluctant to leave them.

Jane had her eyes open, too. The three-year-old grinned, and Heather winked back. Then she closed her eyes just as Mindy finished. Her mother and father hugged each child goodnight before they scattered to their rooms. The older ones could read or play games quietly for another hour, but it was past time for the little ones to be asleep. Heather sat in the hallway, leaning against the cherry wood railings. She watched her father and mother go into each of the younger kids' rooms to tuck them in. Downstairs in the family room, Kathryn had spread her math book, and Aaron was helping her with the last few problems.

Heather arose and went down the hall to her bedroom, listening as silence began to fill the place of the previous bustle. The drawings of Tanner's family home beckoned to her from the easel by the window. She picked up a pencil and added a few lines, but they weren't right so she erased them.

A knock sounded on her door. "Heather?"

"Come in."

Her mother entered with a load of clothes in her arms. "Are these yours? They were in the dryer—don't want you to forget them."

"Thanks." Heather motioned to the bed, and Karalee laid the clothes next to an open suitcase.

Heather replaced her pencil in its box and came over to the bed where her mother was already folding the clothes. Her face was drawn and weary, and Heather wondered how she kept up enough energy to take care of the entire family—especially while she was expecting a new baby.

"You don't have to do that," Heather said. "You should rest."

Karalee sank onto the bed. "I'm fine."

Heather wanted to say that she didn't look fine, but couldn't bring herself to voice the words. Instead, she took a pair of jeans from her mother's hands and sat beside her.

"What is it, Heather? You've been awfully quiet since you got home from dinner. Are you having second thoughts?"

Heather folded the pants neatly in her lap. "I want to go—this is a wonderful opportunity. And it's time I got out on my own."

"You're welcome here for as long as you want. You do know that, don't you?"

"Yes." Heather turned and tossed the folded pants into the suitcase. Forcing a laugh, she added, "But I bet you thought I'd be married by now."

Her mother smiled gently. "Well, actually, I hoped you'd finish your education first. I know how hard you've worked for it, and I also know that I've always wished I'd finished mine."

This surprised Heather. "Really? But why? Do you think your life would have been different?" What she really wanted to ask was if her mother regretted giving up college and painting to marry her dad and have children. But she couldn't ask that. Perhaps she was afraid of the answer.

"Oh, no. Even if I had finished college, I would have been here doing exactly what I'm doing. But I love learning, and there's nothing quite like learning in a college environment. But that's only part of why I've always wanted my daughters to have an education. I've been fortunate to never have been forced to leave you children and earn a living. Many women aren't so lucky. With a degree, you can take care of yourself."

"Didn't you worry about that?"

"Yes, it was a concern when you were younger, but now we're older and have things pretty well planned financially. We'd be okay if something happened to your dad." She laughed. "I guess at least I can look on the bright side of leaving college—I didn't have to take college algebra like you did."

Heather laughed with her. Although all her younger sisters seemed to excel in math, her aversion to the subject was something she shared with her mother. "I only got through it because of Tanner."

"Do any of your doubts have to do with him?" her mother asked, her pale brown eyes searching Heather's face.

"No. I really don't have any doubts about leaving." Heather spoke with confidence. "And Tanner's been nothing but supportive. He's a really great guy. In fact, somehow he heard about me leaving and gave me a sort of special surprise dinner tonight to celebrate."

"Hmm, I wonder how he found out. The kids promised they wouldn't tell anyone, and they're good with secrets. When I talked to Mickelle today, she still had no idea."

Heather shrugged. "Tanner's good that way. He found out, that's all. And whether I'm here or in Boston, we'll always be friends."

"Well, Boston's not that far away nowadays." Karalee sighed. "Still, I must admit, I'm going to miss you."

"Miss me?" Heather asked, putting on her teasing face. "You'll be a little busy for that. Jacob'll be coming home from his mission soon, and then there's the new baby, remember?"

"Oh, I remember." Karalee patted her stomach. "I can't believe it—at my age. I never thought we'd have another one after that last miscarriage. Imagine, eleven children."

"Hey, why not try again and make it an even dozen?"

Karalee laughed. "Oh, no. After this, I'm waiting for grandchildren."

"Well, with eleven children you ought to get at least one or two," Heather said, keeping a straight face.

Her mother chuckled. Then slapping her hands onto her knees, she arose. "I need to get in a load of laundry tonight. I just realized about an hour ago that poor Evan has nothing to wear tomorrow."

Heather felt guilty at the exhaustion so apparent in her mother's face and voice. "Can I help?"

"No, dear. Looks like you have plenty to do here." She gazed pointedly at the pile of clothes on the bed. "Are you going to have enough room?"

"I think so. I'm planning to pay for an extra suitcase. And I had Kevin help me take a few boxes up to the attic for storage—until I decide what to do with them." An almost tangible heaviness entered the room as Heather spoke. She was really going to do it; she was finally leaving home. Though it was a good and natural step—one she had delayed long enough—a part of her was terrified.

Her mother hugged her at that moment, as though sensing some of her emotion. "Whatever happens in the future, honey, your father and I will always be here for you."

"I know, Mom." Heather blinked back tears. The sudden terror faded, replaced by her usual confidence.

"I love you," Karalee said.

"I love you too, Mom."

With a last squeeze, her mother left, and Heather fell to folding and packing her clothes. All too soon, everything was in its place. She hefted the suitcase to the ground, leaving it open for last-minute items such as her hair dryer and makeup. Her room seemed empty now, devoid of the items that had made it uniquely hers. There was only the easel, which would have to go into the attic. The large sketch pad she would take on the plane.

She lay down on the bed, too mentally exhausted to remove her clothing or even pray. After all the things she had said tonight to Tanner about the Church, she wasn't entirely sure her Father in Heaven would even want to hear her prayers. Her eyes shut. Almost immediately Tanner's face popped into her head. She replayed the evening with him, and as she did, she sensed that there had been something strange in his reaction to her news. What was it? After ten more minutes of puzzling, nothing came to mind, so she let it go and thought instead about the exciting future that awaited her in Boston.

Chapter Three

Early Wednesday morning, Heather's family shared a special farewell breakfast before the children went to school. All of her siblings hugged her—even Aaron and Kevin who at fifteen and seventeen were usually too old for such displays of emotion. The younger children wiped away tears, except Jane who was too young to understand what was going on.

At eleven-thirty Tanner arrived at the door, looking more handsome than usual in dark olive dress pants, a lighter shirt of the same color, and an olive and off-white patterned tie. His dark hair was combed neatly except for a patch in the front where it stuck up slightly as though with a mind of its own. Heather smoothed her own brown pantsuit, glad she hadn't chosen jeans for the flight.

She helped Tanner store her suitcases into the Blue Bug, and then kissed her mother goodbye at the front door. She forced herself not to look back.

Since it was during the work week and long after rush hour, traffic was light, and they arrived at the airport with plenty of time to spare. "I'll help you in with the luggage," he said, turning into the short term parking, "and go with you as far as they'll let me."

"You don't have to." She glanced at his strong, angular profile. "You could just drop me off."

"I have time." His voice was clipped, a sure sign of irritation, so she dropped the matter. Truth was, she simply didn't know how she was going to say goodbye to him.

Inside, they waited in the long line to get her ticket and check her bags. "Well, I guess this is it," Heather said to Tanner when they were finished. "You won't be able to go with me beyond the security gate. But I wonder where Lorin is?"

"Over there," he motioned to the line they had recently left. "Checking in her luggage. I just noticed her come in."

Heather sighed. "Good. I was worried. Sometimes she can be a little . . . unpredictable."

"Isn't that a requirement for artists?" His grin showed her he was teasing.

"Exactly." She watched Lorin push her bags up to the counter.

"Uh, Heather."

She turned back to him, mentally steeling herself for his goodbye.

"I have something for you." A muscle in his square jaw twitched.

For the first time she noticed he was fingering a box in the pocket of his dress pants. *What could it be?* she thought. Her heartbeat quickened, though she couldn't explain why. "Oh?" she asked, when he didn't bring it out of his pocket.

He nodded shortly and withdrew his hand. A small fuzzy brown box in the middle of his palm beckoned to her.

"What's this?" For some reason, she remembered the swift kiss he had given her the night before. "You didn't have to get me anything, you know."

Tanner shifted from one foot to the other. "I wanted to. Don't worry, it won't bite."

She took the box, laughing self-consciously. "Of course not. I don't think you've tried to scare me since that snake in my locker in twelfth grade."

"Hey, for the millionth time, I wasn't trying to scare you—I just needed a place to keep it. I knew you weren't scared of snakes."

"Not usually. But when they jump out unexpectedly like that and wrap around your ankle . . ."

"Aren't you going to open it?" His eyes stared into hers and for a moment she couldn't look away.

"I didn't get you anything."

"I'm not going away. You are. You can bring me something when you come back to visit."

She swallowed the lump that had mysteriously appeared in her throat. Slowly, she opened the case. She didn't know what to expect—perhaps earrings or a bracelet—but staring up at her was an anchor made of solid gold. At one and a half inches tall, it was rather large and heavy for a necklace charm, but attached to it was an attractive gold rope necklace that seemed sturdy enough for the job.

"It's beautiful," she murmured. For it was. A smaller gold rope chain wove across the anchor's smooth, shiny surface, reminiscent of one that would have been attached to a real anchor and matching the necklace itself. "Thank you. But . . . well, I'm not sure I understand. Why an anchor?"

She met his eyes, which she had once thought so open and uncomplicated, but today she couldn't read his expression or even guess at his thoughts. A deep melancholy she hadn't yet experienced tugged at her heart.

"I bought it this morning. Took some doing to find, actually. But I thought it fit with our conversation last night." As he was speaking, she pulled the necklace and charm from the box. The weight felt good on her palm.

Tanner paused, and only when she looked up did he continue. "It's just, well, I know you're excited and ready for a whole slew of new experiences, but I also know that sometimes life can be a little confusing. That's why I chose an anchor. I want it to always remind you of your home and your roots. I want it to remind you that it's okay to question your beliefs because the gospel is anchored in truth and is not afraid of questions or doubts. The truth will always remain the truth."

He stopped talking, as though to be sure of her attention. "I want it to remind you that I have a testimony of the gospel, and of our Father, and of Jesus Christ. So even if you find yourself, well, floundering, I want it to remind you that I believe, and that I have faith in you."

He reached out and closed her hand around the necklace, pooling it in the center of her palm. His touch was warm and dry, yet she felt goose bumps ripple up her arm. "Plus," he said in a lighter tone, "I hope you'll wear it always to remember me . . . to remember our friendship."

"Thank you," she said, touched to her core. She was amazed at his thoughtfulness. He had always been considerate, but she felt that today she was seeing a side of him she had only glimpsed before.

His grip on her hand grew tighter. "Heather, I'm here if you need me, okay? Just give me a call—wherever, whenever. I don't care what it is you need, I'll help."

Normally she would have teased his arrogance with a flippant "If you even can help, Mr. Wonderful" but now did not seem the time. Instead she said, "Thanks, Tanner. And if you need me, you know where to find me."

"Well, I have your e-mail address at least." He gave her a smile. "Look, Lorin's coming. I think I'll take my goodbye hug now."

Heather obliged. His touch was at once comforting and confusing. His smell was so familiar, yet she realized she didn't even know the name of his cologne, or if he even wore cologne. He was familiar . . . and yet suddenly strange.

As they parted, his lips brushed her cheek. "Take care of yourself, Heather. Have a good flight."

"Thanks," she said a bit breathlessly.

"Hi, guys," Lorin called.

"Hi, Lorin." Tanner stepped away from Heather. "Nice to see you. Congratulations on your grant."

Lorin's short bleached hair moved slightly as she nodded. "I still can't believe it! When I think of all the others that went with us last Christmas—and us being the ones chosen." Her blue eyes gleamed. "I mean, I could see Heather being chosen, but me? Wow, I still keep wanting to pinch myself."

Tanner laughed at her enthusiasm and honesty. "I'm sure you deserve it. Remind Heather to keep in touch, would you? And go to church at least the first time with her, Lorin. It'll be strange in a new place. Promise?"

"Sure," Lorin said blithely. Heather almost rolled her eyes. No matter how Heather had urged, invited, or pleaded, Lorin hadn't been to church since her last interview with her bishop, which had been required by the university.

Tanner smiled. "I'll leave you two to it, then." He backed up a few steps, then turned and strode away.

When he was out of sight, Lorin sighed, "I really would go to church if I thought that gorgeous hunk would ever look at me."

"Gorgeous hunk?" Still holding the anchor in one hand, Heather slipped the brown jewelry box into the pocket of her suit jacket, where it left a noticeable lump.

"Hey, just because he's like a brother to you doesn't mean I feel sisterly toward him. Why didn't you ever set us up?"

"Oh, Lorin." Heather bent and picked up her flight bag with the hand that didn't contain Tanner's anchor. "You've listened to what I've told you about him. He wants a woman with a testimony, and as much as I love you, I don't think you take religion seriously. Even if you two hit it off at first, you'd drive each other crazy in the end. I care about you and Tanner too much to see you both hurt."

Lorin stuck her lips together in a becoming pout. "Well, I guess I can't take offense at that. Still, religion isn't the only thing that binds people together, you know."

"That's true. But trust me, I know Tanner. We've been friends since before the eleventh grade."

"And never any sparks?"

"Nope." Heather began walking, wondering at the odd feeling the question brought to her heart.

"What's that in your hand?" Lorin pointed to Heather's clenched fist.

"Oh." Heather stopped. She opened her palm and showed Lorin the anchor.

She whistled. "You might think you're just friends, but do friends give presents like that? That cost a thousand bucks if it cost a dime."

Heather didn't dispute the issue. Lorin had worked in a jewelry store for most of her college years and wore at least five gold bracelets on her arm at any given time. The girl knew jewelry.

"I had no idea it cost that much," Heather said, staring at the anchor again, half in horror, half in amazement. "It's probably because he comes from a wealthy family."

"That's right. Then it must be okay."

Heather couldn't tell if Lorin's dry tone was derisive or admiring. They had shared many discussions about wealth, and neither girl had come to a conclusion. The way people spent their money was one more thing that gave Heather doubts about the Mormon culture. There was a lot of talk about sacrifice, but what was sacrifice? She contended that it wasn't giving up something you didn't really need, but something that was important—even vital—to your existence. Most people didn't seem to see it that way. They gave money, time, and effort, but nothing that really cut into their regular lives. Not that she should judge; she was likely guilty of the same thing.

The anchor and necklace weighed even heavier in Heather's hand. She had thought to put it on, but now she wished she hadn't accepted it. She didn't really need a reminder of Tanner or of the gospel. He would always be in her heart, and she had a testimony of the gospel—at least as much as she needed. Besides, what would she do with such an expensive gift? What if she lost it? She fished in her suit pocket where she had placed the small brown box, spilled the jewelry back inside, and closed it with a decisive snap before dropping it into her carry-on luggage.

Lorin eyed her strangely, then smirked as their baggage was searched and the necklace and charm were again brought to light. "It's fate," she whispered. "Besides, shouldn't you put it on? Someone might steal it."

Reluctantly, Heather slipped the chain over her head and tucked the anchor inside her blouse. At first its touch was icy, but gradually the gold heated up to her body temperature. *I'll wear it just until I get there*, she thought.

Later, as their plane soared above the airport, Heather caught a glimpse of the freeway. She wondered if one of the little miniature cars was Tanner's and if he was looking up at her plane.

૭૪

After little over an hour, the plane landed in Denver, where they had barely enough time to use the restroom, grab a soft drink, and change planes. Then after another flight of almost four hours, they arrived at the Logan airport in Boston. Heather stared around in excitement. The people swarming around them in the airport represented a wider cultural diversity than she was accustomed to in Utah. She heard snatches of different languages. *How many of these people live here and how many are only passing through?* she wondered. She had done her homework on the city, and had found that about half the population of Boston was made up of ethnic backgrounds other than Caucasian. She was excited to meet new people and learn about different cultures. Just being in the airport reminded her of Italy and the diversity of its larger cities.

They collected their luggage and exited the airport. "Look," Lorin said, practically knocking Heather aside as she pointed. A man was waiting, holding a white sign with their names written in bold, black letters. He was of average height and indeterminate age. His figure in the three-button gray suit was thin and trim, and every brown hair on his head seemed to be glued into place. The car he stood by wasn't exactly a limo, but in Heather's view the new-looking, silver Cadillac Deville was an excellent substitute.

"Isn't that Mr. Oldham's personal assistant?" Lorin asked. "Lester, or something, wasn't it?" They had met the man on their last trip, and since Mr. Oldham had only addressed him as Lester, neither was certain of his last name.

"I think so. Come on." Pushing a metal cart full of their luggage, they approached Lester, whose thin face took on a crisp smile that warmed his blue eyes. "Ms. Samis and Ms. Roberts?"

"Yes, that's us." Heather answered. "And you're, uh, Les—I mean Mr. Oldham's assistant, aren't you?"

He nodded, his smile reflecting amusement. "Yes. I'm Lester Paddock, but please call me Lester. We'll be seeing a lot of each other." As he spoke, he dropped his R's and used a broad A, making his name sound like "Lestah Pahddock."

Heather smiled. "In that case, I'm Heather." She stuck out her hand.

"And I'm Lorin."

As Heather shook Lester's hand, he grabbed only her fingers, squeezing lightly with a rather limp grip. *No missionary handshake here*, she thought.

"Please get into the cah, and I will store your luggage," Lester said. For a moment, Heather didn't understand, and then she remember that "cah" meant "car." This R-dropping was going to take some getting used to.

"We'll help." Heather grabbed the top case. They quickly filled up the trunk and much of the backseat. Heather gave Lorin a sheepish gaze as she squeezed into the back and left the front bucket seat to her. The whole car smelled of new leather, but the seats were soft and comfortable.

Heather stared with interest as they drove through Boston. Because of the two-hour time difference between Boston and Salt Lake City, it was already twilight, and she couldn't see much. But as she remembered from her past visit, Boston appeared to have a healthy evening life. The newer areas they drove through didn't look much different than any other large city, but as they moved through the older sections, she caught sight of beautiful sweeping trees and the colonial architecture that had so captured her imagination last December.

To think that this two hundred and fifty-year-old city had been the birthplace of the patriots Samuel Adams, Benjamin Franklin, and Paul Revere; the authors Louisa May Alcott and Edgar Allen Poe; the painters John Singleton Copley and Winslow Homer. Even Barbara Walters claimed the city as her own. Heather's heart sang. The city was a historical paradise; she could almost feel how well she would paint here.

At last they arrived at the Oldham Art Gallery. It was just as Heather remembered from their last visit. Like many of the surrounding buildings, the gallery was very old, though perfectly restored and in excellent condition. Subtle modernization had been added with taste to create a historic, yet welcoming atmosphere. The large front courtyard was illuminated by lanterns atop black iron posts, and the walkways were pieced stone and cement—a work of art itself.

"Don't get out," Lester instructed. "I only wanted to show you where the gallery is in relation to your living quarters. You'll have use of the studio in back of the gallery—I'm sure you'll find them ample. And there's a work schedule in your apartment for the times you'll be working in the gallery itself, but it can be adjusted if necessary."

"The gallery is within walking distance?" Heather wondered aloud. The last time they had been invited to Boston, they had actually stayed at a motel, four to a room.

"Yes." With an almost careless glance over his shoulder, Lester moved the car back into traffic. Heather paid close attention as he turned at the corner, drove two more blocks, then turned right. He stopped in front of a house that looked as historic as the museum.

"How beautiful," Heather murmured.

Lester smiled in appreciation. "The second floor's been completely renovated into an apartment for you two. Over there—that building that's a bit separate from the house—is what used to be the carriage house. It's also been redone into an apartment for the male artists. It's too dark to really appreciate now, but I think you will enjoy the house and grounds; you can't beat them for historic appeal."

Heather and Lorin each retrieved a piece of luggage and had only begun to follow Lester up the walk, when two men emerged from the carriage house. "Hi, ladies," called the one in front, taking quick strides to where the girls had paused under the street light. He was a lean, rather tall balding man who sported a trim reddish-brown moustache and goatee. "Lester, are these the other grantees?"

"Yes, they are. Ladies, this is McCahty, from L.A.," Lester said, handing the lead man a suitcase.

"He means *McCarty*, of course," said McCarty, giving them a smile.

Lester's own smile didn't reach his eyes. "Of course."

"Actually my name is Oliver McCarty," the redhead added. "But everyone calls me McCarty."

"Hi, McCarty," chimed Heather and Lorin together.

Lester motioned to the second man, who had caught up to McCarty. "And this is Keith Bybee from Kansas."

Keith was slightly shorter than average height and had a light brown ponytail reaching halfway down his back. "Hello," he said, ducking his head slightly and giving them a shy smile. "Nice to meet you."

"You, too." Heather immediately liked this soft-spoken man. Lorin nodded at him politely.

"And the brooding fellow over there is Nathan Thorne," McCarty said, lifting his chin in the direction of the carriage house. Heather saw that while the introductions had been going on, a third man had appeared and had almost reached them.

"Call me Nate." The third male grantee offered his hand to them, first to Lorin and then to Heather. The stunned look on Lorin's face made Heather want to laugh. With his thick blonde hair, square jaw, and muscular build, Nate was certainly model material. That he looked as though he had forgotten to comb his hair or shave that morning didn't seem to matter to Lorin.

"He's from Michigan," Lester added. To the men he said, "And these ladies, of course, are Heather Samis and Lorin Roberts from Utah. I trust you'll help with their luggage?" The men were willing.

After Lester opened the door to the house with his key, they stepped into a wide entryway, where a flight of mahogany stairs led to the second floor. As promised, this upper part of the house had been redesigned into a modest apartment for Heather and Lorin. The first room they entered was a small sitting room with a television and a DVD player. There was only one bedroom, but it was large enough not to be crowded. Both were delighted to see that the bathroom was equipped with the modern conveniences of a jetted tub and separate shower. But the room that most impressed Heather was the spacious studio she was to share with Lorin. Large easels graced the middle of the rough wood floor, and painting supplies had been set out on a long wooden table that was situated below five large windows spanning the entire back side of the room. A sliding glass door led to a wide balcony where they could paint outside if they wished. Heather had known there was a studio at the gallery—she'd seen it briefly the last time she was in Boston—but she had no idea they'd have a studio in their apartment as well.

McCarty heard Heather's swift intake of breath. "I know," he said. "It's perfect for painting. The carriage house has one, too." He rubbed his goatee.

"Not sure why they felt we needed two studios here, though. We could reach this one well enough by the balcony stairs, and it's large enough to share."

Heather thought she knew why: too often inspiration struck at odd night-time hours, and it would be appropriate—at least in her view—to have separate apartment studios for the men and the women. Though she hadn't expected such courtesy, she was grateful.

"It's so there aren't any distractions," Lorin said, glancing surreptitiously at Nate. "Easier to keep your mind on your work."

McCarty laughed. "Well, now that I've seen you two, I have to agree. We thought they'd be sending out some real—"

Heather scowled at him, not liking where he was going. The balding, red-headed McCarty was too loud and obnoxious for comfort.

"Anyway," McCarty amended quickly. "We're glad you're here."

Lester cleared his throat. "You'll notice that other than the small refrigerator, microwave, and sink in your sitting room, there are no cooking accommodations. This is because Mr. Oldham has hired a housekeeper who will not only supply you with meals in the main dining room downstairs, beginning tomorrow, but will also maintain your quarters. The kitchen below is her domain, but there is a washer and dryer available near the kitchen that you are all permitted to use—provided you prove to Mrs. Silva that you will keep the area neat and supply your own cleaning products. She has a room downstairs, so you are basically in her part of the house when you are using the laundry equipment or eating your meals."

"We'll be respectful," the ponytailed Keith said in his soft voice. "Thank you. And could you thank Mr. Oldham for us?"

"You can do that yourselves tomorrow." Lester walked toward the door of the girls' apartment. "He expects to see you all at the studio in the morning at nine. He'll introduce you to his wife and to Tomás Valencia, the artist who'll be working with you in the studio behind the gallery. After meeting them, you'll follow the gallery work schedule posted here." Lester paused by the TV, lifting a card. "There are also numbers to reach me or the gallery if you have any problems or questions. Please do not contact Mr. Oldham directly unless you are requested to do so. If you find yourself hungry this evening, there are ample foodstuffs and soders in the basket by the sink, or you may go out. There are taxi numbers by the phone. Good evening." With a stiff nod of his head, Lester let himself out.

"That guy is some character," McCarty said, mimicking Lester's accent. "Man, I swear these Bostonians don't speak English at all. Their A's are all funny, they drop their R's, and then add those R's to anything that ends with an A."

"Soder?" asked Lorin, investigating the gift basket by the sink. "He said 'foodstuffs and soders.' At least I think that's what he said. What's a soder?"

"Club soda," translated Keith.

"Ah." Lorin picked up a bottle and studied it briefly before replacing it.

"So, do you guys want to hit the town?" Nate asked. "We were just coming to the house to call a taxi when you arrived. We don't have a phone yet in the carriage house."

"Lucky for us you came when you did," Keith said. "The housekeeper doesn't seem to be here. We couldn't have got in without a key."

"So what about it, ladies?" McCarty asked. "You want to go?"

"Sure," Lorin said.

Heather glanced at her watch, undecided. "It's already after ten."

"Yeah, and that means the night life is just beginning," McCarty said, grinning. "Believe me—we all arrived yesterday and went out last night."

"There's a restaurant nearby," added Nate. "The Lobster Pot. It's casual. We won't stay long."

"Sound great. Just give us ten minutes to wash up." Lorin gave Nate a dazzling smile.

McCarty opened their door. "All right. We'll call the taxi from downstairs."

As the men left the room, Heather sighed and sank down on the couch. "I don't remember any of them from the last time we were here."

Lorin shrugged. "Probably overlooked them—or at least McCarty and Keith." Her eyes turned dreamy. "But not Nate. Him I would have noticed. But I think I heard someone say the Oldhams had several groups of artists out at different times."

"That explains it." Heather kicked off her shoes and stretched her toes. "I certainly would have remembered that loud-mouth McCarty."

"Oh, he's harmless." Lorin yawned. "I think I'll take a quick shower before we go. I know it's only eight to us, but after that flight, I need to wake up a bit. I won't get my hair wet, so it shouldn't take long."

"Go ahead."

Lorin was back in only a few minutes, wearing fresh jeans and a gauzy blouse that barely met the top of her jeans. "I take it jeans are in order, since that's what they were all wearing."

"Except for old loud-mouth," Heather said. "I think he was wearing khakis." Heather herself had changed into a jade green ribbed top and jeans.

Lorin took a few bills from her wallet and shoved them into the front pocket of her pants. "You know, when you think about it, McCarty is actually very distinguished-looking. I love goatees, and that mustache looks great on him. It makes up for the hairline." She grimaced. "But he does come on a little strong."

"Well, that's probably because we don't know him. Come on, they'll be waiting." Heather led the way to the door, tucking the keys Lester had left behind for them into her small purse. She didn't even think to offer them to Lorin; there were some things Lorin wasn't good with, and keys was one of them.

The men and the taxi were already waiting outside. When they arrived at The Lobster Pot, Heather saw the restaurant was indeed a casual place that also had a large bar running the length of the room. In one corner there was a large TV, and in another sat a pool table.

"There's an open table." McCarty led the way.

Heather looked around her at the old photographs of the restaurant in another era. The place was clean, and the delicious smells in the air made her stomach rumble.

The prices on the menu were reasonable, though they had a ten-minute wait before the waitress arrived to take their orders. McCarty, Keith, and Lorin asked for steak, while Nate went with the house lobster. "I'll take the halibut," Heather said. "And a soda."

"The halibut and a soder," echoed the waitress.

McCarty shook his head. "She doesn't mean soda, she wants a tonic."

Too late Heather remembered the club soda back at their apartment. "Yes, anything lemon-lime if you have it," she said with a smile. "Not Coke or Pepsi." The waitress nodded, wrote down the beers the men decided to order, and left the table.

"I tell you, they speak differently here," McCarty said.

"Well, if a tonic is what we call a soda, then what's this?" Lorin pointed to the tonic water on the menu.

Nate made a face. "I'm with McCarty on this one. Tonic water is carbonated, but really bitter—not anything like regular tonics. I guess it's a developed taste."

Heather laughed, amused at the differences between the west and Boston, much of which she had overlooked the last time they were here. Of course, during that visit every second of their time had been planned. They had gone to museums and galleries, as well as famous sites, and their food had been pre-ordered. They hadn't been left alone to discover much about day-to-day Boston life.

By the end of dinner, they were all talking like old friends. Even the shy Keith had opened up enough to tell them a story about a tornado that had nearly taken his parents' house in Kansas.

That was fun, Heather thought as they climbed in their taxi to return home.

Once at the house, she quickly unpacked the clothes in her suitcase that tended to wrinkle. Her eyes felt heavy, and she found it hard to believe it was only eleven back home. Leaving the rest of the unpacking for the next day, she dressed for bed. Only when her head hit the pillow did she realize she was still wearing Tanner's necklace and charm.

I'll put it away tomorrow, she promised herself sleepily.

Chapter Four

The next day Heather's body rebelled at the early morning awakening time—after all, it was barely six back home. Groaning, she pulled herself from bed and stumbled to the shower, making an effort to keep her eyes open. Lorin was even worse off, falling out of bed only after Heather turned off the water.

"We'd better hurry." Heather dragged a comb through her wet hair. "I bet it doesn't take the men long to dress, and I don't want to be trying to find the gallery on our first day alone. At least they know the way."

"We should have come a day early," Lorin complained sleepily.

"I couldn't, remember? Tanner was in Japan."

"And you just couldn't e-mail him a goodbye?"

"No." Heather pressed the switch to her blow dryer. Lorin didn't understand. Tanner was her friend, and as much as she had dreaded telling him of her move, she never could have left without saying goodbye.

She flipped her hair over her head, leaning down to dry the underside to obtain volume. Tanner's necklace banged her in the face. She had been too tired to remove it last night, but as soon as her hair was finished she'd take care of it. She didn't need the constant reminder. She tossed her hair up and over to settle again on her shoulders and down her back. Lorin wasn't anywhere to be seen.

As if reading her mind, Lorin burst through the bathroom door, dressed in a fitted black suit. She had obviously decided to let her shower of the night before suffice for the moment. "The guys are out there knocking," she told Heather. "They say breakfast is ready right now, and we'd better come if we want to eat. Apparently the woman normally serves it at eight-thirty sharp."

Heather shot a jet of hairspray over the top of her hair, fluffing it with her hand. "I'm ready," she said, and hurried from the room.

Downstairs in the dining room they were met by a short, rather stocky, olive-skinned woman with black hair. "Good morning," she said, her smile

45

transforming her dark features. "I so sorry I not here to meet you last night. My daughter has a sick baby, and I go to help."

"This is Mrs. Silva," McCarty said, reaching for a piece of toast from a stack in the center of the table. "She's a wonderful cook."

"Nice to meet you," murmured Heather, slipping into a chair.

Lorin was already scooping eggs onto her plate, barely grunting in acknowledgment.

"She's not a morning person," Heather confided to Mrs. Silva as she opened a napkin on her lap to protect her gray suit. "But it smells absolutely wonderful. Thank you."

Mrs. Silva beamed. "I make plenty. You girls very thin. Need more food."

"I think they look pretty good," volunteered Nate. Today he was clean-shaven and his blonde hair was neatly combed.

"Aw, you American men all alike," Mrs. Silva said, swatting him. "You like toothpicks. Girls like—what's it called?—Olivia Palito."

Mrs. Silva wasn't speaking Italian, but certainly a romance language, and Heather recognized the name. "Oh, you mean Olive Oyl. From Popeye."

"Exactly." Mrs. Silva nodded her head. "Eat, eat." She folded her arms to watch them.

Breakfast was actually Heather's favorite meal of the day. She eagerly downed the toast, eggs, and ham, served with fresh juice and chunks of various kinds of fruit. Afterwards, they thanked Mrs. Silva and began their walk to the gallery.

"A person could get used to meals like that, eh?" McCarty patted his stomach briefly before checking his moustache with the tips of his fingers, making sure no crumbs remained. The others heartily agreed, though Heather had noticed the soft-spoken Keith had eaten only fruit. She asked him about it and found out he was a vegetarian.

Today each of the five grantees had dressed in suits to greet Mr. Oldham. Even Keith—his long ponytail combed and tied neatly back—wore a tweed suit of multi-brown. Unlike the other men, he looked extremely uncomfortable. Heather wondered idly if it took him as long to dry his hair as it did for her. His was almost as long, if not as thick.

Turn, go down two streets, turn again. Heather was relieved to see she had remembered the way from the night before. Still, she was glad to have the men along; they were good company, whereas Lorin had trouble not growling at anyone who spoke to her. Even McCarty quickly learned to let her be.

The brisk morning breeze felt good on Heather's face, and she lifted it to the sky, breathing in the aroma of the summer flowers that were already flourishing in this obviously historic district. Other people were out and about, and each nodded, giving them a warm smile and an occasional second glance. Heather grinned at all of them.

Heather's heart quickened as they reached the gallery courtyard. This would be her first chance to see Mr. Oldham and thank him for this opportunity. She had really been impressed with Mr. Oldham during her last visit and was nervous about the meeting. He had obviously seen something in her that merited this grant; she only hoped she would prove worthy.

The meticulously groomed Lester was waiting inside the gallery foyer. Heather barely had time to glance around at the myriad of paintings and sculptures as he hurried them to a back portion of the gallery where Mr. Oldham waited, dressed in his customary white suit. He was just as Heather remembered: tall and big, and fairly stiff when moving around. He had very pronounced facial features—sunken eyes, large nose, sharp cheekbones, stubborn-looking jaw. His white hair lent him a dignified air that only accompanied the elderly who had led full and confident lives. In his right hand he held an ebony cane.

"Welcome, my young ones. Welcome." He smiled as he shook each of their hands. "I trust that your accommodations are adequate?"

"More than adequate," Heather said, as it was her turn to shake hands. His very blue eyes pierced into hers.

"Good, good." He turned from them to a mature woman behind him, who was apparently absorbed in a gold-framed painting hanging on the wall. Heather recognized her as Ms. Degroot, one of the ladies who had accompanied her group to many art galleries during their last visit. The old lady's gray hair swept gracefully into a loose bun at the back of her head, exposing her delicate neck. She wore a navy blue dress that was typical of her modern good tastes and contrasted nicely with her kind brown eyes. She was shorter than Mr. Oldham by a head, as slender as he was large.

"May I present my wife, Mrs. Amelia Oldham," Mr. Oldham continued. He noted their surprised expressions and added, "You know her as Ms.

Degroot from your last visit. I'm afraid that little deception was necessary to my designs. I needed someone on the inside to observe you."

"I wondered why we never got to meet Mrs. Oldham," Heather mused.

Mrs. Oldham laughed. "It was my idea." She grinned at her husband. "But my maiden name really is Degroot."

Heather's attention shifted to the painting Mrs. Oldham had been studying so intently. The piece was a beautiful rendition of a couple with a small baby boarding a swan-boat in the Lagoon located in Boston's Public Garden. The woman's demeanor was tired, yet as she looked at the infant in her arms, her face radiated excitement, strength, and love. The father's face was partially averted, but the artist had perfectly captured his care and solicitude for his family. Large expanses of grass and enormous willow trees edged the water, adding rich color. Heather would have been proud to have painted such a marvelous piece. Her eyes went to the artist's signature. Signed in bold flourish was the name: Amelia Degroot.

Heather gasped, her eyes going to Mrs. Oldham's face. "This is yours, isn't it?" she said reverently. At once the snatches of conversation around them ceased as the grantees listened for the reply.

"Yes, I've done a little painting in my time." Amelia Oldham smiled, the wrinkles around her large brown eyes becoming more noticeable.

Mr. Oldham chuckled. "My wife is a very talented and renowned artist in her own right. In fact, she is the inspiration for this program. Having been through it ourselves, we understand what sacrifices artists must make for their craft, and we would like to make it easier on at least a few."

"Do you paint, too, Mr. Oldham?" Lorin asked.

"Not a stroke." He smiled. "But I know talent when I see it, and you are all talented artists. What remains to be seen is if you possess the dedication and strength to pursue art as a career. Come." He motioned to them. "We will now go meet Tomás Valencia, who will be your mentor. I know you all became familiar with his works during your previous visit here, though not all of you were fortunate enough to meet him in person."

"He was having an episode," Mrs. Oldham added, but did not elaborate further.

"My wife will also be available to you here," Mr. Oldham continued, "though he will be your chief teacher. I hope you take the opportunity to learn from him. It will not be easy, but what he lacks in social skills, he more than makes up for in talent and dedication."

As he spoke, he led them through a set of double doors at the back of the room. Several smiling employees nodded at them as they passed. "Here is a changing room," Mr. Oldham said, motioning with his hand. "And out here, you have each been given a locker with a key. You may use it to store your painting clothes, if needed, as you will need to dress appropriately while working in the gallery." His eyes scanned them. "Yes, what you all have on now is appropriate, or something similar. You may, of course, return to your apartment to change or to paint. Basically, you have free rein over your time." He raised a finger. "Be warned: use it well. You have six months to show acceptable progress."

"Do we have certain times to study with Mr. Valencia?" McCarty asked, shifting his weight nervously. For the first time, Heather sensed an insecurity in the man.

A grimace touched Mr. Oldham's mouth like a shadow, vanishing almost as soon as it appeared. "Tomás keeps his own hours," he said. "He will likely tell you when to come, but on some days he may not be ready for you. He is, shall we say, controlled at times by his art. We must give him allowances. That is why Amelia—Mrs. Oldham—will also be available."

Heather was growing more and more curious about this Tomás Valencia. She had seen and admired his work many times, though it had impressed her no more than Mrs. Oldham's painting. His style was completely different from Mrs. Oldham's—more abstract than she generally preferred. Still, she was sure he had much to teach her.

"Come." Mr. Oldham was walking away again, stiffly, and leaning heavily on his cane. The grantees followed, exchanging uneasy glances.

They passed through a large storage and shipping area, and into a studio that did not appear to have been used often. Shelves of supplies were neatly organized and new-looking, and the cement floor unspotted by spilled paint. Heather couldn't see any canvasses, but the tall cupboards at the far side were large enough to conceal them. Floor to ceiling windows at the back let in natural light, and there were numerous overhead lights as well. Also at the back of the room, huge sheets had been attached to rollers on the ceiling. By pulling the sheets forward, they could serve as temporary walls if they should need a modicum of privacy.

"This is where you will work, except when you are with Tomás or at your apartments," Mr. Oldham said without slowing his walk. They followed him outside to a small courtyard containing a picnic table and several medium-sized trees. On the other side of the back courtyard was another building, smaller than the studio they had just left.

Lester was waiting at the door to this second studio. He nodded at Mr. Oldham, whose face seemed to relax slightly—at least to Heather; as far as she could tell, no one else noticed the exchange.

Inside, the studio was rather stark, with long, bare white walls. Unused canvasses stacked against the far side, while painted canvasses—most turned to the wall—lined up singly against the back of the room. Several large easels held canvasses covered by white sheets. One of these canvasses was taller than Heather herself. The cement floor was spattered with bits of color, and here and there were tubes of used paint. Despite the rather bleak and messy atmosphere, the light coming through the large windows was better here than in the larger studio, and Heather understood why Mr. Oldham's pet artist would choose this for his personal work space.

All this Heather took in at a glance, for it was Tomás Valencia himself who drew her main attention. The artist was sitting on a very high stool in front of a canvas whose front was facing away from them. He had very black hair cut to his chin, and his eyes gleamed green in his white face. He was dressed in black from head to toe; only the skin of his hands and face were exposed. By no means could he be called handsome, yet there was something incredibly arresting about the man.

With a slow, deliberate motion, he set down his brush on a nearby table, heavily stained with bits of paint from previous projects. "Hello." After three steps, he paused and bowed to them. His lithe body and graceful movements hinted at great strength or passion barely held in check, calling to Heather's mind a caged panther.

"These are your students," Mr. Oldham said without preamble. "I will leave you all together now. Work out what you may. Make them great, Tomás." With that, Mr. Oldham started for the door, the *click, click, click* of his ebony cane the only sound in the room.

Tomás's eyes followed their benefactor to the door. Then his gaze shifted to them, studying each in succession. When her turn came, Heather felt his eyes boring into her, seeming to examine parts of her inner self that she did not care to have examined by a stranger. She met his gaze steadily, with her chin high.

"You will pose for me," Tomás said to her with a flick of one finger. "You, too," he said to Lorin. His gaze shifted back to the men. "I do not usually paint men, but we'll see."

Heather was more than a little offended. She had come to paint, not to pose for a man who apparently had no respect for fellow artists. It wasn't like she was a beginner—she had her art degree to prove that.

"Easy," Lorin offered softly, but Heather had come too far, had given up too much to waste time.

"No," she said, clenching and unclenching her hands.

Tomás looked at her, as did the others. No one seemed to breathe.

"No?" There was a slight accent in the single word, more noticeable than in all the others he had spoken. Heather couldn't place it—almost Spanish, yet not quite.

"I will be glad to learn from you, Mr. Valencia," she said, keeping her voice polite but firm. "But I am an artist, not a model."

He stared at her; she met the stare without blinking. Sweat beaded on the back of her neck.

All at once he looked away. "Go," he said making a shooing motion with his hands as though they were dogs. "All of you go. I do not want to see you again today."

Heather turned to leave with the others, feeling her face flush with humiliation.

"Not you," Tomás commanded. "You, artist, will stay and learn art."

Heather swallowed hard, not knowing if she should feel triumph or fear. Why was he singling her out? Had she just ruined her chance to succeed here? *Me and my big mouth*, she thought. Yet she found it hard to be truly sorry. One of the advantages of coming from a large family, she had learned long ago that if she wanted something, she had to fight for it.

"And you, Redbeard," Tomás called after the departing group. "You come tomorrow. At six in the morning—sharp. Longhair, you come at noon tomorrow. The others come on Saturday. I don't care who comes first." The group silently nodded their assent and left the room.

Heather was alone with Tomás—or at least she thought so until Mrs. Oldham suddenly stepped into view from behind a large easel. "Here, dear," she said to Heather. "You will need this frock to cover your suit." Heather accepted the gray painting frock with gratitude.

Tomás shifted impatiently, but didn't say a word. Mrs. Oldham smiled at Heather. "Don't back down," she said in a whisper. Louder, she added, "I'll see you both later. Behave yourself now, Tomás." With a spryness that belied her age, she moved toward the door. Heather had the impression that she was laughing.

Tomás strode at once to his deserted canvas, while Heather removed her suit jacket and slipped the painting frock on over her white blouse and gray dress pants. It was long enough to cover all but the bottom foot of her pants; if she was careful, she wouldn't get any paint on them at all. Tomás cleared his throat impatiently. Heather went to his side.

"You want to paint," he said. "Then paint. Show me what you can do." Again she detected his slight accent, but more obvious was the challenge in his voice.

He handed her a brush and a palette from the small paint-spattered table. "Paint," he urged again, motioning to his own canvas.

Her gaze shifted from his face to the canvas that had been prepared with a slather of white paint, streaked with yellow. *So he had been planning to teach today*, she thought.

"Paint," he commanded.

Heather didn't know what to paint. So many things had already happened to her since arriving in Boston. She could paint the restaurant where they had gone last night, or the renovated house that now held her apartment, or even the historic streets she had walked on that morning. But those she would prefer to paint with a photograph.

"Photograph?" he asked before she realized she had mumbled something aloud. "Bah, photographs are a crutch! Real artists must learn to paint from their hearts. Use a sketch when you must get the proportions right, use photographs to compare color, but throw it all away to find the feeling."

The way he said the last word made Heather's heart ache. Feeling. She had felt so much leaving Tanner and her family. She almost groaned aloud with the guilt.

Guilt? Where did that come from? And what right did her family or Tanner have to make her feel guilty for following her dreams?

Dreams? something inside her scoffed. *Your supposed mentor wants to paint you, for crying out loud.*

Heather gripped the brush, dipped it in yellow and began to paint.

"That's right, paint," came Tomás's voice. "Paint what you feel."

Heather painted. She formed the outline, paused to mix in gold. Then a little black. With the ease of long habit she mixed paints and experimented with the shades. Several times, she painted over the object again with yellow.

"Feel," Tomás would say at these times. Once he grunted in disgust, took the brush from her and blotted out an entire portion of the painting before giving her a lecture on how an artist should find his true voice.

Practically growling at him, she seized the brush and began again.

Occasionally, Tomás would grab her hand, dip it in a mixture of paint, and guide it along the canvas.

"Yes," she said, seeing at once the depth he wanted her to achieve. Before, she had always trusted photographs to show her what to paint; now she had to trust her memory and feelings.

On she painted, stopping only once when a cloud temporarily blocked out the light from the sun. Then she found that the lack of light added to this particular painting, and she turned the easel away from the windows.

Tomás had now retreated to his stool with a sketchbook in hand. He didn't look at her.

Heather continued to paint. She was tempted to measure the object and verify its size, but she knew Tomás wouldn't allow that. So she painted only from memory.

An anchor, she thought with a slight snort. *I am not a child. I know where I'm from and where I want to go.*

Of course, the problem was she didn't know how to get there.

That made her furious. Why was Tanner always right? What did he have that she didn't? After a while, the answer came: *He's a man. And that's the difference. He will never know what it is to give up his career to have eleven children.*

Heather changed brushes, slathering the new one with cobalt blue, dotted with black. With bold strokes driven by her frustration, she swept the brush across the entire canvas. Not a thick layer, but just enough. Then came the eyes. They seemed to appear without her permission. White, green, a little brown—swirl it. Add the black, more white. Black again. Then the larger fan brush filled with the blue. There was more to be done—shadows there, a gleam here. White slithered with gold. *Yes, that's it.*

Heather stood back from her painting, chest rising and falling rapidly as though she had been running instead of standing for hours in the same position. She couldn't believe it was finished. The painting might not be the best she'd ever done, but it was certainly the fastest.

"See?" Tomás came up from behind her. "This is painting. This is *feeling.*"

Heather blinked, suddenly exhausted. "What time is it?" By the long shadows in the courtyard and the growling in her belly, it must be very late.

Tomás shrugged. "I do not keep a watch in here. Watches have no place in a studio."

Heather wasn't sure what to make of that. If an artist didn't keep time, how could she function in the world?

Tomás handed her his sketchbook. She noticed that her hands were spotted and smeared with paint, while his had barely a trace of charcoal. The book held sketches of her as she was painting. But not quite her, really. The hair seemed messier, the frock more fitting, and the eyes reflected unrealized dreams. She swallowed hard. "I see you got what you wanted."

To her surprise, he shook his head. "I could not help but to draw you. The feeling, it is in your hand. You are right: you are not a model, you are an artist." He turned away. "But only if I can make you forget half of what you learned in school."

She laughed at that, though where she found the energy, she didn't know. "I'd better go," she said.

He didn't reply, but began sketching something on his pad.

Okay, she thought. *I guess I'm dismissed.*

Carefully, she picked up her jacket and her painting and started for the door. Every muscle in her body screamed in protest. She paused to stretch her neck, knowing she was going to pay dearly for her hours of happy oblivion.

Chapter Five

When she entered the gallery studio, Lorin and Mrs. Oldham looked up from a bench situated next to the orderly shelves. None of the men were around, but the four easels spread out in the studio suggested the others had also been painting today.

"Thank heaven," Lorin said, standing. "I was beginning to worry. Another few minutes and we were going in after you."

"Oh, Tomás may be a little strange, but Heather was perfectly safe." Mrs. Oldham arose more slowly than Lorin had.

Heather smiled wryly, lowering her painting to rest on the ground. She set her suit jacket on a nearby stool. "What a day! I don't think I've ever been so tired after a day of painting. I feel like I've just run the Boston Marathon. And I'm so hungry, I could eat enough for ten."

"Well, it's nearly eight," Lorin said. "The gallery is closed, and the others already went back for dinner—served precisely at eight, according to McCarty. They promised to ask Mrs. Silva to save us something."

"The gallery . . ." Heather's mouth opened in dismay. She had been scheduled from ten to noon. "My two-hour shift. I didn't—"

"Oh, don't worry about that." Mrs. Oldham waved her hand. "Everyone here knows how Tomás is. You're excused when you're with him. Someone else will fill in."

"Actually, Keith took your shift," Lorin said. "He hoped you'd do the same for him tomorrow since he'll likely be with Tomás during his time."

Heather sighed with relief. "Oh, of course I will."

"See? It's all taken care of." Mrs. Oldham smoothed the skirt of her navy dress.

"I may be too tired to eat once I get to the house," Heather said with a small groan. Her neck and the back of her legs were aching. "I might just throw myself on that bed and go to sleep."

Mrs. Oldham appeared amused. "So I take it you're happy with your apartment?"

"Oh, yes," Lorin answered. "Especially the studio."

"We were glad to have one separate from the men," Heather explained.

"I thought you would be pleased." Mrs. Oldham turned to the shelves and picked up a bottle of paint remover. "That was my idea. The men might not care what they're wearing or who's watching when they paint, but I always did."

"Too right," Lorin said. "Thank you so much."

Heather voiced her thanks, too, but Mrs. Oldham's comment reminded Heather of something that had been bothering her. "The men," she began, "are all from different states. I've been thinking it's just a little strange for us—well, you know, we're both from Utah *and* the same university."

Mrs. Oldham turned to face them, the bottle of liquid still in her hand. "That, too, was my idea. Yes, there were many qualified young women we could have chosen, but I was impressed with the friendship between you two. We women have to give up a lot in life to pursue our dreams, and I thought keeping you together would be a good thing. Especially since you have to share a bedroom."

"But, but . . ." Heather couldn't finish. The idea that she and Lorin had won their grants only on the merits of their friendship made her feel discouraged.

"Oh, don't worry, I wouldn't have chosen you if I hadn't been impressed with your individual abilities." Mrs. Oldham reached for a folded rag on the shelf. "That's why we had you bring portfolios. And I believe either of you could have gotten along well enough with others, but I liked the two of you. And I felt that—I don't know. There was just something about you."

Heather wondered what that something was. Could it be the gospel? She had always heard that the light of Christ shone in the features of those who believed, but a few others from her class had also been believers—some certainly much more so than Lorin.

"Here." Mrs. Oldham offered her the bottle and the cloth. "You might want to get that paint off your hands."

"If we can get her to let go of that painting long enough," added Lorin. "What it is you painted anyway? Can we see it?"

Heather hadn't realized she was gripping the edges of the painting so tightly, or that she would feel as reluctant as she did to show anyone her work.

"You don't have to, dear." Mrs. Oldham still held out the paint remover and cloth. "But you will have to set it up to dry. The canvas cupboards over there should have enough space, if you don't want anyone to see it yet."

"Oh, I don't mind," Heather lied, unable to find a valid reason not to show them the painting. She stepped back, securing the canvas with only one hand. "Come and look, if you'd like." With her free fingers, she twisted a lock of her hair.

"Wow." Lorin blinked. "It's really good. But not at all like your usual style."

"It is rather abstract," Heather agreed. She stared at the painting of the anchor, now seeing a million places where she could touch up and improve. Her fingers yearned to do so right now, but the rest of her aching body rebelled.

"Looks like you've thrown it into a dirty stream," Lorin said. "I like that big rock and the way the chain is hooked over it. And the anchor itself almost seems to be, not floating, but knocked about by the flow of the water."

"It is very good." Mrs. Oldham studied the painting closely. "I like the feeling."

Lorin frowned. "Except, well, it's kind of depressing. Those bodiless eyes, floating there above the anchor. Like a drowning victim in a lake or something. Not that depressing isn't good—it certainly sells well nowadays."

Heather wasn't offended; she and Lorin were accustomed to critiquing each other's work.

Mrs. Oldham tucked the cloth she still carried under her arm and brought her hand to her chin. "I don't see it like that at all. The anchor is holding the eyes in place, don't you see? So they won't float away. The emotion behind it—not despair—but one of holding, of searching." She turned to Heather. "Isn't that right?"

Heather shrugged. "I don't really know."

Mrs. Oldham smiled. "That's the very best kind of painting—the one we learn about after we've finished."

"It's not done," Heather ventured.

"Good. That will give you time to learn what it's about." With that, Mrs. Oldham put the paint remover and the cloth in Heather's free hand and then relieved her of the painting. "I'll just put this on an easel over here while you clean up."

Heather wasn't unhappy to see her take the painting; it disturbed her as much as it pleased her. Nor did she worry about Mrs. Oldham smearing it; as an artist herself, she would be careful.

"There's a sink over here." Lorin led the way, and Heather followed, grateful to alleviate her suddenly itching skin from its encasing of paint flecks.

Mrs. Oldham returned as Heather was removing her painting frock. "Well, you girls should be getting along home. It'll be dark soon. Better yet, let me give you a lift. I'm on my way home as well. Usually, Lester drives me, but he left earlier with my husband. They will wonder what took me so long." She smiled. "Of course, my husband is accustomed to my forgetting the time."

Heather chuckled. "Yes, you're an artist after all."

"Tell that to a crying baby," Mrs. Oldham said as she led the way through the gallery. "Or a husband waiting for dinner."

"How many children do you have?" Heather wanted to know.

Mrs. Oldham waited until the night watchman let them out of the front gallery door. "I have four children. Of course, they're all grown with families of their own now, but there was a time it seemed I could barely get in a brush stroke between diaper changes."

"Sounds like my mom," Heather said so softly that neither of the other women heard.

"But you've done really well," Lorin was saying. "You have six paintings in this gallery alone, and those price tags aren't cheap. One of the salesmen told me that you've become quite a big name here in New England."

"Don't forget about Switzerland," Mrs. Oldham said with a smile. "I'm really big there."

Lorin slid into the front seat. "No way."

"Yes. It's very strange, but true. For some reason they really like my work there." The words were spoken with simplicity, not with the spirit of bragging. Heather realized that here was a woman who was completely comfortable with who she was and where she was going.

But how had she done it? Why hadn't her children brought a halt to her dreams as it had her mother's? Yes, there was a large difference between having four and ten—no, almost eleven—children. But given the opportunity, could her mother have been so successful?

Heather didn't have an answer.

℞

Not only had the men been able to convince Mrs. Silva to set aside the girls' dinner, but she had also kept it warm on the stove. "We're just about finished," McCarty said as they sat down, "but we saved you some wine."

"No, thanks," Heather said. She was glad to see that Lorin didn't accept either, for all she claimed not to believe in the Word of Wisdom.

Mrs. Silva brought in huge bowls of stew and a plate filled with warm biscuits, all the while clucking at the injustice the girls had endured to be kept so long at the gallery. Heather tried to reassure the woman, but she just shook her head and muttered, "Wicked, it's wicked."

"Don't worry," McCarty whispered, when Mrs. Silva finally disappeared from the dining room with an armload of the men's used dishes. "Wicked seems to be sort of a saying here. Must have heard it a hundred times in the gallery today. 'What a wicked painting. That's a wicked price, isn't it?' Or my personal favorite: 'That artist certainly has a wicked way with the brush.' Too amusing, these Bostonians. I think I'm going to like it here."

Keith stood up from the table. "Glad you made it back. If you don't mind, I think I'll go to the carriage house now. I have some drawings I want to work on."

"You don't want to go to the bah tonight?" asked McCarty.

"The bah—oh, you mean the bar." Keith shook his head. "No. I think I want to get some ideas of what I want to paint. I don't like the one I started today at the gallery."

Heather swallowed a bite of potato that contained more flavor that any potato she had ever eaten. Mrs. Silva was certainly a good cook. "Don't worry, you'll think of something tomorrow with Tomás, that's for sure. He makes you think."

"Oh?" Nate asked. Everyone at the table turned toward her, waiting expectantly. Keith paused by the door.

Heather realized they were curious about her day, but had been too polite to ask. "Well," she began. "It was—"

Mrs. Silva took that moment to reappear. This time she was carrying cake topped with chocolate. "No one go anywhere," she said to Keith. "Sit down. I make Boston cream pie for you."

"Looks like a cake," McCarty commented.

"I know, I know. I say same thing to my daughter when we come here from Portugal twenty years ago. I say, 'This is no pie, it is cake.' She say, 'It is their country, so they call it what they want.' Smart girl for only six years old."

Heather laughed as she spooned up more of her stew. Pie or cake, the dessert looked wonderful.

"It is my own special recipe because I not like some I have tasted," Mrs. Silva added. "Everyone say my cake is lightest they ever eat, my filling the best. Maybe you will agree." She cut them each a large slab of the two-layer sponge cake divided with a layer of custard filling. Heather bit into it with relish.

"I've died and gone to heaven," McCarty said with a sigh.

Everyone murmured agreement.

Nate held up his plate. "Can I have another piece?" Mrs. Silva beamed with pleasure.

"So tell us about Tomás," Keith urged a short time later as Heather finished her last bite of pie. "If you don't mind."

"There's nothing really to tell." Heather set down her fork. "The guy is an arrogant, overbearing jerk, but he's also very talented. He kept bugging me and forcing me to search for my feelings. I don't usually paint that way. I mean, I'd rather see a photograph—even better than a live model. But it was good, too."

"Any advice for us?" Keith asked.

"Only not to give in to him. We have to remember that we're artists—good ones. We may be at a different stage than he is, but we all have talent."

Keith was nodding, as were McCarty and Lorin, but Nate grimaced. "I hope you're right," he said. "Either way we only have six months to prove it. McCarty, I don't think I'll be going out tonight, either. I have work to do."

"Yeah," McCarty agreed. "Besides, I have to be at the gallery at six. Can you believe it?"

"It's one of the best times to paint," Heather offered.

"Yeah, but I'm from L.A. To me it'll be three in the morning!"

Lorin laughed. "All the better to turn in early, I'd say."

Calling their thanks to Mrs. Silva, the men took Lorin's advice and left, taking with them the unfinished bottle of wine. Heather gulped the rest of her water and automatically began clearing the table. Mrs. Silva came in from the kitchen. "Oh, no. This my job. I get money to do this. You are very tired. Need to go to bed."

Heather didn't wait to be asked again. Her body was so weary and achy that she doubted she would ever be the same again. Inside their room, she collapsed on her bed without removing her suit.

"Oh, no," Lorin said, sounding oddly like Mrs. Silva. "You need a hot bath first or your muscles are going to feel even worse tomorrow."

"Leave me alone," muttered Heather.

"And have that gorgeous hunk, Tanner, kill me at your funeral? I don't think so. You'd do the same for me."

Heather heard the water running, and in what seemed like less than a second Lorin was back, dragging her to the bathtub. "Get in," Lorin ordered. "I'll hang up your clothes—actually they'll probably need dry-cleaning after today."

Heather removed Tanner's necklace, setting it carefully on the edge of the porcelain sink across from the tub. Then she gingerly stuck her foot in the water—and jerked it back. "Ow." But she eased her sore body in and began to soak. Gradually, the ache in her muscles abated, chased away by the hot water. The bath had been a wonderful idea. Sighing, she reached for her lilac shampoo and conditioner.

When her bath was complete, she climbed from the tub and wrapped her white robe around her. In front of the mirror, she splashed her face with cold water. As she did so, the gold anchor fell into the water, the chain hooked around the bar of hand soap on the edge of the sink. In the water the anchor resembled her painting more than ever. Heather studied it, noting the way the water bent the light hitting the anchor. She'd have to check her painting tomorrow to make sure she had it right.

She picked up the anchor, rubbing it between her fingers. By depicting Tanner's gift cast away in a river, had she been acting out her desire to get rid of it? Had she been trying to distance herself from the values and memories it represented? Or did her portrayal mean she felt she needed an anchor as much as someone cast afloat in a dangerous current? Heather simply didn't know enough about her feelings or her new situation to decide.

Whatever the meaning, maybe she'd better wear the anchor until she found out for sure.

"Thanks, Tanner," she whispered as she slipped the chain over her head. "I think."

𝛀

The next day Heather's muscles were sore, but she felt much better than the previous night. Joyfully, she threw herself into her work. In between painting and working at the gallery, she had no time to think of home or Tanner.

After touching up her first painting, she decided to find a stream and take photographs of the anchor in the water. During lunch hour, Bridget, one of the gallery employees, took her to her mother's house where a small stream meandered through the back yard. Heather found a large, black stone that she could wrap the chain around. Following Heather's directions, Bridget squatted near the bank upstream and made the water murky by running a hand through the mud. Heather snapped pictures avidly. Then she hurried to find some place to develop them before she had to be back at the gallery to fill in for Keith.

When the two-hour shift ended at four o'clock, she picked up her developed photographs and used them to add detail to her painting. She still was not satisfied, so she began on a new canvas, copying one of her photographs. She worked on it until dinner, and then again in the studio at the apartment. Lorin was also there, working silently on one of her own paintings.

On Saturday after Heather's ten-to-twelve shift at the gallery, she went home and spent the rest of the day painting. Since Lorin had a session with Tomás, she was alone. She didn't mind; in fact, she was grateful for the solitude. Time had no meaning when she was painting, and Heather was content.

However, the second painting didn't turn out as expected. Though perfect in every detail, it lacked the emotion of the first. At midnight on Saturday, she threw her brush in a jar of paint thinner and decided to let it go until Monday. There had to be some way to incorporate the feeling of the first, with the details of the second. Perhaps a day's rest would give her enough distance to identify the problem.

By one o'clock in the morning, Lorin had still not returned. She had gone to paint with Tomás at two, and Heather had not seen her since. Heather kept listening for her, but the house was utterly silent. Mrs. Silva had gone to spend Saturday evening and Sunday with her daughter and grandchild, as she had informed them was her custom, leaving the grantees ample leftovers to heat in their own apartments.

Feeling alone, an emotion Heather had not often experienced in a family with so many children, she began to pace from one end of the apartment to the other. Finally, she ended up on the balcony where she could see a myriad of lights and the taller buildings of the more modern part of the city. There was also a light on in the carriage house, but it came from the men's studio and Heather was loath to interrupt anyone who might be painting in the middle of the night. Besides, she hardly knew them.

At last she heard the sound of a bell. *That's right, I have the keys.* Heather made a mental note to make a few copies for Lorin the next week. That way even if Lorin lost one, she could give her another. Heather flew downstairs to the door of the house, nearly tripping over her feet in her hurry.

Lorin grinned at her from the other side of the door. "Oh, good. I was afraid you were asleep." Behind her, the dark car that had obviously dropped her off, sped into the night. "That was Tomás," Lorin said with a sigh. "Boy, is he something. I think I'm in love."

"You've got to be kidding!" Heather grabbed her arm and helped her inside.

"I posed for him today. That's what took me so long. He said that painting people is how he comes to know them best. That's why he wanted to do it—so he'll know how to teach us better." She giggled. "But I was strong like you said to be. I made him pose for me first. Have you ever noticed his eyes? I don't think I've ever seen any so green."

Heather locked the door. "Come on, let's get you into a hot bath."

"I *am* tired. Very tired." Lorin leaned on her heavily as they went up the stairs. Heather couldn't be sure, but she thought she smelled alcohol on her friend's breath.

Heather ran Lorin's bath water, as her friend had done for her days earlier. Though she felt exhausted herself, she waited in the sitting room for Lorin to finish.

"At least I got something to eat," Lorin said as she came from the bathroom, wrapped in her blue robe. "Tomás made me a dish that his mom used to make—kind of like spaghetti, but without the tomato sauce like we use here."

"So you're not hungry? I saved you dinner, just in case."

"Nope. Couldn't eat a thing." Lorin sank to the couch. "You know, Tomás has a very interesting heritage."

"Oh?" The artist's personal background was not something Heather had discussed with Tomás.

"Tomás's father is from Italy." Lorin stretched out on the couch, while Heather settled on the carpet next to her. "He was part Yugoslavian, part Italian. His mother is from Bolivia, but is also part German. They met in America when they were both here to study. They married, but before they finished school, his father died of lung cancer. Apparently, the father's parents had been heavy smokers, and he had taken in all that second-hand smoke over the years, plus he started smoking himself as a teen. About that time, his mother's visa expired and she returned to Bolivia, where her German mother still lived. Tomás grew up there, painting with anything he could get his hands on. He was eventually befriended by an American missionary couple—Baptists, I think—and when he was older, they sent him to America to college. He met the Oldhams at an art exhibit and has been here ever since."

"That explains his odd accent. I couldn't place it."

"Well, he grew up speaking a mixture of German and Spanish, and he also spoke some Italian when he was very young. Problem is, his father's Italian was heavily accented with whatever it is they speak in Yugoslavia. All that affects his English."

"Does he speak any Italian now?" If he did, Heather would practice with him.

"Nope. Says he understands a lot of it. I told him you'd gone there on a mission." Lorin gave a dreamy sigh. "He obviously got that dark hair from both his parents, but his lighter skin and those green eyes—maybe they're from his German grandmother."

"Could be." Heather felt a little sad at Tomás's rather confusing background. Who would she be if she hadn't been raised by her parents and surrounded by siblings?

"Whatever, it's a great combination." Lorin shut her eyes. "I wonder if he's seeing anyone?"

"It might not be a good idea to get involved with him," Heather cautioned. "Everything we've heard indicates that he's a little different."

"He's just dedicated, that's all. And even artists need to be loved. But don't worry. After all, I'm here to work."

Heather climbed wearily to her feet. "Well, it's definitely past my bedtime."

"I'm so glad it's Sunday tomorrow," Lorin muttered without moving or opening her eyes. "I'm going to sleep all morning. And maybe paint a little in the afternoon."

Heather froze. She hadn't even considered painting on Sunday. Painting was her chosen profession, and except for doodles in her church notebook, working on Sunday had never been an option. Her parents would have been shocked. Of course, it wasn't likely the other grantees shared her compulsion to keep the Sabbath holy. Would that put her at a disadvantage in gaining a continuance for her grant?

And even if she chose not to paint, would it matter if she didn't go to church just one day? She was tired—exhausted even. She hadn't had so much as a minute these past few days to look up the address of the nearest chapel in the phonebook.

"Maybe I won't go to church tomorrow, either," she said, expecting Lorin's approval. "There's plenty of time to find where it is next week."

Lorin's right eye came open. "I never thought I see the day when *you* missed church." She shut her eye again and grinned. "What would your parents say? Or your boyfriend, Tanner?"

"He's not my boyfriend, just a friend. And I'm not a child. And you know as well as I do that attending church doesn't automatically make you a good person, does it? We've talked about that before. Remember, it's not what you're wearing or what calling you have, it's what's in your heart that counts."

"I also remember you always telling me that it's a commandment to go. Remember that?"

"Of course. But I'm not saying I'll never go again. I'm just tired *this* time."

Lorin shrugged. "Look, don't get mad at me. I don't care what you decide. I know exactly how you feel. I haven't been to church more than a couple times since I left home. Believe me, it gets easier not to go."

Heather frowned. She was *not* like Lorin. Though she had questions and even doubts about certain aspect of what she viewed as Mormon culture, she believed in the Church and the gospel. She had even told Tanner so.

And he had bought her the anchor.

Did that mean he hadn't believed her?

"Speaking of church," Heather said, "you told Tanner you'd go with me the first time. Do you remember that?"

She was answered by a loud snore from the couch.

Heather retrieved the phone book from the shelf underneath the coffee table and easily found the address of the nearest chapel. She wasn't sure what time it would start, but probably at nine. Likely, there was a later meeting as well.

The clock on the wall now read almost two in the morning. If she hurried to bed, she might get a few hours of sleep before she had to find her way downtown.

CR

It seemed but a minute before the jangling sound of her alarm clock dragged her from a sound sleep. She moaned and hit the off button.

One missed day won't matter at all.

She was drifting off again when she had the sensation of something pulling at her neck. Groaning, she rolled over, but the strangling worsened. *What's going on?* She clawed at her throat and found Tanner's chain digging into her flesh. The heavy anchor had gotten caught behind her neck and was pulling the chain tight.

Sighing, she freed the anchor. "Stupid thing's so darn heavy," she muttered. Lying back on the pillow, she shut her eyes, but this time sleep eluded her. With a long sigh, she sat up and swung her feet to the floor. "If you were here right now, Tanner, you'd be a dead man."

Stumbling into the small sitting room, she found Lorin asleep on the couch. She walked over and shook her shoulder. "Time to wake up," she called. "No way am I going to find this place alone. You promised. And a promise is a promise."

"Go away," Lorin growled.

"Nope." With an ungentle shove, she rolled Lorin off the couch.

"Ow!" Lorin rubbed her thigh. "All right, all right. I'll get up. But you're going to regret this. Once they know you're here, you'll never be able to sleep in on Sunday again."

Chapter Six

*T*he knock on the door took Tanner's attention away from his small, battery-operated television set—not that he was really watching the program in the first place. The reality show couldn't hold his attention. In fact, it was too hot in his condo for *anything*. He had been seriously considering going back to the office to work, and maybe even to sleep.

He took his time walking to the door. The knock sounded again, more impatiently. He swung the door open without checking the peephole, and his cousin Savannah Hergarter pushed her way inside.

"It's about time. Do you know how long I've been out there waiting?" She flipped her long white-blonde hair back to emphasize her annoyance. "I kept ringing and ringing, and you didn't come. But I knew you were in here. I could hear your TV."

"The electricity's out," he explained, "so I guess the doorbell here must use electricity because it didn't ring."

She gave a disgusted sigh and stomped toward his couch. "Yeah, right, try another excuse. I said that I heard your TV."

"It's battery-operated—you know, the one I always take camping when there's a game I want to see."

She glared at him, but he pointed to the adjoining kitchen, where the TV still blared. She followed his motion, then looked toward his entertainment center where his large-screen TV was blank.

"Honestly, Savvy," he said, using her nickname, "the electricity's out. That's why it's so hot in here. The air conditioning isn't working either."

"Oh." Her frown was gone in an instant. "For a moment I thought you were avoiding me."

"Not my favorite cousin." He gave her a mocking smile and sat down on the other side of the couch.

"And don't you forget it." She kicked off her shoes and turned in his direction, pulling one foot up under her. She smiled then, making her face radiant. Not for the first time, Tanner noticed that his young cousin was exceptionally pretty. She had very blue eyes the color of the sky on a bright summer day, and her skin was smooth and unblemished. Her short stature made her prone to ample curves that only added to her attractiveness. Soon to begin her first year in college, he suspected she would be chased by a variety of college men looking for a spouse. He was happy for her, but the knowledge made his own loneliness stand out rather blatantly.

"So, what's with the electricity?"

"Construction workers cut the line—they're building more condos next door where those old houses used to be. They're fixing it, but I don't know how long they'll be."

"So why don't you just go to your parents'? It's not like they don't have room."

"Too lazy, I suppose." He placed his stockinged feet on the coffee table. "So, why're you here? You're not in school, so you can't need help with homework."

"Hey, do I have to have a reason to visit?"

"No, but usually you do."

Savvy frowned. "Okay, you win. I'm here because I'm worried about you. And Aunt Mickelle is worried about you, too. In fact, only yesterday she asked me to talk with you—which I was planning to do anyway. Don't think I haven't noticed that you've done nothing but mope around for the past . . . I don't know, month maybe. Everyone at work's noticed it."

Tanner couldn't dispute her words. She worked at Hospital's Choice like he did, since her father was his father's partner in the business, and she had access to company gossip.

"So what's wrong?" she pressed.

He sighed and shrugged.

"Look, I know just the thing." She leaned toward him, and her long hair fell forward over her shoulders. "I have a friend, and I'll set you up."

"Is she even old enough?" he quipped.

"Of course. She's starting her second year in college. I know you'll like her." Savvy sat back abruptly. "Actually, I'm not sure of that, but she's a lot of fun. She'll make you laugh. Of course, you'll have to send those pants to the dry cleaners, and probably the jacket as well, if it looks as bad. She's got kind of a thing about rumpled suits."

Tanner smiled at her honesty. He waited for her to say more, but she was apparently through. Rising, he went across the room and up the two carpeted steps to the kitchen counter where he had been pouring himself a ready-made salad from a bag. The images on the TV distracted him for a minute, and he stared at them.

Savvy followed him. With an impatient flip, she silenced the TV. "Tanner," she urged, "talk to me."

He met her eyes. "I don't want to go out with your friend, Savvy. In fact, I'm sick of dating—especially people who have a thing with rumpled suits. I just want to go on with my life." He drew in a large breath and held it. "I probably wouldn't admit it to anyone except you, but the truth is I want to get married. I want to have a family." *At one time I would have told Heather, too*, he thought with more than a little bitterness.

"Married?" Savvy blinked once, then again. "Well, I'm not sure our parents will be expecting this, but I guess since you and I are not really blood cousins, me being related to your stepmother and all, but if you really think it's the right thing to do, then I guess we can get married." She looked at him with a sweet, innocent smile on her face. He stared back, first surprised and then confused. Her smiled widened.

He shook his head as laughter bubbled out. Savvy joined him. "You should have seen your face," she said, as she clung to the counter. "Oh, my. It was priceless!" She giggled harder, losing her grip on the counter and sinking to the floor. She scooted to perch on the top step leading down to his sitting room. Tanner sat beside her, still laughing. He couldn't remember the last time he had laughed so hard.

After some minutes they began to calm down. "I really wish it could be that simple," Tanner said. "You and me getting married, I mean."

"Well, if something had been going to happen between us, it would have happened a long time ago," Savvy said. "Besides, you're like five years older than I am—ancient."

"I know. And you see me as a brother."

"No more than you see me as a sister."

Tanner sighed. "You're right. But it's always possible. Sometimes you don't see things that are right before your nose—or at least not until it's too late."

Savvy cocked her head, considering him silently. He began to feel uncomfortable and turned away.

"Okay, who is she?"

Tanner whipped his face toward her. "What?"

"Call me stupid that it took me this long, but I finally figured it out. It's obvious. You're moping about, saying incomprehensible things like"—her voice lowered to mimic his own—" 'Sometimes you don't see things that are right before your nose.' " Her voice returned to normal. "And that all adds up to one thing: you, my dear cousin, are in love. So, who is she?" Savvy waited expectantly.

"Look, I don't know what you're talking about."

Savvy held up her hand. "No, let me guess. You've been like this a whole month or more. It's someone who's been right under your nose—and it's not me, because I'm not *that* blind. And it can't be any of the secretaries at work, although maybe that new woman in sales . . . Hmm. But then you said something about it being 'too late' and it couldn't be too late with her if she's still around and single. That means maybe it's someone who's left the company. Or maybe someone in this complex who's moved away. But you haven't mentioned anyone like that." Abruptly, her blue eyes grew very wide. "Oh, I really *have* been blind. It's Heather!" Her face flushed with triumph. "I should have seen it all along!"

"*You* should have seen it? What about *me*?" Tanner placed his elbows on his knees and let his head sink into his hands.

"Oh, so you're not denying it."

"Why should I? It's true. And you're not going to tell anyone."

"Does she know?"

He shook his head miserably. "I was going to tell her, but then she sprang that Boston thing on me. I had set up a special dinner and everything in the conference room at work."

"In the conference room?" Savvy wrinkled her nose. "You couldn't think of anywhere more romantic to confess your undying love?"

He lifted his head from his hands. "Not where we wouldn't be interrupted. And what's wrong with the conference room, anyway? It was decorated. It looked great."

"But you didn't tell her."

"No." Tanner sighed. "She thinks I had the dinner to celebrate her grant. I didn't want to lie to her, but I didn't know how to tell her after that. She wanted to leave so badly—I could tell."

"She wanted to leave Utah? Or the conference room? Or you?"

"Not me in particular. But certainly the culture, the Mormons. I think she's having a crisis in faith, and I couldn't even help her with that."

Savvy put a hand on his knee, which was bouncing up and down slightly but rapidly with his tension. "I'm sorry, Tanner. But Heather's a good girl from a good family. She'll be okay—you have to believe that."

"I don't know. I guess I can understand why she's having doubts. She talked about how the Church keeps us so busy that we don't have time to excel in our careers. I don't see that much with the men—although I suppose that may be more true with artistic types—but she's right about the women. They give up a lot of potential to raise families."

"I don't know that it's giving up so much, but rather it's a trade," Savvy said. "At least according to my mom. But, yes, it's something I've thought a lot about. I want a family—I love what my parents have—yet at the same time, I'm afraid of losing *me*. My dreams, my goals."

"So what are you going to do?" Maybe if Tanner could understand his cousin, he could begin to fathom Heather.

"Finish my education, get married, have a family. Not necessarily in that order. So far, I plan to keep working after I marry, if I feel like it. I'm lucky my dad owns a business and can trust me to get things done at home. Eventually, though, I'd like to teach college when my children are older. I don't think it'll be easy raising a family, but I believe it'll be every bit as important as what I can do in the world. Or more."

Tanner nodded. "That's what I've always thought—still think. But there's a basis of truth in what Heather says. What if we married and she became so busy with kids and, say, a Cub Scout calling, that she didn't have time to paint? I know her well enough to know it would kill her inside."

"But she can still paint. That's the point. She'll just have to *make* time. And you're discounting the fulfillment that being a mother gives—and that's a lot, if any of the women I know count. And having a calling also has its rewards." Savvy patted his arm. "Like I said, it's a trade."

Tanner let his head sink into his hands again, rubbing his fingers against his skull. While his cousin made some good points, he didn't think Savvy was even close to understanding how deeply Heather felt compelled to paint. It had taken years before he had understood.

With another loud sigh he faced his cousin again. "I guess it's all a matter of what a person wants. I mean, I've done nothing these past two years but pursue my career, and up until last Christmas my work and my activity in the Church filled all my needs and desires. But now it's not enough. I want a relationship. I want a family." He stared down at his tan carpet. "I want Heather."

Savvy stood, looking down at him. "Well, the first thing you need to do is tell her, don't you think? You may believe she has everything she needs and wants right now, but it's possible she's feeling just as confused as you are. What isn't fair is that you're not giving her an option. You have to let her know how you feel so that when she makes a decision, she has all the information she needs. That's what I'd want if I were Heather."

"And what if . . ." He couldn't complete the words.

Savvy shrugged. "Then at least you'll go through life without regrets. Tell me, if Heather married someone else or never married, wouldn't you always wonder what *could* have happened if you'd told her how you felt? This way, you know you tried and can put it behind you—one way or the other."

Tanner arose and began pacing from the stairs to the couch. Abruptly, he stopped. "I don't know if I can do that. I want to, but oh, Savvy, if you saw the look in her eyes. Her dreams were coming true. She wants to be in Boston."

"Well, you never gave her any other option, did you?"

Tanner didn't answer.

"Have you talked to her at all since she left?"

He shook his head. "Not even over the e-mail. I know I could have sent one, but I keep waiting for her to make the first move."

"Well, that's stupid." Savvy clicked her tongue. "I don't care how liberated we are, women hate to be the first one to make a move."

"It's not like I didn't try to give her a hint," Tanner protested. "I bought her a necklace with a charm before she left. She could have thanked me for it, or something. And I guess I felt that if she needed me or missed me at all, she'd call."

Savvy rolled her eyes. "I declare, for having two sisters, a ton of gorgeous female cousins, including *moi*, and claiming to be Heather's best friend, you know nothing about women. Nothing. You know, you almost deserve not to hear from her."

"It's been six weeks! She should have at least let me know she's okay."

"You never asked."

"Well, then she should wonder how I'm doing."

"She knows how you're doing. You're not the one in a new environment. She probably thinks you're too busy building your career and dating gorgeous women to write."

"I'm doing nothing of the kind—at least the women part. It's her I can't get out of my head."

"Then tell her. You can't let pride stand in the way."

"Pride? Is that what you think this is?" He resumed his pacing. "Maybe, maybe. But what I think is closer to the truth is that I'm afraid she's going to rip out my heart and throw it away."

There was silence for a long minute and Tanner was glad. It wasn't every day he opened up this way—even to someone as close to him as Savvy.

"There's another thing you can do," Savvy said. "Look, stop pacing for two minutes so we can finish this conversation. What is it with you, always pacing or jiggling your foot or something? No wonder you stay so fit. I bet you burn a lot of calories that way."

Tanner halted his movements. "Okay, I'm stopped. What's your great idea?"

She reached into the pocket of her jeans and pulled out a scrap of folded paper. "I can understand your not wanting to get hurt, so maybe you should forget everything I said about talking to her and go out with someone else." She crossed the space between them and thrust the paper into his hands.

"Your friend?" Tanner asked, feeling suddenly very weary.

"No. Actually, this is *your* friend. Remember Amanda Huntington? Green eyes, blonde hair, nice build—your girlfriend in high school? Any of this ringing a bell?"

"She wasn't exactly my girlfriend. We just went out a lot—at least until our senior year when she met that guy over Christmas break. Last I heard they were engaged. She's probably married with a couple of kids by now."

Savvy smiled triumphantly. "Well, that's where you're wrong. I ran into her the other day at a singles dance here in town. She lives in the same stake that I'll be moving into next month. Apparently, she never did get married. They broke up, and she ended up going on a mission. She's been back about a year now. She's at BYU, finishing a teaching degree."

"She'd be a good teacher," Tanner said, remembering what a great student she'd been. Her face came into his mind as though he'd seen her yesterday. Amanda, with her beautiful green eyes and doll-like face. He had really liked her once. Maybe this was the path he should pursue.

But what about Heather? Was he willing to let her go forever? He wasn't so naive to think that there was only one person in the world meant for him. No, he believed that people who claimed to feel that way would be just as happy with someone else who was equally compatible. But he and Heather had a lot of history—memories—between them. And no matter what her feelings for him, he loved her. It wouldn't be fair to call Amanda and open up that past chapter unless he was sure of his own direction—unless he was no longer waiting for Heather to return. Because that was exactly what he was doing.

Tanner strode to the coffee table and pulled out the phone book, placing the paper with Amanda's number in its stead. He picked up the phone.

"Who are you calling?" Savvy asked, coming to his side.

"An airline. With the Fourth of July holiday coming up, I think it's the perfect time for me to visit Boston."

"That a boy," Savvy said. "And don't worry, from all accounts that heart-ripping thing doesn't hurt as much as you might think."

"Oh, that's encouraging." He put down the phone.

"I didn't mean it!" Savvy's pretty face wrinkled in dismay. "Tanner, this is Heather—she's your friend. Whatever may or may not be between you romantically, she's not going to be a bear about it."

Tanner grinned at her consternation. "Relax, Savvy. It's not that. The phone, it's a cordless. Doesn't work without electricity."

Savvy sighed with relief.

"Now if I could only remember where I put my cell phone." Tanner brought his hand to his chin. "I know, it's in the jacket of that suit—the one you're sure is as rumpled as these pants. Hope it's charged." With another grin for his cousin, he went to find his phone.

Chapter Seven

Heather stood back and contemplated her new anchor painting. It had turned out very nicely, if she did say so herself. Much better than the first two she had done. Of course, the work on those had helped her with this current painting, which was all but finished. She couldn't wait to show it to Mrs. Oldham, who was a frequent visitor in the gallery studio and who was quickly becoming a friend. But maybe she ought to take another look at the three anchor paintings together, just to make sure she had captured the emotions she desired.

She set the other two up on easels on either side of her new painting. Yesterday Mr. Oldham had expressed a desire to sell the third anchor painting in the gallery, which excited Heather a great deal. Her first major painting in a prestigious gallery! Of course, the gallery would keep a portion of the proceeds, but she would put the rest in the bank. First, she'd have a print made for her records.

"Harder than you think to let it go, isn't it?" Nate asked from behind her.

Heather smiled, motioning him to come stand at her side. "When I began college, I used to think I could never part with my originals," she told him, "but I think this is one painting I'll be glad to see the backside of."

"What will you do with the other two?"

"Store them away, I guess. They were good learning tools."

She studied the three together. The first anchor painting, the one she'd done with Tomás, was full of emotion, but more abstract than she liked. The second, copied from her photographs, was too perfect, starched of any real feeling. The third, however, had been the charm, as she combined the proportions of the second, with the feeling and the disembodied eyes of the first.

"When you become famous, they'll sell anyway," Nate said. "You'll have every collector in the country trying to become the owner of all three."

She laughed. "*If* I become famous."

His arm slipped around her shoulders in a comfortable gesture; they had become close over the past six and a half weeks. "I don't think you have to worry about that."

"Well, I'm still having trouble getting the proportions right. Even with photographs or a model."

"And I'd still rather paint people than trees."

Heather smiled. Nate was right. All the grantees had their strengths and weaknesses. Nate was a genius at portraiture, but he didn't do as well with backgrounds. It would take him longer to paint a simple tree than it did a person. Keith, on the other hand, could paint landscapes and animals in his sleep, but avoided painting people at all. Lorin had a particular talent with buildings, while McCarty was quickly becoming a master at abstract or interpretational paintings like Tomás. Heather felt she was best at close-up details of just about anything, though she struggled with proportions. Her painting goals included integrating more emotion into her work, while at the same time making the depictions more realistic.

Besides the anchor paintings, she was currently working on one other painting that was now drying on an easel some distance to the right side of the anchor canvasses. This one contained children, and she found she had enjoyed painting them, as she had not in the past. Some of this she felt was because she missed her siblings more than she wanted to admit.

From the open window came a brief, high burst of female laughter, drawing Heather's thoughts back to the studio. The laughter came again. Lorin. She was painting with Tomás in the courtyard. Heather frowned, thinking of Tomás. "You know, maybe being famous isn't exactly my goal."

Nate nodded knowingly, his well-formed mouth twisting into a wry smile. "I hear you. That guy drips talent, but he has the social skills of a mosquito."

Heather bit her tongue, not wanting to voice her agreement. She had learned a great deal from Tomás these past weeks, and she admired his dedication to his work. But when it came right down to it, he was eccentric, undependable, irrational, smug, cold, and downright obnoxious. She didn't understand what Lorin saw in him. McCarty was worse, nearly worshiping the man and emulating not only his style but also his attitude. At least Nate and Keith seemed to have their heads on straight.

"Are you finished with your painting?" she asked Nate, changing the subject.

"Yes, two of them, actually. But I don't know if my client will like one. When he asked me to paint a portrait of his wife, flattering her, well, it just sort of went against my sense of truth. So I did two instead. Why don't you come and tell me what you think?" His arm slid from her shoulders to her back, as he led her to his two easels.

On the first was a painting of a pretty, yet ordinary woman. Her nose was a little large, her hair too thin, and her eyes too small for real beauty. Her face showed signs of a long life. The portrait was what Heather would call a realistic painting, done in harsh, unforgiving light.

The second painting portrayed the same woman. This time her nose was smaller, hair slightly thicker, eyes larger, and the wrinkles smoothed. The softened light around her made her features almost ethereal. She was beautiful. Heather knew that any woman would prefer the second painting, though she personally found more to admire in the first.

"You'll have to give your client that one," she said, pointing to the second.

Nate ran a hand through his thick, blonde hair. "Yeah, I know. Mr. Oldham was quite adamant when he introduced me to the client that I give him exactly what he wanted. But I'm loath to separate the two. There's such a feeling here."

"You're right, there is. But you have no choice about this particular painting. Its commission means thousands of dollars in your pocket." Heather studied the two again. "I have an idea. How about giving the one to your client as planned, storing away the other, and then choosing another model and doing the same thing—one realistic painting, one made more beautiful? You could call the pair Eye of the Beholder. I think it might be something Mr. Oldham would be anxious to sell in the gallery."

Nate nodded. "Hmm, I never thought of that. I'd have to choose someone about the same age for the wrinkles, pay for her to model . . ."

"Well, I'd volunteer, but I'm rather busy."

Nate looked at her, amused. "You're nowhere near her age, and besides, I couldn't paint two different paintings of you, Heather. I have to see both sides to paint them—eye of the beholder, and all." His voice became soft. "I'm afraid that I see only one side of you."

Heather blinked in surprise. She knew exactly what he was hinting at, but hadn't expected such a revelation. She purposely made her tone light. "Yes, but which painting do you see?"

Whatever Nate was going to reply was lost as Bridget, the gallery employee who had helped Heather take the photographs of the anchor, entered the studio. "You have a visitor up front to see you, Heather." She winked. "Tall, dark, and handsome. Says he's a friend of yours."

Heather knew no one in Boston fitting that description except Tomás, whom she didn't exactly consider handsome or a friend. She glanced down at her paint-covered smock. "I'm a little messy to go out in the gallery," she said. "And I have shorts on under this. I'll have to change first."

"Don't bother. I can have him come back here, if you want."

"Is that allowed?"

"Yes, if he really is a friend."

"Well, bring him on back," Nate said. "We'll see soon enough."

"All right." Bridget left them.

Nate began to remove his own painting smock. "It's almost time for me to relieve Keith in the gallery. I'd better clean up."

"No, wait a minute, would you?" Heather put a hand on his arm. "What if I don't know this guy?"

Nate raised his arm, making a show of his well-formed muscles. "Then I'll send him packing."

Heather giggled. "Thanks, Nate." She gave him a little hug as Bridget reentered the studio with someone Heather immediately recognized, though his brown hair was slightly longer than she remembered.

"Tanner!" she screamed, launching herself at him. "Oh, Tanner! I can't believe you're here! Why didn't you tell me you were coming? Oh, I'm so happy to see you!" His arms tightened about her, and she squeezed back as hard as she could.

"I wanted to surprise you," Tanner said. "Surprise!"

Bridget grinned. "I guess you know him. I'll be getting back to my customers. You see him out, okay?"

"Sure." Heather drew back, but held onto Tanner's hands.

"Guess I'll be getting cleaned up," Nate said, stepping away from them.

"Oh, Nate, first you have to meet my very best friend in the whole world from Utah."

"But I thought Lorin was your friend from Utah," Nate teased.

"Not my best." Heather dropped one of Tanner's hands and pulled him with the other toward Nate. "Tanner, this is Nathan Thorne, one of the other artists. He's from Michigan, and a very good painter—as you can see from these canvasses here. And Nate, this is Tanner Wolfe, my next door neighbor and best friend since I was sixteen. He works as an executive officer at Hospital's Choice Inc. They do software for hospitals, and he's the head of their Japanese division."

Tanner and Nate shook hands. "Nice to meet you," they mumbled. Heather thought both of them sounded anything but pleased. She didn't protest as Nate excused himself.

She focused her attention on Tanner, looking so handsome in his dark suit, unable to believe he was really standing before her. Only now did she realize exactly how much she'd missed him.

"So am I interrupting your work?" Tanner asked. "Because I can come back tomorrow."

"Actually, you've come at a good time. I was just going to get lunch."

"But it's nearly four."

She shrugged and gave him a crooked smile. "We eat when we're hungry here."

"Or more likely when you remember." Tanner shook his dark head. "But you don't look any worse for it—in fact, you look absolutely beautiful."

Heather flushed. Since when had Tanner ever paid her such compliments? And sound like he meant every word? She turned from him. "We have a landlady who makes sure we get enough calories, believe me. Now, I need to take care of my brushes, and then we can go somewhere to eat. I'll have to call a taxi, though."

"I rented a car. It's out front."

"Oh, good."

Tanner followed her back to her canvasses, where she began gathering her supplies. She hesitated when she found Tanner studying her paintings. Nervously she waited, unable to ask him if he liked them. Could he see that in the first one, the anchor looked thrown aside rather than used as security? Did he notice the third contained even more ambivalence? Could he tell that the disembodied eyes were hers?

"This is the final one, isn't it?" he said, pointing to the middle painting. "It's very good. *Very* good."

"Thank you. And yes, it's the last one I did. Sort of a composite of the others."

"I can see that. The light's better and so is the shape—more realistic—but the feeling is better than the one on the right. That looks more like a plain photograph."

Heather was pleased that he'd caught those details. She would have liked to tell him more about how the anchor was needed, yet unwanted, but for some reason she couldn't admit such a thing to him.

"It's perfect," he said with sincerity, but his voice was also tinged with a sadness Heather couldn't identify.

"Is that yours, too?" He motioned to the painting to the far right of the three anchors. Heather nodded as he walked over to examine it.

For what seemed an indeterminable time, he stood there silently. Heather found herself trying to swallow a sudden lump in her throat. What must he think about this latest effort, the one she had been so proud of only a few moments before? She stepped to his side, trying to see the painting as it must appear to him.

The mother was the central figure. She was not slender, yet not large. Not well-dressed, but obviously not poor. Her hair was neatly cut, but her body bent and weak-looking, her face worn. Her thin hands were roughened and red. She was surrounded by seven children of differing ages, each of them looking to her for their needs. One girl held a clumsily drawn picture in her hand, a boy a piano book, and another child of indefinite gender held a pencil and a math book. One little girl was crying, clutching a doll. Another boy with his back toward them carried something that could be a scout book; the boy next to him sported a basketball. The smallest child wore only a T-shirt and diaper which bagged around her waist as though in need of a change.

She had used her own photo album and the faces of her family for the mother and children. To get the bodies and proportions correct, always her greatest challenge, she had visited parks and taken photographs of children—with their parents' permission, of course—and had also visited a preschool. Seeing the children playing Ring Around the Rosies with their teacher had inspired her to encircle the mother as she had with her painted children.

Tomás had supervised several initial sketches for the painting, helping her to place the children to best advantage. Later, he had helped her experiment with a few models and spotlights to obtain the gray shadows on the backs of the children in the forefront of the painting—shadows that had given Heather the appearance of the metal bars she had desired. That the children made up the mother's prison was the most significant and perhaps tragic symbol in the painting.

Tomás had suggested making the children's faces more cruel, but she had refused. She had never believed children to be purposely cruel; they were innocent. Certainly her siblings had never meant any harm to her mother. So each of the seven children depicted were beautiful to Heather, and yet their innocent eyes begged—even demanded—attention, which the mother, radiating submission, gave to them willingly, never trying to break free.

Experiencing the painting now, Heather could feel the resentment in the hand that had painted it. Did Tanner notice? And did he recognize that the mother was her own?

Without looking at her, Tanner reached out and took her hand in his. His fingers were strong, but his skin soft from office work. She became all too aware of how her own hands had become chapped by the solution she used each day to scrub them clean of paint. He turned toward her; she waited without breathing.

His deep brown eyes delved deeply into her own. "I knew you were talented, but this . . . it's incredible." His voice was so gentle she felt like crying. "Come on, you need to eat. Can I help you clean the brushes?"

She accepted his help, glad he had not chosen to challenge her choice of subject. Perhaps he hadn't noticed how the children trapped the mother so completely.

After brushing her long hair and changing from her shorts to the blue print dress she'd worn in the gallery earlier that day, Heather felt more relaxed. By all appearances, she and Tanner were a well-dressed couple ready for a nice outing. They went through the gallery, passing Keith on their way out. Heather stopped to introduce him, and she could tell that Tanner immediately liked him. Nate was talking to a customer, and he glanced in their direction, nodding briefly before continuing his conversation.

"Where to?" Tanner asked when they were in his white rental BMW. At once Heather felt nostalgic for his Blue Bug.

She pointed down the road, intending to take him to The Lobster Pot, the restaurant where she had eaten on her first night in Boston. It had become the grantees' favorite haunt—one she could always be assured of finding without a map.

Tanner put the car in drive. "So, I'm assuming the gallery is closed tomorrow for the Fourth of July and that you'll be taking a day off. But I also assume you have plans. I don't want to be an annoyance or anything. You go ahead and do whatever it is you've planned, while I take in a few sights. Then we can spend Sunday together. My plane doesn't leave until Monday morning."

"What do you mean?" Heather punched him in the arm. "I wouldn't hear of you seeing the sights by yourself! You'll spend the whole day with me tomorrow, I hope, after coming so far. And actually, the gallery stays open for a lot of holidays—sometimes that's when they're the busiest. But the Fourth happens to be an exception, so you picked a good time to come." Then she had another thought. "You're not here on business, are you?"

"Nope. I came just to see you." He said it matter-of-factly, but suddenly she realized how strange it was that he should fly clear across the U.S. to visit her. He could have called or e-mailed. Not that she had written to him. Had he become worried because of her silence? How could she explain that not only had she been very busy, but that when she sat down at her computer to write, she had missed him so much that she hadn't been able to continue?

"I've heard there's a huge celebration here for the Fourth," she said into the lull of their conversation. "Which stands to reason since this is Boston, the so-called cradle of the American independence, the birthplace of the nation." She smiled. "I can't tell you how many times I've heard *that* here. The Bostonians are a wonderful people, and very proud of their heritage. Anyway," she began ticking events off on her fingers, "they have a reading of the *Declaration of Independence* from the balcony of the Old State House tomorrow, waterfront activities with the USS Constitution, and an outdoor concert at the Hatch Memorial Shell with cannons and fireworks. I think it'll be fun."

Tanner nodded in agreement but kept his attention on the road. "Man, these drivers are aggressive. All this weaving in an out and the tailgating. Reminds me of New York."

She laughed. "You get used to it. But they are pretty accident prone." She pointed to two cars at the side of the road that had obviously been in an accident. "Good, looks like no one is hurt."

"I'd love to see Chinatown and Little Italy while I'm here, if we have time." Without taking his eyes from the road, he pulled out a guide book from under his seat and handed it to her. "And the Boston Tea Party exhibit sounds interesting."

"I've been to Chinatown, but I'd like to go again. You'll love how colorful it is. And Paul Revere actually had a house they've kept up—the oldest house in downtown Boston. I've passed by, but never been inside. They say it's just like it was when he lived there."

"Sounds interesting."

"Pull over up there by that blue van," Heather directed. "I think you'll like this restaurant. Serves both lobster, steak, and southern type foods like fried chicken. But if you want a soda, remember to ask for a tonic."

"Got it."

They went inside together. The awkwardness Heather had felt so acutely when viewing her paintings was completely gone, and she was grateful. After they ordered fried chicken with all the fixings, Tanner tapped the guide book she had brought from the car.

"I read that Boston has sixty colleges and more PhDs and medical doctors per capita than any other U.S. city."

"There are a lot of colleges."

"So, I've been wondering. With all these colleges, why did your benefactor go outside Boston to find artists? Surely there were many good ones here."

"Oh, yes," Heather said. "McCarty—that's one of the others you haven't met yet—wondered the same thing. When he asked, Mrs. Oldham said they had wanted to bring people here who hadn't been living in Boston. Basically, they wanted an outsider's view because they felt we would see what those who already lived here overlooked." She grimaced. "But I'm afraid that's more with landscape paintings and historical stuff. I haven't done any of that kind of painting yet. I was thinking that tomorrow I'd take pictures of some of the activities. Maybe I can find something to paint that interests me."

"That's the really important thing." Tanner's eyes didn't leave her face. "To paint what interests you."

Heather smiled and took his hand. "Tanner, it's so good to see you. I'm glad you came."

His brown eyes became serious. "I wasn't sure if you'd be happy to see me." He paused and then added, "Why didn't you write?"

"I guess it's because I've been so busy." She saw the disbelief in his eyes and continued, "What I meant was that each time I sat down at the computer to write, I'd be so tired that I'd dash off a quick e-mail to my mom to let her know I was okay, but when it came to writing you . . . well, there was so much I wanted to say that I would have been on the computer all night." She tore her eyes away from his. "I guess it made me too sad. Sometimes it's a little lonely here." *At least when I'm not painting*, she added silently.

"Well, from now on if you don't write, I'm calling," he said.

"Hey, you didn't write me either."

He gave her the grin she adored. "You're right, I should have. Look, here comes our meal." He picked up his fork. "I think I'm hungry enough to eat a horse."

 C3

Later that evening, Tanner and Heather left his rental car outside her place and went to a movie using the subway. Tanner didn't pay much attention to the film as he thought about Heather and the work she had been doing. He had enjoyed the anchor paintings and had been proud that Mr. Oldham would be selling one of them in the gallery, but the Mother and Children painting had disturbed him deeply. He loved Heather—he had no doubts there—but the painting helped him understand how conflicted she felt. She loved children, that was clear in each line of the innocent faces, but she was also more aware than most unmarried women of the challenges and the demands of being a mother. He had not missed the positioning of the children, or the dark metallic shadows on those in the forefront, as though they formed a boundary the mother could never pass.

The most disturbing thing to him was that though the mother in the painting had short blonde hair like Heather's own mother, she had Heather's striking hazel eyes instead of Karalee's soft brown ones; and the lines of the face were Heather's in some future era, not Karalee's rounder curves. Heather didn't seem to be aware of the resemblance, but if she felt this way about rearing children—even subconsciously—how could he profess his love and ask her to share a life with him? A life he also wanted to share with their children? His heart suffered with the pain and confusion she must feel. Did he have a right to add to her inner chaos?

Yet she had a right to know how he felt. As Savvy had suggested, if he kept the feelings of his heart a secret, she wouldn't even realize she had a choice. Was it better for her to know? Or worse? He didn't know. What he did understand was the way he felt, the way his arms ached to hold her.

Tentatively, he reached out and took her hand in the darkened theater. She glanced over at him, smiled, and returned her attention to the film. She didn't pull away.

Tanner knew then that he had to talk with her before he went home. He would plant the seeds and be patient. As for his own heart, his cousin was right: Heather was his friend and would not purposely hurt him. Even if things didn't work out, they would remain friends.

At least that's what he told himself.

There was another worry on his mind. When he had entered the studio, Heather and her artist friend, Nate, had been quite close, and he could not miss the intimacy between them. Though Tanner had been reassured by her enthusiastic and sincere greeting, the image of them together was burned into his mind, as was the expression on Nate's face. The artist liked Heather—liked her a lot. Tanner didn't know if that affection was returned. Though Nate wasn't a believer or member of their church, Tanner wasn't sure if that was a strike for or against him at this point. That would depend on how far Heather had strayed and whether or not she had genuinely lost her testimony.

Tanner's hand tightened on hers. He wished he didn't ever have to let go.

Chapter Eight

*T*he next day turned out to be beautiful and sunny, though not as hot as Tanner and Heather were accustomed to in Utah. Heather wore her camera around her neck, planning to snap photographs at every opportunity. The other grantees also had their cameras, except Keith, who carried a thick drawing pad and who was sketching almost constantly. Tanner caught a glimpse of his work over his shoulder and was amazed at the quiet man's talent.

Lorin had come along with them only after Heather had dragged her out of bed, and by the bleary look in her eyes Tanner suspected she had been drinking the night before. That worried him, but Lorin perked up after the parade and became her usual amusing self.

Tanner was not the only addition to their little group. McCarty had a young woman with him whom he'd met a few nights before—a college girl named Andrea who was as soft-spoken as McCarty was loud. She was obviously daunted by her date's volume, and Heather and Tanner exchanged sympathetic glances behind Andrea's back.

After the parade they went a little out of their way to the site of the Boston Massacre, and then to the Old State House for the reading of the *Declaration of Independence*. Tanner was impressed with the costumes and the accompanying pomp. Heather snapped photographs, as did most of the others—even Lorin was interested in the building, if not the reading itself.

Next, they made their way over to Paul Revere's house, grabbing a quick bite to eat afterward.

"I'm amazed at all the differences in architecture here," Tanner said, munching a hamburger. "On one hand they have these beautiful old buildings, really majestic in their own right, but then just over there they have these modern skyscrapers. It's such a contrast."

"Boston is full of such contrasts," McCarty said in his know-it-all tone. "For instance, Boston is unquestionably the medical capital of America, yet it's also home to the huge Christian Science Complex."

"Aren't those the guys who don't believe in using most medicines and medical procedures?" asked Nate.

"Exactly. It's just one example of the paradoxes that are a part of this city."

Despite his rather obnoxious air, McCarty was a wealth of information, and Tanner discussed many things with him. He found that behind the man's urge to be the center of attention lurked an inferiority complex that left him vulnerable to extremes. He was constantly mocking the Bostonian accent, until his date, a native to Boston, overcame her shyness enough to order him to stop. Surprised, he complied.

They made their way to the Waterfront where earlier there had been a turnaround of the USS Constitution, followed by the national twenty-one gun salute. Though they had missed the actual event, Tanner found "Old Ironsides" as impressive as he had hoped.

"They turn it around once a year to keep it weathered evenly," McCarty informed them. That took some of the romance out of the idea for Tanner, but he didn't comment.

On their way to the outdoor concert at the Hatch Memorial Shell situated on the banks of the Charles River, they stopped at the Public Garden for a ride on the swan boats. Andrea and McCarty got into a disagreement—Tanner never knew what about—and McCarty almost ended up in the water. The teen piloting the boat kicked McCarty off, and after that his date kept as far away from him as she could. However, Tanner noticed that she was talking a lot with Keith, who had finally put aside his sketch pad.

When that adventure concluded, they bought more food from an outdoor vendor near the concert. Only Heather and Tanner weren't eating this time as the next day was fast Sunday, and they had begun their fast shortly after noon.

Heather had brought a large but very thin blanket in her handbag, and they stretched it out on the grass to eat and to watch the gathering crowd. Though it was still early, many people were already staking out their places for the concert. Tanner was glad they hadn't waited any later—they might not have found a place.

"McCarty and I are going to walk around a bit," Nate said to Heather when their food was gone. "We'll see you later."

"Yeah, we're going to check out all the wo—the people," McCarty added.

That was when Tanner noticed McCarty's date and Keith were nowhere to be seen.

"So where's Keith?" Heather asked, apparently noticing the same thing.

"I asked him to take Andrea home—or wherever she wants to go. Things weren't clicking with us." McCarty shrugged. "She's more his type anyway."

Lorin smirked. "That's really nice of you, McCarty," she said with false sweetness. "You know as well as I do that's the only way Keith would ever ask a girl out. I don't think I give you enough credit."

"When you're good, you're good," McCarty said, playing along.

Lorin rolled her eyes. "I wouldn't go that far. Even if you're being nice, you're still killing two birds with one stone—getting rid of Andrea *and* helping Keith."

McCarty shrugged and gave her a grin. "If we don't catch up to you guys here, we'll see you tomorrow."

"Sounds fine by me."

McCarty and Nate wandered off, leaving Heather, Tanner, and Lorin. Heather lay back on the blanket, extending her legs. "Oh, what a day! I think my calves are a little burnt—and I even put sunscreen on this morning. I probably should have worn long pants."

Tanner sat beside her, lifting her lower leg slightly for perusal. "You are burned, but it doesn't look bad." She was staring at him oddly, so he dropped her leg and stretched out beside her.

"It's like old times," he said. "Remember how we'd go to all the activities back home?"

"My favorite was the park and the fireworks. I guess that's where my family is now." For an instant, she sounded wistful. Then he tickled her side, and the melancholy was gone.

"Hey," Lorin said, checking her watch. "I just remembered I promised to meet someone right about now. Enjoy the concert and fireworks, 'kay? I'll meet you back at the house."

Heather nodded but frowned as she watched Lorin disappear into the crowd. "I wonder if she's really going to meet someone. If so, I hope it's not Tomás. I don't think he's good for her. You know, in the past few weeks she hasn't painted nearly as well as she did before. It's like she's preoccupied or something."

"What about? Doesn't she tell you anything?"

Heather sat up, pulling her legs to her chest. "No. But there's nothing really I can do about it."

Tanner nodded and a comfortable silence fell between them. Tanner was relieved to finally be alone with Heather. While he enjoyed the company of her friends—except Nate whom he felt was constantly staring at him—there had been little time for private talk. Now, for a while at least, he could pretend he and Heather were any other couple in love.

The concert was fabulous, culminating with cannons and fireworks. Since the air had cooled considerably, they had been forced to cuddle in Heather's blanket for warmth. Tanner had never been so content.

They arrived home after eleven, never having run into any of the others. Tanner walked Heather to her door. "I had a wonderful day," she said, echoing his own feelings.

"I'm glad. It was unusual. I really like Boston."

"You could move here," she teased. Or was that a note of seriousness?

He shook his head. "I know where I belong, Heather." Almost immediately he regretted his words.

"I wish I did," she said softly.

His arms seemed to go around her without his willing them to. She rested her cheek on his shoulder. "Thanks for coming."

"What are friends for?" Again he could have kicked himself. What he wanted was to tell her how much he loved her. Why couldn't he seem to break the habit of friendship and confess his real feelings?

She drew away from him, covering a yawn with her hand. "Well, see you tomorrow. Can you find your way to your hotel?"

"It's a bed and breakfast, actually," he said. "It's not far. I can find it." He hesitated. "Do you want me to pick you up for church?"

"That would be nice."

"What time?"

She gazed at him sleepily. Her long, light brown hair was mussed and she looked adorable. "Hmm. Eight-thirty ought to give us enough time."

"Okay. I'll be here."

ෙ

Heather shut the door behind her, locking it. Then she peered through the spy hole and watched Tanner walk to his car. She felt a loss she couldn't name as he drove away. For no reason at all she thought of her final night in Utah and how he had kissed her at the door.

"What, now you want him to kiss you?" she said aloud. The idea was ridiculous . . . wasn't it?

Their day together had been wonderful, one straight out of the past. Tanner was such good company, despite the mistrusting looks he had given all day to Nate. In a way, spending time with him here made her Boston experience complete.

I should have written to him. Why was I afraid?

She turned from the door. The house was quiet as Mrs. Silva had gone to her daughter's that morning. Her apartment was even quieter.

Where was Lorin?

Heather hoped her friend had better sense than becoming romantically involved with Tomás. With what Heather had gleaned from the regular gallery employees, Tomás was lucky enough when he remembered he had a current girlfriend, much less her name, and the word loyalty simply wasn't in his vocabulary. He was too distracted to remember important dates or to even pay his bills. Apparently Lester Paddock took care of those duties. Tomás had an apartment somewhere in town, but he often slept in his studio, painting at odd hours. Occasionally, he would disappear for days, only to turn up again, unshaven and wild-eyed. It was then that he would paint his best. Heather didn't understand it—was afraid to understand it.

Did all true painters lose sight of reality? History was rife with examples, yet there were good examples as well—she just couldn't remember any at the moment.

Heather sank to the couch, her eyes falling on a paper perched on the edge of the coffee table. "Oh, no," she moaned. The teacher in Relief Society had asked her to share an experience from her mission, and she had completely forgotten.

"No way I could go crazy like Tomás," she muttered. "I have too many responsibilities." She grabbed the paper and a stray pen and began to write. A half hour later she was satisfied that she wouldn't make a fool of herself.

Lorin had still not come home, but she had one of their spare keys. Heather hoped Lorin hadn't lost it because she was going to bed. If she didn't sleep now, she might not wake up in time for church. So far she hadn't missed a meeting, though Lorin hadn't come with her since that first day. In turn, their visiting teachers, home teachers, and the bishopric had all visited their apartment. Not a week went by without someone calling to offer support or encouragement. Whether Heather admitted it or not, she appreciated their efforts. Maybe she even needed them. She was deeply grateful she hadn't missed church that first Sunday; it might have been too easy to have put off going indefinitely.

On her way to bed, she spied the open door to the studio she and Lorin shared. Her fingers itched to paint, but she resisted the urge. It was late and her body needed rest.

Hours later, something awoke Heather. "Lorin?" she called.

No answer.

She turned on the lamp by her bed. Lorin's bed, still unmade from that morning, was empty. Heather checked the rest of the apartment, but there was no sign of her friend. At last she turned out the light again and returned to bed.

Chapter Nine

*A*t precisely eight-thirty the next morning, Tanner was on her doorstep. Heather answered just as promptly. Lorin was still not home, and Heather found herself sharing her worry with Tanner.

"If she's not there by the time we get out of church, maybe we should go to the police," he suggested as he held open the door to his rental car.

Heather agreed. "I know she's an adult and she was probably just out too late and crashed somewhere. But sometimes she's not very . . . well, practical."

"And you are?" He grinned. "This from the girl who once stayed up for three nights in a row to see how it would influence her painting?"

Heather laughed, grateful he could get her mind off Lorin. "Well, those were some of best abstract paintings I've ever done."

"No wonder your Tomás is so famous."

"Well, he's not exactly my idol, but he has taught me a lot."

Tanner sobered. "I believe that—I saw your paintings." After that he didn't speak, but followed her directions wordlessly. When they arrived in the church parking lot, he said, "So, how do these Bostonians saints measure up—do they subscribe to the so-called Mormon Checklist?"

Their conversation of her last night in Utah came back to her vividly. She smiled. "Well, they still have the checklist, but I think they're not as afraid to show some of their grayer parts. It might just be me, but they seem more accepting of people who aren't outwardly perfect. And it's refreshing to see leaders of different ethnic backgrounds. In Utah, I never saw that."

Tanner hopped out of the car and ran around to open her door. "So, maybe what we were talking about before is more Utah culture than Mormon culture."

"Yeah, I guess you're right."

"Everyone here is trying." He gestured around him at the people walking toward the church building. "And so are the people back home. That's all anyone can do."

She stopped walking. "You think I judged everyone back home too harshly, don't you?"

He shrugged. "Maybe. I don't know, Heather." He reached for her hand. "I just know that I miss you. That's all." Without another word he started up the walk again, and she went with him, pulled along by his hand.

During the sacrament meeting, Heather sat next to Tanner. As usual, his foot was pumping up and down as though his body contained too much energy. Smiling, she put a hand on his knee to still the movement.

He grinned at her. "Savannah says that's what keeps me so fit," he whispered.

"She's probably right. Or maybe your blood pressure's too high."

"It is when I'm with you." The way his eyes widened after he said it told her he hadn't meant to let the words out. He turned his head toward the speaker, refocusing his attention. Heather's hand snaked up, grabbed a lock of hair from the base of her skull, and began twirling it. A warmth she didn't recognize filled her heart.

After church they headed to her apartment to find something to break their fast. "Don't worry, Mrs. Silva always leaves us plenty of food for Sundays," Heather told Tanner.

To Heather's relief, when they arrived at the apartment they found Lorin eating cold cereal straight from the box. "Where have you been?" Lorin asked.

"We could ask you the same thing," Heather replied.

Lorin swallowed her mouthful of Froot Loops. "Well, I got back pretty late. I forgot my key—"

"You mean you lost it?"

Lorin shook her head and continued, "So I rang downstairs, but you must have been asleep. I noticed the guys still had lights on, so I ran over there. McCarty was up and he let me crash on their couch. Then this morning, he found my key in my purse, and I came home. You know, McCarty's not half bad when he doesn't have an audience."

Heather remembered being awakened in the middle of the night. "You should have kept ringing or gone around to the balcony. I would have heard you eventually."

"Oh, well. I was tired."

"So where were you before going to the carriage house?"

"With Tomás. And believe it or not, we were painting." Lorin gave a disgusted sigh. "That's all he ever thinks about, you know. I mean, he can hold something else in his mind for a few minutes, but it always comes back to the painting. It's like he's obsessed."

Tanner had stayed quiet during their conversation. Now he spoke up. "But isn't that what painting's all about? Being focused?"

"Focused, yes," Heather said, "but not obsessed."

"How do you know the difference?"

"Well . . ." Lorin began, but Heather took up his challenge. She suspected where he was headed.

"You know, when you do it to the exclusion of most anything else," she said.

"Yet sometimes that's appropriate," he countered. "Like now. During the period of your grant."

"Yes. But it's not something you can keep up for—" Heather stopped abruptly. What had she been going to say? She *wanted* to stay here indefinitely. She *wanted* to continue to focus solely on her painting for as long as possible. Did that mean she was obsessed?

Lorin flounced down on the couch and began laughing. "Don't worry, Tanner, we find plenty of opportunities to focus on other things. For instance, we work in the gallery where we sell paintings, we visit other galleries and museums to see more paintings, we often go out and take pictures of things to paint, and we even have books about paintings that we read in our spare time."

Heather gave Lorin a withering look. "We also go see the sights like we did yesterday. We go swimming and work out at the gym a few times a week. We go out to eat and dancing."

"Dancing?" Tanner asked. "That sounds interesting."

"You only did that once," Lorin put in. "And I think you only went to the gym for a half-hour each week this past month."

Heather ignored her. "I go to church. I'll probably even get a calling soon."

"That's something," Lorin said, barely keeping a straight face.

Tanner nodded. "It sounds like you have it all covered." All at once his grin widened. "Speaking of swimming, do you know what I did last weekend? Savvy and I took my sisters and some of your siblings up to Deer

Creek. We went jet skiing. It was great. You should have seen Jennie Anne—that's one of my sisters, Lorin. Anyway, at first she was afraid, but then we couldn't get her off the jet ski. And your brothers, Heather, they were just as bad. Next time I think we'll have to rent a few more jet skis. I promised we'd go again."

Heather felt a sudden wave of homesickness as she vividly remembered similar jet skiing trips. "Kevin and Aaron should rent their own," she said. "They both have summer jobs; they can afford it."

"I'll keep that in mind."

"Who's Savvy?" Lorin asked.

"My cousin," Tanner answered. "Well, actually my stepmom is her aunt. There's no blood between us."

"Ah-ha." With a knowing smile, Lorin turned to Heather. "There'll be wedding bells soon, mark my words."

Heather laughed aloud at the ridiculousness of the idea. Savvy was just a kid, and she was more like a sister than a cousin. *And I'm more like a sister than a next door neighbor*, she thought. Though it was true, for some reason the idea rankled.

"Actually, the other day she did ask me to marry her," Tanner said gravely. "But I had to turn her down." He cracked a smile. "I'm kidding. Savvy and I are just friends."

Heather didn't respond to Tanner's comment, but busied herself heating up the beans, ham, chicken, and sausage mixture Mrs. Silva had left for them. The *feijoada* was a traditional Portuguese dish that Heather was rather fond of—at least since she had convinced Mrs. Silva to forego the addition of pigs' feet and ears. She was relieved when neither Tanner or Lorin pursued the subject of his cousin.

They spent the afternoon and a good portion of the evening talking and playing a few board games. At a little after eight someone rang downstairs. "Must be the guys," Lorin said. "They said they wanted to go out for ice cream tonight. I told them to come and get me when they were ready." She went out the door and down the stairs to let them in.

"So," Tanner said casually, "do they do that a lot?"

Heather's anger flared. "You mean break the Sabbath? Tanner, your checklist is showing."

"Hey, in this case it's not my checklist, it's the Lord's."

He was right, but she still glared. "They're not members—not even Lorin, really. They aren't accountable."

He nodded. "Well, you could argue that the Bible is for everyone who believes in Christ, not just members, but that's not what I'm getting at. I was just thinking that if they do that a lot, it must be really hard on you."

Heather felt her anger seep away. He was right. In the beginning it had been very hard on her, and she had often felt left out. But the truth was they had quit asking her to go with them weeks ago. "They're good people," she said.

"I know. I was with them yesterday. I'm not judging them, Heather—I'm not. I do wish I could make them see the importance of keeping the Sabbath holy, but I know they haven't had the same background I have."

His eyes were sincere and Heather felt guilty. She had accused him of judging, yet it had been her who had judged him.

Lorin came into the room with the others, saving Heather from further comment. "Hi, Heather, Tanner," the guys said. Tanner went to shake hands with them.

"Did you hear Lorin had to sleep at our place?" McCarty asked. "You must sleep like a stone, Heather."

Heather snorted. "You could have called. Last I heard Mr. Oldham had a phone installed for you."

"We didn't want to wake you," McCarty said.

"Hey, Keith and I were already asleep," Nate volunteered. "So don't blame us." He kept near the door, as though anxious to leave. Occasionally, Nate would stay home with her when the others went out on Sundays, but today she knew he would make no such offer. Heather didn't mind; tonight was for Tanner. Many more months might pass until she saw him again.

"We're going for some ice cream," McCarty told Tanner. "With jimmies."

Tanner's brow rose. "Jimmies?"

"He means sprinkles," Lorin said. "He's just showing off. And if you want to talk obsessive, you should see these Bostonians with their ice cream. Sometimes we have to wait in line for twenty minutes to get a chance at the counter. Especially when it's warm like tonight."

McCarty put his arm around her shoulders. "More time for you to be with us handsome males."

Lorin rolled her eyes, but she let him lead her to the door.

Keith lifted a hand in farewell. "We'd ask you to go," he said to Tanner, "but Heather doesn't—"

"That's okay. I don't either. We'll be fine. We still have a lot of catching up to do."

"Well, if we don't see you before you leave, have a good flight."

"Thanks," Tanner said.

Keith smiled and followed the others out the door.

"And don't lose your key!" Heather called after Lorin.

Once they had gone, she sat again on the couch, stretching her legs and resting them on the coffee table. "So what shall we do? Are you hungry?"

"No. I think that bean dish will still keep me for some time. Maybe I shouldn't have eaten so much. I'll tell you one thing, your housekeeper is a great cook." He sat next to her on the couch, but on the edge instead of settling in. Heather sensed a nervousness about him, and her own heartbeat quickened. Why was he suddenly nervous to be alone with her?

She leapt to her feet, unable to stay still in the silence. "I think I'll have another piece of Mrs. Silva's bread."

"Okay, and then why don't we go for a walk?"

"Good idea." Heather slathered the bread with butter and then motioned to him. "I'm ready."

"Keys?" He handed them to her.

"Oh, I almost forgot. Thanks. I'd never live that down with Lorin." Heather's fingers brushed his hand as she took the keys, causing her a rush of inexplicable confusion—the same confusion she had felt when he had examined the sunburn on her calf at the outdoor concert.

They walked for a long while. The muscles in Heather's legs were slightly sore from the day before, but she didn't complain. The evening was perfect, the residential area calm. After a few blocks, they found a small neighborhood park where they sat on a bench and rested. The sun had set, and the bench was the perfect place to study the brilliant reds, oranges, and yellows reflected in the few wispy clouds in the west. Several small children were playing frisbee, and a man was walking his dog, but besides that they were alone.

They watched in comfortable silence until the brightest lights in the clouds had faded. The children finally left for home, and the man with the dog was long gone.

Tanner took her hand in his and began tracing the fine veins showing through her skin. Heather stared, fascinated, but for the life of her, she couldn't pull away. What was happening between them? The Tanner she knew from the past would have sooner tackled her than stroked her so softly.

Finally, she managed to look up into his eyes, which she found fixed on her face. She opened her mouth to ask him what he was thinking. "Tanner, I—"

He put his finger gently over her lips to still any further words. "I need to talk to you, Heather. I've needed to for some time. That's why I came." He fell silent and she waited. "I know this is going to come as a surprise," he said. "It did to me—at first. But then, well, it was just so right."

Her mind raced. So he *had* come to tell her he was getting married. All that joking today foreshadowed this revelation. Why hadn't she understood that? Of course, he had to tell her. They were best friends, and one of them getting married would necessarily change all that. Heather felt a lump rise in her throat. *Who is she?* She felt an unreasonable jealousy toward the woman—probably someone she hadn't even met. Or could it be his young cousin after all?

"I—uh—well . . ." Tanner was having difficulty speaking. Heather wanted to shout at him to spit it out. In the past he had never been so inarticulate when sharing his secrets.

He was very close to her now, their faces separated only by inches. "Heather, I tried to tell you the last night you were in Utah. I know you think that dinner I set up was to celebrate your grant, but I didn't even know about it yet. And then I couldn't tell you because I didn't want you to feel you had to stay because of me." He closed the last inch between them, and their lips met. Heather instantly recalled the quick brush of a kiss he had given her that last night in Utah and how it had shaken her. This kiss was much deeper, full of feeling and meaning.

Questions whirled in Heather's mind even as she responded to his touch. She cared so much about him, and kissing him felt oddly right. His hands slipped around to cradle her head; her own hands rested against his chest. She wanted the moment to continue forever.

Then her senses returned from wherever his touch had sent them. She pushed against his chest, drawing away at the same time. Immediately, he lifted his head, breaking contact, though she saw the reluctance in his eyes.

"Why?" she asked, wanting to say more, but unable to speak past the pounding of her heart.

"I love you, Heather," he said simply. His hands had fallen to her shoulders when they had separated, and now one of them traced the curve of her neck to her hairline, where it tangled in her hair.

She swallowed hard, barely understanding. He hadn't come to tell her of his engagement at all, but to confess his love for her! Shaking her head, she said, "But we're friends. We've always been friends."

"I know. I never expected to feel this way. All this time I've looked for someone—and you've been right there." His dark eyes were intense. "I've fought against this since December, didn't really believe, but then I realized something—who better to fall in love with than your best friend?"

"But I don't . . ." She trailed off, not able to say that she didn't feel the same, because all at once she didn't know how she felt—except that she longed to have him kiss her again.

He must have read the thought in her eyes, because his face again came closer. At first his touch was tentative, but as she responded, he grew more confident. They were both breathless when they drew apart, arms still embracing one another.

"Heather, come back to Utah. Marry me."

Thoughts tumbled about in her mind. All at once she was tempted to follow this budding relationship to see where it led. But what about her life here? What about her art? The response that came to her lips was not the one she knew he wanted to hear. "I can't leave—there's the grant. And I want to paint."

"But what about us?"

A vision of her Mother and Children painting at the gallery flashed into her mind, giving her strength. She pushed away from him and stood up from the bench, shaking her head. "Tanner, please try to understand. I can't. Not now, maybe not ever. I have to paint. I *have* to! And you . . ." Her eyes begged him to understand. "I know what you want. I can't be that for you. I don't even know who I am anymore." Tears spilled down her cheeks.

He had arisen with her and now took a step forward, taking her reluctant hand. "I know you're really confused right now. I felt the same way when this hit me out of the blue. But Heather, I won't rush you. I won't, believe me. I want you to be happy with whatever you choose. The last thing I want is to cause you pain or to make you confused, but I had to let you know how I felt. I had to see if maybe you returned that feeling."

She didn't answer. To confirm his words would cause her to lose the battle. To deny would cause him pain—and she cared about him too much to hurt him. With her free hand she dabbed at her tears.

"You don't have to say anything," he said after a long silence. "I know you well enough to tell how you feel about me—or at least how you're beginning to feel. But this really isn't about us, is it?"

She shook her head.

"I thought so. This is about you and your dreams . . . and your relationship with your Heavenly Father. About the gospel."

"I believe it's true," she whispered.

"I know. And that's what gives me hope. I think you'll find your way."

"You could move out here," she said, almost hoping he would. If he were here, she suspected she would not be able to resist his charms for long. "You could open a new branch, or work at another company."

"No." His voice was resolute. "I'll be home—waiting for you."

She thought that rather selfish of him. He wanted her to give up everything, but was not willing to do the same for her.

"Heather," he said more gently. "I love you, and I want to do anything to make you happy, but it has to be your choice. I won't force you—not even by my presence."

Turning abruptly from him, she began walking in the direction of her apartment. Tears streamed down her face. She didn't know why she felt so terrible. She *wanted* to stay in Boston and paint. Doing so was a dream come true. She didn't need Tanner around to mess things up. She didn't need him at all!

After a while, her tears dried and she slowed, allowing Tanner to catch up to her. They walked silently the rest of the way. At her door, he hugged her tightly.

"Take care of yourself, Heather. Remember, if you ever need me for anything, I'll be on the first flight over. And please write." He pulled away, giving her a weak smile. She had thought he might try to kiss her again—a part of her even hoped that he would—but he turned and sauntered down the walk.

At his car he paused. "I love you, Heather Samis. Don't forget! And I'm not giving up on you." He opened the door, started the engine, and sped away.

Once again Heather stared after him.

Chapter Ten

Heather didn't see Tanner again before he returned to Utah. When she called the place he was staying the next morning, he had already checked out, though it was still early for his flight. She wondered if he was going to stop by Chinatown since they hadn't been able to visit on Saturday. She didn't know if she should be angry at him for not including her or relieved that she wouldn't have to face him again. All night in her dreams she had seen nothing but his handsome, earnest face and the love that was so apparent she didn't understand how she could have missed it before.

She cared for him, too; there was no denying it. Perhaps she even loved him in the way he desired. Somewhere in the past few days her feelings of friendship had certainly changed. Was it when he had held her hand at the movie? Or when they had cuddled under her blanket at the fireworks? Or had it been when he had shown concern about the influence of her friends? Certainly, their relationship had changed before he had kissed her in the park. Her response had proven that.

Yet her feelings for him were shadowed by her goals and aspirations. The idea that her artistic gift would fade as she lived Tanner's dream was like a knife cutting into her soul. She had witnessed a similar sacrifice in her mother and could not bear to follow the same path. She adored painting. The urge to paint was like fire in her veins, and she believed her gift had come from a loving Father who wanted her to develop it. So why all this confusion? Why in her free hours did she miss Tanner so desperately? Why did she continue to wear his anchor charm?

Heather let out a long sigh and began searching for her keys. Lately, she'd been as disorganized as Lorin. She found them at last by the small microwave.

"Are you ready?" Lorin asked from behind her. She had not returned until late Sunday evening, and this morning was still in her pajama shorts and shirt. "We'd better hurry down for breakfast. I wonder what marvel our Mrs. Silva has prepared today."

Lorin was much more chipper than she normally was in the morning, but Heather scarcely noticed. She was staring at the keys in her hand, recalling how Tanner had looked at her in the park. Had there ever been anyone who cared so much about her? She couldn't believe so. He had always been there for her, and now what he offered . . . well, once it might have fit in with her dreams. Oh, why couldn't she be normal? Why did her ambition have to stand in the way of accepting the love of a wonderful man?

Lorin stopped at the door to their apartment. "Aren't you going to tell me to get dressed first? Not that there's anything wrong with what I'm wearing. These shorts are quite modest, in case you didn't notice. Heather? Heather! I'm talking to you."

"Huh?" Heather looked up, shaken from her reverie.

Lorin walked toward her. "Is something wrong?"

"No, I was just thinking."

"About?"

Heather grimaced. "About Tanner. He asked me to marry him last night." She hadn't meant to tell anyone, but it was a relief to say the words.

Lorin's jaw dropped "Oh my gosh! I knew there was something between you two—I knew it! Why didn't you tell me before?"

"There was nothing to tell," Heather practically wailed. "We were friends—we've always been just friends. Yes, I care about him, but I knew it wasn't anything that . . . well, I knew it was—" She broke off.

"Safe," Lorin finished for her. "But he wasn't safe after all, was he?"

"It wasn't supposed to happen this way," Heather said miserably. "Somewhere the lines got blurred. I still don't know when it happened. I—" Clutching the keys, she held her hand to her heart.

"Do you love him?"

"No," Heather hurried to say, and then, "At least I don't think so. But last night all these emotions came to me. I've never felt that way before, Lorin— never! Oh, I've been so blind, haven't I?"

"I'd say it's clear you've both been as blind as bats," Lorin said matter-of-factly. "But what remains unknown is what you're going to do now."

Heather was silent a long moment. Then she took a deep breath. "I'm going downstairs to eat breakfast, and then I'm going to the gallery. I'm painting with Tomás today."

"Go girl!" Lorin grinned and gave her the thumbs up signal. "Work will cure what ails you, if anything can. And just remember this: a husband and family—that would really put an end to your career, wouldn't it?"

Heather nodded. Lorin was right; they were both right. Heather only wished she didn't have to hurt Tanner in the process. Marriage for her was not in the near future, and though she cared deeply about Tanner, she wouldn't give up her dream for his.

"Although, you're kinda good for each other," Lorin added in an undertone. "You both believe in the Church for one, and I hear his father's rich."

Ignoring her friend, Heather hurried to the door. "I'll tell them you're changing," she said over her shoulder. "If you come down like that, Mrs. Silva will either kick the men out or she'll wrap you up in one of those huge aprons she wears."

"Okay, okay." Lorin rolled her eyes and retreated into the bedroom.

CR

Heather and Nate were the only grantees going to the gallery that morning. She had a session with Tomás, and Nate had promised to fill in her hours at the gallery. Later that day she would take his shift—if Tomás allowed her to leave by four. They always had to bow to his whims.

Heather quickly changed into her painting clothes. On her way out to Tomás's studio, she paused a few seconds at her paintings, still standing where she had left them to dry last Friday. Sometimes when she took quick peeks, an idea to enhance the work would come to her mind. Not today, however. Today, she could only think of Tanner and how impressed he had been with her work, even though the symbolic meaning of the Mother and Children could not have pleased him.

I've chosen the right thing by leaving Utah, she assured herself.

Tomás was staring at several of his paintings as she came into his studio. He was dressed in his usual meticulous black, and though unstained with paint, they were wrinkled. The black hair that hung halfway down his neck was uncombed. His green eyes flicked to hers and then back to his paintings. They were duller than usual and almost looked past her, as though staring at something only he could see.

Without waiting to be invited, Heather went to stand beside him, noting the sour smell of alcohol and unwashed male body. Yet almost immediately, the paintings took over her attention. The features were rather vague, as was normal with Tomás's style, but one of the paintings portrayed Heather in a yellow print dress she often wore to the gallery. The skirt, however, was long and flowing, unlike the real cut of the dress. A wind blew it all about the canvas, yet her modesty was retained, only her ankles and calves exposed. The woman's hair in the painting was also longer, teased to a fullness Heather used only when going somewhere special. Tomás must have seen her the night they went dancing. The woman wasn't smiling, but her partially open lips portrayed wonder. Her overly large hazel eyes held a sense of mystery.

The painting was good—very good, and Heather found herself flattered, though the painting was more an interpretation than an accurate rendition of Heather's qualities. The woman Tomás saw was apparently as unattainable as a butterfly, an imaginary, abstract princess who walked among fields as magical as her own self.

The second painting was of Lorin and an obvious contrast to the first. She wore only a shawl of midnight black looped around her torso, exposing shoulders, arms, and legs to the stormy elements that surrounded her. The ends of the shawl blew out behind her like a dark shadow. Her smile was wide and inviting, almost too revealing, wanton, like an evil enchantress out for souls. Heather was offended.

Why would he paint Lorin this way? Heather knew how much it would hurt her friend, who practically worshiped Tomás. Her gaze shifted to the artist. One hand was on his chin, the other supporting the elbow. He ignored her completely.

"Are we painting today?" she asked. "I have some sketches I did this morning of the fireworks. I wanted to paint the Hatch Shell. You know, to come up with something more Bostonian for the gallery."

He didn't reply.

Heather walked to a stool, sat down, and began to sketch. Sometimes this was the way to deal with Tomás. She quickly outlined the entire painting, wishing she'd had time to develop her photographs first. Without them it would mean more work in the long run, since she struggled with proportions. But at least she would have begun.

At last Tomás glanced over and spoke. "I have studied them all morning; there is nothing to be added. They are perfect."

Heather bought time by closing her notebook. "They are very good," she answered honestly.

He smiled in satisfaction and turned back to the paintings.

But she wasn't through. "I don't like the one of Lorin, though, no matter how perfect it may seem. Tomás, how could you be so cruel?"

He stiffened, then whirled on her. "Cruel? Cruel? I am not cruel." His odd accent was stronger than Heather had ever heard it, and his expression showed genuine fury. "This is the face she shows to me—or wants to show. She posed for me; this is what I saw."

"But she's your friend. She trusts you!" Heather stood up, not liking how dwarfed she felt sitting on the stool.

"Feelings do not matter," Tomás said, his green eyes flashing anger. He was so close, she recoiled from the odor of his sour breath. "Paintings are what's important. *Nothing* means more, *nothing* takes precedence. Painting is all there is." He brought one hand forward under her nose, fingers pointing upward and squeezed tightly together. "It is something you must find and capture. Nothing else has real meaning. A great artist has no friends, no family. Relationships are only for pleasure or for painting. That is all!"

He turned and stood before his canvasses again, hands clutched behind his back, indignant anger emanating from every line of his lank body. "Leave me. I will not teach you today. Go. And think! Decide what is important, or you will never be an artist." The disgust in his voice pierced Heather's heart, and she bit back tears as she gathered her materials and fled from his studio.

When she arrived in the main gallery studio, Nate was standing before his paintings, though dressed to work in the gallery. He looked up at her in surprise. "Done so soon?"

"You won't need to take my shift," she said bitterly. "Tomás doesn't want to teach me today."

He came toward her, concerned. "Did something happen, or is he just in one of his moods?"

"No, it was me. I told him I didn't like his painting of Lorin—have you seen it?"

"No. What's it like?"

She described it. "It's abstract, of course, like most of his work, and maybe strangers won't even be able to tell it's Lorin, but it's just . . . well, I know Lorin. She has her moments, but she's not the evil, wanton creature Tomás has drawn. If he was going to change her so, why didn't he use some model? Why Lorin? He has to work with her."

Nate's arm went around her in a brief, comforting squeeze, then dropped to his side. "All I can say is that's Tomás for you. He thinks he's his own law. But, you know, Lorin may not be as upset about this as you are."

"She practically worships him."

"Exactly. And she's not the only one." Nate grimaced and shook his head. "You ought to see what McCarty's painting at the house. Better yet, you shouldn't. Looks just like something Tomás would do. He's had half clad models posing all week."

Heather closed her eyes for a moment. "Well, I'd better get changed if I'm going to get started in the gallery."

"We can still change shifts," he offered.

"Well, if it's all the same to you, I'd rather work out there now. It'll take my mind off everything. And maybe Tomás will let you go in this morning." Heather twirled a lock of hair.

Nate looked at her hand and smiled. "It's not just Tomás, is it?"

Heather wondered how she had never recognized how intuitive Nate was to her feelings. "No," she said with a sigh. "It's not just Tomás. I had a bit of a falling out with my friend last night. But we'll be okay. We've been friends a long time."

"Well, if you ever want to talk, I'm here."

"Thanks. I appreciate that." Giving him a smile, she went to change.

❧

Heather kept busy and the days passed. As Nate predicted, Lorin didn't mind Tomás's painting and was even amused that he had portrayed her that way. "I look like a beautiful, exotic sorceress or something," she said. Pacified by Lorin's response, the artist passed both paintings over to Mr. Oldham, who would eventually auction them to the highest bidder.

On Friday, Tomás called Heather in and helped with her painting of the Hatch Memorial Shell. He showed no trace of animosity toward her, and Heather tried to put the incident behind them as well. Whatever his faults, she had to admit that he knew his way around a canvas.

After arriving home on Friday night and eating dinner, she plugged her laptop into the phone jack and sat on her bed. She had written Tanner a brief e-mail earlier in the week, expressing hope that he arrived home safely, but she hadn't been able to check e-mail since. There was one from him waiting for her now.

Dear Heather,

The flight was long and tedious, but I did arrive safely. Thank you for asking and for writing. I worried that you wouldn't. You have to admit, though, that what happened between us is not a complete surprise—we have been headed this way for a while, even if we didn't recognize it.

I went to my parents' for dinner last night. Jeremy and I played basketball (boy, that kid is good!). It came to me that I was playing on that same slab of cement the day you moved in next door. You know, when we went in my car for ice cream after moving all those boxes, I looked into your eyes and I noticed they were the most beautiful eyes that I had ever seen. I wonder now if things would have developed differently between us if I had told you. Or if on the night of our senior prom your mother hadn't given birth to your little sister. Remember how we ended up at the hospital instead of the dance? I didn't mind then, but I do now. I wish we'd had that night. But then, I cherish our friendship more than I can say. I believe that all serious relationships should be built on such a solid base. I'm not trying to rush you, I just want you to know that I meant every word I said to you last Sunday.

I hope everything is all right with you. I hope your painting is going well. I'm sure it is, if what I saw was any indication. I am proud of your accomplishments as if they were my own.

Next week I'm going to Japan for another week. I have e-mail access there so you shouldn't notice any difference. Someday I'd like to take you to Japan with me. You will likely find it as strange as I found Boston!

There is more I would like to say, but I'd better stop now. You know how I feel, and that's enough. Have a good day, Heather. Paint lots!

All my love,
Tanner

Heather re-read the e-mail slowly. What was she going to do about him? She missed him—there was no way around that, but she had worked hard for this opportunity. Then again, she wouldn't be honest if she didn't admit there was a part of her that was flattered by his attention. Despite their previous "friends only" relationship, she had always been aware of how attractive he was. Their kiss on Sunday had opened her eyes to many other feelings she had secretly harbored.

The customary bi-weekly e-mail from her mother had also arrived, detailing family events. Heather found herself smiling wistfully, but she knew they were doing well without her. However, an e-mail from her thirteen-year-old sister Kathryn brought worry.

Dear Heather,

Mom has been very, very sick. She's supposed to be long over that part of it now, but she's not. I'm beginning to believe she is really too old to have another baby. She mostly just stays in bed. She can help the little children with their homework, but she can't make food or clean or anything else. Kevin and Aaron think I ought to cook since I'm a girl. That makes me so mad 'cuz they're older. So I heat up stuff in the microwave before they get home or when they're in their rooms and I feed the little kids. I don't save any for them. Dad cooks half the time, though, so they're not starving. As if they would! They have hands and know how to push buttons.

Tanner's mom comes over a lot to help. She's the one who sends for the groceries. Mom says she'll be better soon, like she always has before, but I just keep thinking of the other baby she lost when you came home from your mission. It's scary. I wish you were here. I know you're painting a lot and I'm glad. But can't you paint here just as well? You can have your old room back. And I promise not to ask you to make dinner! It would just be nice to talk to you. Alison and the little girls aren't much company.

Anyway, besides Mom, we're okay. Tanner brought us some pictures of you. I didn't know he went to see you. Alison says traveling all that way means he's in love with you, but she's only ten and doesn't know anything. Or does she? Is there something you should tell us about Tanner?

I wish I could come to see you in Boston. How long are you staying there? Mom says probably for a few years, at least. It's strange to think you might not be here when the new baby comes in December. (I hope it's another girl 'cuz boys are a real pain.) She won't even know you at all. That's okay, I'll tell her all about you. You will come home for Christmas, won't you? We're hoping Jacob will come off his mission by then. He's supposed to come home at the end of November, but he might not come until January if he gets permission to stay in the Philippines longer. I guess he likes his mission.

I'd better go. But one more thing. Remember Cody? Well, he's been calling me a lot lately. I know I said he had a big nose, but I don't mind it now. He is so nice. Don't worry, we're just friends. I know I can't date until I'm sixteen. Bye now.

I love you,
Kathryn

Heather frowned. Her mother hadn't mentioned she was sick in any of her e-mails. Of course, self sacrifice was common fare for her mother. She had spent her life sheltering and caring for others, never minding the cost to herself. While Heather admired the example, her mother's actions only made her feel more inadequate. *Oh, why can't I just be normal! Why do I care so much about painting?*

With a long sigh, Heather briefly answered the e-mails from her family. Then she began to tell Tanner about Tomás and the painting of Lorin, but she ended up erasing the entire thing. The story made artists sound unreliable and crazy—and not every artist was as out-of-touch as Tomás. Telling Tanner would only support his suggestion that she return home. Yet not long ago, she wouldn't have hesitated to confide in him. She might have even confessed her own growing obsession, hoping he might help her find balance. But that was when they were only friends. Sadness filled her heart. Had this new aspect of their relationship cost her Tanner's friendship? She didn't want to believe that, but it seemed now she had to choose between all or nothing.

Leaving Tanner's reply for the next day, Heather donned her painting clothes—try as she might she could never paint so fastidiously as Tomás—and went to the apartment studio. Her painting of the Hatch Memorial Shell was in the gallery studio, but she didn't feel like working on it anyway. Thumbing through her sketches, she found the ones she had done of Tanner's parents' house. Somewhere she also had the photographs.

Yes, tonight this was what she wanted to do. The feelings were right, and she couldn't rest until she put them on the canvas. Never mind that she was already exhausted from a day of painting with Tomás. The familiar fire coursed through her veins, bringing energy that would give her hours to pursue her dream.

Chapter Eleven

ore days streamed into weeks. Heather was so busy and content with her work, she rarely had time to think about her family or Tanner. Only at night when she checked her e-mail—something she had begun to do more often since his visit more than a month ago—did they come vividly to mind. She and Tanner had exchanged many short missives. She kept hers light, and he matched her tone, though he always mentioned something about their relationship and how he felt, even if it was in a simple closing. She understood instinctively that he didn't want to push her, yet also didn't want her to forget his love.

Heather felt guilty, though she couldn't exactly say why. She craved hearing from him, yet lately, she had begun responding to fewer of his e-mails, claiming that she was very busy.

And she was. Mr. Oldham had placed her painting of Tanner's anchor in the gallery and had requested her Mother and Children painting when she finished the details she planned to add. Mr. Oldham also arranged several family portraits for her to paint over the next few months, since she did so well with children. Her painting of the Hatch Memorial Shell was coming along more slowly, but she was confident she would find the right touch that would make it a triumph.

She had never felt so successful and confident. No longer did she hold doubts of being able to earn a living as an artist. This chance had been everything she had hoped for. Day and night she ate, drank, and breathed painting. The only day of rest was Sunday, which she kept religiously, though much of the afternoon she spent catching up on rest lost during the week of work.

The other grantees were following a similar pattern. Each of them had settled into a routine that involved furious painting around the clock and then a day or two of sleeping it off. McCarty, however, seemed to work the most. Heather rarely saw him anymore as he passed all of his time either with Tomás or painting in the carriage house studio. He skipped so many of his shifts at the gallery that they lost count. Mr. Oldham didn't seem to mind, but

Heather worried about McCarty. Every time she ran into him he seemed distracted and silent, almost sullen. Heather found she missed his old boisterous, annoying self. His style had grown more and more abstract by the day, and though Heather much preferred Keith's landscapes, Nate's portraits, or even Lorin's buildings, she recognized his talent.

Heather also saw Mrs. Oldham less than before, and she wondered why. Finally, she decided the older woman was likely painting as well. It was odd not seeing her around the gallery, and on the rare occasion that she appeared, Heather made it a point to spend time with her. In fact, it was Mrs. Oldham who helped Heather pinpoint that the lack of life in her Hatch painting was partly due to the absence of children playing in the Fourth of July crowd in the foreground. Heather painted white over several of the figures and began again. She decided to add a few pets as well.

Not everything was going as smoothly as Heather's painting. She and Lorin had grown apart over the past month. Lorin drank alcohol openly now during their meals and often didn't sleep at their apartment. She rarely gave Heather any explanation for her absences. Unsure how to respond, Heather did the only thing she could think of—she begged Lorin to go to church with her. Lorin only laughed and told her she was much too busy painting.

As for Heather, Sundays and church in particular had become a refuge. No longer did she have to stop herself from painting on Sunday. Rather, it became a relief because it was the one day she *couldn't* paint. Blessings came in the form of good health and fewer weekdays spent in bed because of exhaustion. Many times she felt inspiration while painting, and she attributed it to the fact that the Lord helped her because of her willingness to keep His commandment. When she tried to explain this to the other grantees, only Keith understood what she meant by a spiritual inspiration; for the others, inspiration was derived from substance abuse, lack of sleep, or plain determination. Not even Nate believed there was any such thing as divine help. Heather couldn't doubt—not when she was having so much success.

At the end of the first week in August, when she had been in Boston for almost three months, Lorin came into their apartment, glassy-eyed from painting all day with Tomás at the gallery. She kicked off her shoes and lay down on the couch, her short, sleeveless summer dress bunching up slightly around her thighs.

"How'd it go?" Heather asked, sitting on the coffee table. She had just finished working on her painting of Tanner's childhood home, which, uncharacteristically, wasn't going as well as she had expected—probably because she was tired. She was definitely looking forward to the Sabbath the next day.

Lorin's face was pale under the tan she had obtained painting in the back gallery courtyard with Tomás. "Great."

"I saved you some dinner, in case you didn't get a chance to eat."

"I'm not hungry." Lorin shut her eyes.

"I'm glad you're home. I've missed seeing you around."

"Hmm."

"Is something wrong? You've been acting very strange lately. I'm here for you if you need me, you know."

"I'm fine."

Heather knew her friend wasn't fine. Not only had she lost weight, but the deep circles under her eyes told of little sleep and too much work.

Heather leaned forward. "Come on, talk to me."

"I just want to sleep," Lorin muttered.

"Well, hey, how about going to church with me tomorrow? They keep asking about you." Heather hoped that if Lorin accepted, they might, if only for a few hours, regain the comradery they used to share.

"No. Heather, I'm going to sleep in. Can't you see that I'm about dead? I'm sorry if you want to talk. I just can't right now. I'm exhausted."

"Okay, okay. You should rest. In fact, you should probably come home earlier, maybe not stay out so late."

Lorin's eyes popped open. "Oh, for crying out loud, Heather. You're not my mother! And I'm sick to death of your suggestions. Why do you think I spend so much time away from here?"

Heather had thought it was because Lorin felt guilty about her lifestyle, but she didn't dare say so now.

"I'll tell you why—because I'm tired of you looking down on me. No, I don't go to church, but that hasn't hurt me a bit. And yes, I've been drinking. It helps me paint. If you'd try it, maybe you wouldn't be so uptight all the time. Why do you think no one invites you out to party anymore?"

"Party? We're all too busy to party."

"*You're* too busy, you and McCarty. But the rest of us find time. We just don't tell you."

Heather was hurt at the revelation; she didn't think she had been so noticeably different from the others.

Lorin sat up and swung her feet down to the carpet. "And before you begin preaching to me, little Miss Perfect, maybe you ought to look at your own life. You say you believe in honesty, and yet you keep Tanner on a string even though you have no intention of ever marrying him. Admit it. You love painting more than you love him. But why not have a rich boyfriend hanging around just in case things don't pan out?"

This was too much. "Oh, it's okay for you to have a boyfriend, but not me." Heather had suspected for some time that Lorin was seeing someone secretly—probably Tomás. Or perhaps Lorin was simply jealous of her relationship with Tanner.

Lorin stood, her blue eyes bright. "It's different with me. The men I date know where I stand, and they feel the same way. But as you've told me so many times, Tanner wants the perfect Mormon wife—which you don't want to be. You have no intention of letting your talent go to waste in order to care for a houseful of his brats. If you were really honest, you'd let him go so he could find someone else. *Before* he gets seriously hurt." Lorin glared at her, fists clenched.

Stunned by her friend's outburst, Heather sat where she was on the coffee table, unable to move or speak.

Lorin wasn't through. "I like my life here. I love what I'm doing. *You're* the one who's confused. *You're* the one who has one foot in one world and the other in another. You want to have your cake and eat it too."

Heather swallowed hard. "I've been honest with Tanner. He knows my goals."

"Does he? Then why is he still in Utah waiting for you to come home?"

"I shouldn't have to choose!" The words were ripped from Heather's very soul.

"Well, you do," Lorin said flatly. "So get over it. Like Tomás says: the painting requires everything. Tanner can never understand that."

Heather stifled tears, wishing Lorin would leave. "Stop," she begged.

"Oh, don't worry, I'm finished." Lorin turned quickly, marching to the door of their apartment. Abruptly, she paused, a hand going to her head. She wavered and then sank to the carpet with a muffled *thump*! Heather stared for a moment, then rushed to Lorin's side, her heart pounding furiously. Lorin was unconscious.

"Lorin, Lorin!" Heather gently slapped the sides of her face. "Please, wake up. What's wrong?"

For a few long seconds Lorin didn't respond. Thoughts of calling an ambulance raced through Heather's mind. She leaned over to check if Lorin was still breathing, and a faint aroma of alcohol reached her nose. *Well, she's breathing.* "Come on, Lorin," she urged, rubbing her friend's cheeks.

"Uhhhh," Lorin muttered, eyes fluttering.

"Can you hear me, Lorin?"

At last her eyes opened. "Wh—what happened?"

"You fainted, I think. Do you want me to call an ambulance? Maybe we should go to the doctor."

Lorin shook her head. "No. I'm okay. I'm just tired. Didn't eat much today. Can you help me to bed?"

"Sure."

Heather put her arms around Lorin and practically dragged her to the bedroom. Lorin had always been petite, yet now she seemed almost childlike. Heather pulled back the blanket on Lorin's bed. "Here, get in."

Lorin obeyed. As Heather tucked the thin blanket around her, Lorin closed her eyes and lay still. Heather stayed by her side, making sure her friend was breathing normally. Finally satisfied, she turned off the light and went to sit on her own bed, feeling more numb than anything else.

"I'm sorry, Heather," came a soft, sleepy voice. "I didn't mean any of it. I know you want the best for me. And there haven't been so many parties— we've all been working. Everyone likes you. Please forgive me."

"It's okay." Heather waited to see if Lorin would speak again, but after a few moments she heard soft snores.

She pulled her knees up to her chest, wrapping her arms around them. Lorin might have been wrong in some of the things she said, but Heather knew she was right about Tanner. Though not in so many words, Heather had been leading him along by allowing him any hope in their relationship. At the moment she had no intention of going back to Utah; and no matter how much she cared for him, she had no right to allow him to think she was considering it. Their lives were going along different paths. If she loved him, she had to let him go.

With determination she arose and retrieved her laptop from their small corner desk. Going into the sitting room, she plugged the computer into the phone jack, sat down on the couch, and pulled up her e-mail. There was a huge emptiness in her chest as she wrote Tanner for what might be the last time. Surely he wouldn't be her friend after reading it, but someday he would realize she had done it for him as well as for herself. There simply wasn't room in her life for two passions.

Dear Tanner,

It's so difficult for me to write this letter. Your friendship over the past years has been a constant in my life and I value it deeply. I'm afraid that after this e-mail our friendship will be over. I know it's only what I deserve.

Tanner, I've been flattered by your attention, and the fact that you would consider me worthy of your love. Knowing you as I do, I understand that the emotion and commitment did not come easily. But I have thought about this intensely during the past month and have come to the conclusion that your romantic love is something I cannot return. As I tried to tell you your last night in Boston, I must be true to my own dreams, and marriage and children aren't a part of that right now. I honestly don't know if it will ever be—at least not in the way that it has been for my parents. If I had children, I think my duty and desire would be with them—and rightly so.

I know we've been given a commandment to marry, but I was also given a commandment in my patriarchal blessing to magnify the gift of painting I've been given. I don't feel I can do both, and while I care so much for you, I must paint. It's like breathing to me. Please try to understand, though I know it's difficult to accept this final word. If I ever would marry anyone, I'd want it to be you. But I can't. You want something I can't give you.

I want you to go on with your life. I want to see you happy. You deserve it. I know there is a young woman prepared for you, and that you will find her. Please don't talk to me of love and marriage anymore; it is an impossibility for us. I must find my own life. Forgive me if you can.

I'm sorry,
Heather

When she was finished, hot tears streamed down her cheeks. But this was energy she knew how to use. Shutting her laptop, she returned to the studio and began to paint.

Chapter Twelve

On Sunday after church, Tanner stared at Heather's e-mail with an overwhelming urge to scream, cry, and break something. She had rejected him! Waves of hurt and despair flooded his entire being. For what seemed like hours, he stared at the screen, seeing the words, but unable to read them.

It was over. Heather hadn't even given them a chance. He had been worried about leaving her there alone, and he'd been careful to keep up a continuous dialogue over the e-mail, sharing with her his feelings and his vision of their future. At times her answers had seemed so positive that he felt they were making real progress.

All that was over now. She didn't love him—at least not enough. Certainly not as much as she loved painting.

Without thinking, he reached for the phone on the desk, pushing the button that would automatically dial his cousin's number. Savvy had finally moved into her nearby apartment and should be home from church by now.

She answered on the second ring. "Hello?"

He was grateful she had answered instead of one of her roommates. "Savvy," he said, barely managing the word.

"Tanner? Is that you? What's wrong?"

He swallowed hard, trying to speak past the huge lump of pain.

"Tanner?"

"Can you come over?" he managed.

"I'll be right there." The phone went dead. Tanner replaced it in the cradle and went to the sitting room to wait. The urge to cry had left; now he only felt a numb emptiness that was almost worse than the previous pain.

Tanner opened the door to Savvy five minutes later. She rushed in, blue eyes searching his face. "Oh, Tanner. You're so pale. What happened?"

He led her to the second room in the condo that served as his office. With a tap of his finger, he removed the screen saver and brought up the e-mail. His cousin sat at the desk, scanned Heather's words rapidly, and then turned to him. "I'm so sorry."

"I just don't understand," he said, running a hand through his hair. "Things were coming along well. I thought . . . Oh, Savvy, why does she think it has to be me or her art? I wouldn't dream of taking that away from her—ever."

Savvy shook her head. "It's not you taking it away, it's the demands of life, of motherhood. You may not see it, but I do. My mother never finished college because she got married. That was fine for her. She's really happy with her life. But for me—there's just so much I want to learn and do. I'd hate it if I couldn't finish my astronomy classes. Unlike you, I don't want to work at our fathers' company for the rest of my life."

"I know, you want to teach."

"Yes, at a college. That's the best way for me to keep up on new developments in the field. So I want to do that at least part time when my children are in school. I won't be able to if I don't get a degree."

"But you can do both—learn and have a family. You want to do both, don't you?" Tanner was feeling very confused. Once, gender roles, especially in the Church, had seemed so easily defined. Prophets had urged women to stay home, and that was that.

"Oh yes, but I'd be a fool if I thought it was going to be easy." Savvy stood up from his leather chair. "If I find Mr. Right and get married before I'm done with school, it'd be hard juggling any children we might have with my classes. And then even though I want to stay home with my children while they're young, I'll need to keep my skills updated. That means more classes over the years to assure that I'll be able to teach someday."

"But you're willing to do the extra work." Tanner paced to the door.

"That's because it's something I believe in."

He turned, ready to pace back across the room, but Savvy had followed him. "And Heather doesn't?" he asked. "She was raised the same way you were. She's been in the Church her entire life."

"I don't have the answer. I'm as confused as you are." Savvy's brow furrowed. "It's plain she cares about you. You can't look at this like she's choosing her art over her love for you. That's not the problem. It's her basic beliefs."

"I know that's how it seems," he replied, frustrated. "But I'm just not sure anymore."

Savvy's eyes bore into his. "You have to get your ego out of this. You love Heather because of who she is, and her experiences made her that way—the same experiences that are causing her confusion."

With Savvy in front of him, there was nowhere to pace, but Tanner had to keep moving. He pivoted on his foot and stalked into the sitting room. "I've been over this time and time again in my mind. Heather's going to church, and I believe she has a testimony. Everything I know about her says that she should be able to put her trust in the Lord and follow what He requires of her, believing that her painting won't suffer."

Savvy sat down on an easy chair and watched him pace. "Well, there is her mother, and the fact that she gave up painting to have all those children."

"It was her choice!" Tanner exploded. "And never, ever have I told Heather or even implied that I'd expect her to have eleven children. That's a decision we'd make through prayer."

"Hey, don't yell at me, I'm only here to help."

"I know, Savvy. Sorry." He walked over and sat on the couch. "But it all seems to come down to the fact that either Heather doesn't have a testimony of the Church, or maybe . . ." He paused and took a deep breath. He noticed his foot was bouncing up and down again, releasing his nervous tension. Consciously, he stilled it. "Maybe we're wrong about how we think she feels about me. She might actually believe I'm not the right man for her and is trying to let me down easy. I mean, if she honestly loved and trusted me, she would believe as I do that we could make it through anything and be happy. She'd know that I'd bend over backward to help her reach her goals. She'd come home and give us a chance."

"I don't know." Savvy shook her head. "That seems a little too pat to me—too black-and-white. Put yourself in her position. What if you had to give up working at the company to stay home and take care of children and a house?"

"Hey, if Heather would support me, why not?"

Savvy snorted. "Yeah, right. I've seen you at work. I know how much you enjoy it. The truth is, you know you can do both so it doesn't worry you. You'll have a wife taking care of the homefront, while you're working."

"Okay, okay, maybe there's some truth in that. I admit that I've seen Heather with her brothers and sisters. She'd make a great mom."

"But it's still a lot of work. Being the oldest in her family, she's obviously seen just how much work it really is."

"Heather's not afraid of work."

"No, but she does seem to be afraid of losing a chance to reach her own goals."

"But shouldn't a family *be* her goal? It is for you." His foot was moving again; he let it continue.

Savvy sighed. "I don't know. That might be part of the problem. From what I see, she does want a family—or believes she should want one—but she also believes she couldn't be a good mom and paint at the same time. So that means a choice. It's as simple as that."

"But all that boils down to faith." Tanner felt like he was dying inside.

"How so?"

"With God *all* things are possible. I believe that. He wouldn't give us a commandment, and then not make it possible for us to fulfill it."

Savvy sighed. "That's easy for you to say—you're a man. Your challenges are so different."

Tanner glared at her without speaking. She shrugged and added, "The point remains—what are you going to do about this?"

"I don't know. She's made herself very clear." He dropped his head into his hands. "There's a part of me that thinks it's time to give up."

"Or maybe give her more time."

"How much?" he asked miserably. "A year? Two? Three? Ten?"

"I get it," Savvy said.

"She won't even consider letting us continue as before. She thinks it's stringing me along."

"And maybe it would be. I'll say this for her: she's honest."

Tanner wasn't sure he cared for honesty at this point. "I guess that's true. And I also guess I have no choice."

"Actually, you do. You can still be her friend or not. And you can try to go on with your life and see what happens. Maybe she'll come around in the future. Or, if Heather isn't right for you, there's still a host of girls out there who could be right. You just need to find one of them."

What Savvy said made sense. But it hurt—really hurt. Tanner had known this outcome was a possibility all along, but there in Boston when Heather had returned his kisses, he had felt sure they could jump any obstacles thrown at them. He hadn't fooled himself that it would be easy, but together they'd find a way. Now, Heather had refused to even try, and he couldn't force her.

Tanner was quiet for a long time. He had almost forgotten Savvy was in the room. "You don't need to stay," he told her when he became aware of her presence again. "I'll be okay."

"You shouldn't be alone. Why don't you come over to my apartment for a bite to eat, and then there's a single adult fireside for my stake tonight. I'd love for you to come with me."

He shook his head, then nodded. "Maybe you're right. I need to get away from here. But first I have to do something. Wait here, okay?"

"Okay."

He went back to his computer and sat down. He stared at Heather's e-mail for a long time. Then he quickly typed in his response and sent it before his heart broke all over again.

Heather, I will always be your friend. Nothing can change that. Tanner

ଓଃ

Tanner barely heard the speaker at the fireside that evening. He was going over everything he and Heather had said to each other since his trip to Boston. With a sinking feeling, he realized that she had never really given him any hope, but had been honest about her intentions from the beginning. Yes, some of her e-mails had seemed loving and hopeful, but without hearing her actual voice, he could have interpreted almost anything into them. Perhaps the progress they were making had all been in his mind. *She probably recognized from my e-mails that I still had hopes of winning her, and she didn't want me to get hurt.* That would mean it was him she didn't want.

Agony sliced through the protective numbness, making it difficult to breathe.

Then why all that business about her painting?

Tanner clenched his jaw. There was just no way around these seesawing emotions. It hurt him deeply to think that she didn't return his romantic love, but at least that was something he could understand. He was beginning to believe the painting issue might just be an excuse, as he had suggested earlier to Savvy—an excuse Heather used so she didn't have to hurt him further. Yet if he was wrong, and the painting was the real reason she couldn't return his love, maybe he shouldn't give up on her. He should pray, offer support, and remain her friend until everything worked out. Tanner felt paralyzed. He simply didn't know what to do. To risk his heart further seemed out of the question.

"Tanner, it's over."

Tanner jerked and looked in surprise at Savvy, who was standing beside him. She tugged at his arm. "Wow, that was one of the best talks I've heard in a long time."

"Yeah," he said, coming to his feet. He watched the singles file out. Somehow he felt much older than the rest, though he wasn't even twenty-four until November. True, many LDS men his age were married or engaged, but that had never bothered him before. Heather's rejection, it seemed, had evoked a lot of previously unknown emotions.

"Tanner? Tanner Wolfe?" came a voice as they left the chapel. "Is that you?"

Tanner looked around the foyer to see a striking woman in a loosely fitted green dress coming toward them. She had long blonde hair, swinging freely about her shoulders, and very green eyes. He'd know those eyes anywhere. "Amanda?"

"Yes, it's me!" she said, holding out her hands. "It's been soooo long."

Tanner took her hands and squeezed them, throwing a questioning glance at Savvy. She shrugged. "I told you I was moving into Amanda's stake, remember?"

He remembered now. "That's right. You did." He returned his attention to Amanda. "Good to see you. You look great!"

"Me? Tanner, you're the one who looks wonderful!"

Tanner knew women considered him good-looking, and nothing they said to that effect usually phased him, but for some reason he felt himself blushing. Was it because he had grown to think of himself as attached this past month and therefore flirting was off-limits? He let go of Amanda's hands. "So, what've you been up to?"

"Oh, Savvy probably told you I never did get married." Amanda looked around for Savvy, but his cousin had disappeared into the crowd of singles. "It just didn't work out. I ended up going on a mission to Georgia. Then I came back to school. Just finishing up."

"Savvy said you were a teacher."

"Almost."

"I'm glad you're doing something you love."

"I do love it. And it's something I can do part time later. Or take a few years off for family if I need to."

"Savvy was saying just the same thing today. She wants to be a teacher too—in college, though." Tanner felt uncomfortable. Here Amanda was practically telling him she would gladly take time off to have a family, when Heather ran away at the very thought.

"I bet you're working at your dad's company. Have you taken over yet?" She smiled as she spoke.

He chuckled, beginning to relax. "Not yet. Just the Japanese division."

"That's where you went on your mission, isn't it?"

"Yeah. I'm surprised you remember."

"I remember a lot of stuff," she said with a wink.

Tanner's chuckle became a full-blown laugh. "I'll bet. Hope it's not the time I got the days messed up for one of our dates."

"Oh, no. It's the good things—like junior prom. That was fun."

"It was," he agreed.

An awkward silence fell between them.

"Well," Tanner said. "It's good seeing you. I guess I'd better find Savvy and haul her away from whatever crowd of guys she's in."

Amanda laughed. "She certainly has grown up."

"Yeah, tell me about it." He took a step backward. "Well, see you around."

"Hey, Tanner," Amanda said, stopping his flight. "It just occurred to me that maybe our meeting wasn't a coincidence."

"What?" He didn't hide his surprise. Was she making hints about a possible future for them? While Amanda was certainly a smart, beautiful woman, he wasn't yet up to even considering a relationship with someone who wasn't Heather.

"Well, I'm student-teaching summer school at a private school, and right now we're beginning a short section on Japan. Do you think you would be able to swing by the school and give us a presentation and answer some questions?"

Tanner felt like an idiot. *Of course, it's not you she's interested in, but your expertise.* To cover up he spoke quickly, "Uh, sure. When?"

"Any day next week, at any time you can make it. Our schedule is adjustable. But later in the week would be better so that I can cover some of the material first."

He took out the thin, electronic organizer he carried in his suit coat. "How about Thursday? I have a meeting until noon that could run a little late, but I could come over after that."

"Great!" Amanda was enthusiastic. "About one-thirty then?"

"Okay." He put the information in.

"If you run later than expected or something else comes up, call me." She took a business card from her purse and scribbled a number. "That's my direct number at the school."

Tanner looked at the card before slipping it and his organizer back into his pocket. When he looked up, a man he didn't recognize had come up beside Amanda. "You about ready?" he asked her.

"Yes. But you have to meet my friend Tanner. Tanner, this is Gerry. Gerry, this is Tanner. We went to high school together."

"Nice to meet you," Tanner said, offering his hand. Now he really felt stupid. Amanda hadn't been making any hints about them getting together. For all he knew these two were almost engaged, and her innuendos regarding a family—if there had been any—were likely meant for Gerry. "Well, I'd better round up Savvy. See you around." Tanner smiled and turned away.

"Until Thursday," Amanda called after him.

He walked to the end of the foyer before glancing behind him. Amanda and Gerry were exiting the double glass doors in the front of the church building, Gerry with a protective hand on the middle of her back.

"There you are." Savvy came up behind him. "So how did it go with Amanda?"

Tanner stared at her suspiciously. "You set me up."

"No, I didn't. Yeah, I knew she'd be here, but I also knew you weren't interested or you would have called her by now. You just ran into her, that's all."

"Well, I just said goodbye to her and her date, Gerry."

Savvy shrugged. "Hey, he's just a date. They aren't engaged or anything."

"So you *did* set me up!"

"No, you idiot." Savvy's face became red with frustration. "But you know what? I can tell that you *are* interested, for all that you deny it. Or you wouldn't be making such a fuss." She turned on her heel and stomped toward the back exit where she had parked her car.

Tanner groaned. What was wrong with him? Just because he felt so terrible inside, he didn't have the right to take it out on Savvy. She had done nothing but try to comfort him, and despite her completely erroneous assumption about his interest for Amanda, he needed to apologize. He hurried out the door after her.

ʘʘ

On Thursday afternoon, Tanner was running late as he reached Amanda's school. After checking in with the office, he power-walked toward the fourth grade, carrying his large box of displays. He tried to come to a stop outside the room, but he was moving so quickly that he slid a few feet past. Two children sitting in the hallway in front of the next classroom snickered. Grinning, Tanner shook his head and sighed. He definitely did not miss being in school.

Amanda looked up as he walked hesitantly through the open door to her classroom. She put down the whiteboard marker she was using. "And here is our guest speaker now," she said. "Students say hello to Mr. Wolfe."

"Hello, Mr. Wolfe," twenty-seven children said obediently.

"Hi, guys." Tanner smiled at them.

Their regular teacher waved a greeting to him from the back of the room. She mouthed something to Amanda about going to talk with the principal and left. Tanner was relieved to have one less adult around to judge his performance. Taking a deep breath, he began to speak.

An hour and a half later, Tanner let out a long sigh of relief as the bell rang. As the children collected their belongings and scattered, he slumped to the table where he had arranged his displays. "Whew! They're much tougher than any client I've had to make presentations for."

She gazed at him with an amused smile. "Well, your clients probably sit still. But you were wonderful with them. I can tell you have a lot of experience with kids."

"Not really. My neighbors have a lot of young kids—I used to spend a lot of time there." He frowned. The last thing he wanted to do was think of Heather and her siblings right now.

"Oh, yeah, I remember. That was Heather's family, wasn't it? You two were always great friends." Amanda arose from her desk and came to stand

127

beside him. "I have to admit that used to bother me a little when we dated."

He hadn't realized that. "We're just friends," he said as the familiar sadness welled in his heart. "Still are. She's in Boston now, studying painting."

"That's nice," Amanda said politely. "So, if you're not busy tonight, would you like to have dinner? I make a mean spaghetti sauce, and my garlic bread is, well, out of this world, if I do say so myself. After such a great presentation, you deserve it."

"Well," he hesitated.

Her smile wavered. "You're probably seeing someone," she said quickly.

"No, actually I'm not. But I thought you were. What about Gerry?"

"We're dating, but we have no firm commitment. We both date other people." Her beautiful smile returned like the sun from behind a cloud. "So how about it? For old time's sake?"

"I'd love to." And suddenly he was telling the truth. His heart still missed Heather, but obviously he had to start considering a future without her. Perhaps running into Amanda again was the Lord's way of encouraging him to begin that future. "But don't worry about cooking, Amanda—especially after what had to be a long day of teaching all those kids. I know just the restaurant for us."

ॐ

Tanner picked Amanda up a few hours later at her apartment and drove his Blue Bug to the Pizza Factory in Lindon. Amanda grinned when she saw the restaurant. "Oh, I haven't been here since the old days. This is perfect! You have another Blue Bug *and* we're eating here. I feel like we're back in high school."

"Not quite. This car is a new model Bug, though I still have the old one we used to putter around in."

"You don't!" Her face was animated in the way that had once made him so attracted to her.

"Yep. It's at my parents'. Can't bear to get rid of it."

"We'll have to go for a ride sometime! We just have to!"

He laughed at her enthusiasm. "Sure. Why not?"

Inside the restaurant, they both ordered spaghetti and garlic bread, as had been their custom. The conversation came easily, and Tanner felt his wounded heart slowly begin to mend. After their meal they drove to Alpine and retrieved his old car to drive Amanda home. She reverently slid her fingers along the shiny blue paint. "Boy, does this hold a lot of memories."

"Yeah," he agreed. The first day he had met Heather came sharply to mind, followed by dates with Amanda and outings with his friends.

"I'm almost sorry I have to teach tomorrow," she said. "Remember how we used to drive up to Salt Lake and go dancing?"

"Oh, yeah. I remember—especially that night we missed your curfew. Ooh, I never saw a man so angry as your dad that night."

Amanda laughed. "But we were never late again!"

"I didn't want to die an early death."

All too soon they arrived at Amanda's. Tanner walked her to the door. "Thanks, Amanda. I really had a good time."

"Me, too." The moonlight reflected from her features, making her more beautiful than before.

"It meant a lot to me." He looked away, embarrassed to be telling her this. "It's just, well, I've had a rough time lately—mostly my own fault—and it's nice to forget all that for a while."

When he looked back at her, he found Amanda watching him. "I ran into Savvy yesterday," she said. "We had a stake Enrichment activity. Anyway, she didn't tell me a lot, but said that you'd recently had your heart broken. I'm really sorry, Tanner. I know exactly how you feel."

"But you at least had a reason to expect something in the future—you were engaged. I never even got that far. So maybe I'm just . . ." *A darn fool,* he wanted to say. "Maybe I'm just taking it too hard."

"There's no scale for things of the heart. You'll be okay. Believe me."

"I do."

There was a tension between them now. Tanner realized that he was at the door with a stunning woman who seemed to like him and who had eased the pain in his heart considerably with her warm heart and ready smiles. Was she expecting him to kiss her? He didn't think he was ready for that yet. Not when Heather was still so prominently in his heart.

Smiling gently, Amanda reached up and gave him a soft kiss on the cheek. "Goodnight, Tanner. Call me if you want. I'd love to go out with you again." She opened the apartment door and went inside, gently shutting it behind her.

Tanner stood on the small cement porch for a minute pondering his options. He had to admit that tonight had been the best he'd spent since the Fourth of July nearly six weeks ago.

Almost of its own volition, his hand knocked on the door. After a brief wait, Amanda answered with a puzzled look on her face.

"Hey," he said. "I was wondering—you want to go dancing tomorrow night?"

A smile lit her face. "I can't tomorrow, but how about Saturday?"

"Great. We can eat first. I'll pick you up at seven."

Chapter Thirteen

*H*eather tingled all over with joy. The months had flown by, and it was now the first Monday in November, two weeks before her grant was due to expire. She had been sleepless the past few days, wondering if she would be offered an extension. Only yesterday Mr. Oldham had announced that all the artists had been offered a six-month extension. Heather was so happy that she felt if she came down even a little, her toes would barely brush the clouds.

There was only one thing marring her contentment. After two weeks of silence following Tanner's brief reply to her e-mail, he had finally e-mailed her again at the end of August. His communication had been light and noncommittal, almost like old times. For a reason she couldn't define, she had burst into tears. She thought she had resolved her feelings with her supposedly final e-mail, but once again her heart felt torn.

Tanner had e-mailed her a least once a week after that in the ensuing months and though she returned the e-mails faithfully, neither of them included anything deep or personal. And then, about a month ago, he mentioned that he was dating—of all people—Amanda Huntington, whom he had dated in high school. Apparently he had run into her back in August.

Probably right after I sent that e-mail, Heather thought bitterly. The idea of them together hurt her, though she had absolutely no right to feel that way. Tanner hadn't said anything more about Amanda since—and Heather didn't ask. She tried to be happy that he was seeing someone, but the emptiness in her heart when she thought about him betrayed her.

Heather coped by burying herself in work, and her bank account was beginning to show the result. Her painting of the anchor had sold, and the portraits she had been commissioned to do had been well received by the clients. Mr. Oldham had put her painting of the Hatch Memorial Shell in the gallery and was eagerly awaiting the Mother and Children painting as well. But Heather still felt it lacked something vital. So it had sat for months on the easel, and each day she studied it for at least a half hour.

She was studying the Mother and Children early that morning when Mrs. Oldham came into the gallery studio. Keith was also working in the studio, but he had the curtains pulled, which signaled a request for privacy. Heather had been about to do the same, since she was working on several other paintings, but when Mrs. Oldham came in, she smiled and motioned her over.

"Are you still hanging on to that?" Mrs. Oldham asked with a smile.

Heather frowned. "I guess I think if I stare at it enough, I'll know what's wrong. Do you have any ideas?"

The older lady came forward, tilting her head gracefully to study the painting. As usual, her gray hair was swept into a bun on her head, revealing the neck that seemed even more delicate than usual. Heather noticed that Mrs. Oldham's clothes also seemed looser. Had the old woman lost weight? If so, it could signal that she had spent days painting. Heather's own weight fluctuated by as much as ten pounds during her most intent painting days.

"Ah," breathed Mrs. Oldham, smiling at the painting. "I remember days like this. Days when everybody needed me, and I felt I had nothing left to give. Yes, sometimes it can be just like that. And I had only four children, not the seven you have in this painting. But I wonder that you should see such things so clearly—not being a mother yet yourself."

Heather didn't remind her that she had nine—soon ten—younger siblings. She had already changed more diapers than many mothers with only a few children would ever change.

"So what's missing?" Heather asked. "Why don't I feel satisfied with it?"

Mrs. Oldham studied the painting a few more minutes before saying, "The painting for what it is seems complete to me. But you are the only one who can judge that with certainty. You know what they say—that there are never really finished paintings, but only paintings that have been abandoned. Maybe it's time for you to let this one go."

"I can't—not yet."

Mrs. Oldham turned back to the painting, nodding slightly as though she hadn't heard Heather's reply.

"Oh yes, I remember days like these. But they don't last forever. And suddenly I find I miss them." Moisture gathered in her eyes. She brought a hand to her head and grimaced.

"Are you all right?" Heather asked, placing a hand on the woman's back.

"Yes, yes. Just a little dizziness." The words were weak and unconvincing.

"Come over here. Sit down." Heather led her to the bench next to the supply shelves. "May I get you some water?"

"No thanks. It passes." Mrs. Oldham sounded stronger now. Her brown eyes met Heather's without wavering.

"Have you been painting?" Heather couldn't help but ask.

A faint smile came to Mrs. Oldham's lips. "No, dear. There is a time not to paint, and for me this is that time. But I have been very busy. My children have been visiting, you know. I like to see the grandchildren."

This took Heather by surprise. She could never imagine a time when her soul would not crave to take up the brush and create. There was something about filling the white canvas that always filled her soul.

At that moment, Keith came out of the curtained area, smiled at them as he picked up a brush near the sink, and then disappeared again.

"Keith will not be staying," Mrs. Oldham said, looking after him.

"What?"

"That's right. He told us last night."

"But I heard him the other day saying how much he's learned, and how grateful he was to have been chosen."

Mrs. Oldham patted her leg. "That's still all true. Sometimes there is more than just a single truth, Heather. He also misses his family and Kansas. And apparently, he's been dating a girl here. He wants to get married and settle down."

"I knew he was dating. She's a girl McCarty actually went out with once. Ever since she met Keith, they've been going out. But I didn't know it was serious."

"It might not be. It's still early."

Heather shook her head. "I never thought he'd give this up. He loves painting."

"Oh, he's not giving it up. He'll just learn in another way." Mrs. Oldham smiled. "Besides, his work is lovely. He doesn't need Tomás anymore. He needs to practice and to further develop his own style."

"Is that what you did?"

Mrs. Oldham took her hand. "Oh, Heather, you ask me the strangest questions. I'm so glad you're here. You've been like a daughter to me. I'm sorry we've not had more time together."

"I think you've taught me more than Tomás," Heather confessed, feeling a rush of love for the older lady. "And I'm sure glad you don't have his inclination for fits."

Mrs. Oldham laughed. "Me, too."

Heather sobered. "But I'm sorry there hasn't been another painting by Amelia Degroot. Is it partly because we've taken up so much of your time?"

"Perhaps," the old lady said thoughtfully. "But if so it has been my own choosing. Life has given me so much; I wanted to give something back."

"You have, believe me. I've learned more these past five and a half months than in all my years of college."

Mrs. Oldham studied her silently for a long moment. "About painting, yes. But what about life?"

"My life is painting," Heather said simply.

"But you cannot hug a painting."

Heather didn't know how to respond to that. The secret place in her heart that held her emotions for Tanner suddenly ached. "Don't worry, I try to be well-rounded," she said lightly. "Hey, I went to church yesterday—I go every Sunday."

"Ah. That's good. And what does your God think about your painting?"

Heather frowned in concentration, seeking an answer to satisfy both herself and Mrs. Oldham. "I think He wants me to develop my talent. Beyond that, I don't really know."

"When I was young," Mrs. Oldham said, "I never went to church. For me attending church meant resisting the urge to paint the night before because I would have to get up early to make it to the chapel on time—and what if that night was the one I would paint the masterpiece?" She snorted lightly in self-deprecation. "I didn't understand that the muse would always return refreshed after a day of worship—just as I did."

Heather nodded. "That's what I've learned. I really do feel it helps."

"Then you're fortunate. You've learned that much earlier that I did. I think your parents must have had something to do with that. I would like to meet them one day. Anyone who can be the parents of eleven children—and such good children as I can see from you—must be very special."

"They are," Heather admitted. "But they gave up a lot to have so many children."

"I'm sure they did." Mrs. Oldham put her hand on the back of the bench, using it to help herself rise. "Well, I had best be getting home."

Heather watched her walk to the door leading into the gallery. She moved with grace, and yet there was a hesitancy Heather had never before noticed in her step. Was it simply advancing age? The woman Heather had first met last December had been spry and eager to go; now she seemed worn and tired.

She just didn't sleep well, Heather told herself. *And apparently she's had a lot of visitors coming and going with her children and grandchildren around. Tomorrow, she'll feel better.*

Heather placed a cloth over her Mother and Children painting to protect it from dust and light. Then she pulled her privacy curtain and picked up a tube of paint. She still had another hour before she was supposed to work in the gallery that morning, and if she began now, she might be able to add some desperately needed details to her newest painting of two children playing frisbee at the park near her apartment.

She had only dipped her brush into the green when Mrs. Oldham peeked around the curtain. "Heather, I'm sorry to disturb you, but there's a man on the phone out there. I told Bridget to tell him you were working, but he insists that it's important."

Heather put down her brush. "Well, I guess I'd better see what he wants. I hope it's not Mr. Kennison again saying that another one of his children took a brush to the family painting I did for them. That wasn't fun to clean up."

Mrs. Oldham chuckled. "I hope not, either."

Together they walked through the studio. Nate had arrived and was setting up his equipment. He gave her a wave. Though he was always friendly, he had kept well away since Tanner's visit. Heather missed him, but had been relieved; while she really liked Nate, a relationship with him was even more impossible than one with Tanner. If she worried about having children with one parent as an artist, how much more would she worry with two? Besides, he didn't share her faith, and that meant more to her than she was willing to admit to the other grantees.

Of course, Lorin had pointed out during one of their now-rare conversations that a relationship didn't necessarily mean children, that people were married all the time and chose not to have them. To Heather, whose parents had always taught her that having children was a primary reason to be married, Lorin's philosophy was strange. Not that any of it mattered in the end. She was focused on her work, and that meant relationships had to be put aside—at least for now.

"Thanks, Bridget," Heather said as she picked up the phone. "Hello?"

"Thank heaven!" came Tanner's voice. "I was worried that I'd have to wait for my e-mail to reach you."

"Is something wrong?" It was a stupid question; she could tell something was very wrong.

"It's your mom. Your dad asked me to call you. They took her to the hospital in American Fork last night. Then they transferred her to Utah Valley Regional Medical Center in Provo."

Heather felt a lump form in her throat. "Is it the baby?" Her mother had at least four weeks left in her pregnancy.

"Yes. They tried to stop labor all night, but she's coming anyway right this minute."

"She?" Her parents had wanted to leave the gender of the baby a surprise.

"Yes, they found out last night that's it's a girl."

"Is she going to be all right?"

"They had time to give your mom a drug that would help the baby's lungs develop faster. There have been complications, but they're hopeful." Tanner paused before rushing on. "But it's your mother they're really worried about. Heather, she might not make it. She's lost a lot of blood."

Heather couldn't speak. Her mother might not make it? How could this be happening?

"I've arranged a ticket for you. Will you come?"

"Of course I'll come. Of course." Heather was crying now, and her head whirled so much that she could no longer hear what Tanner was saying.

Mrs. Oldham gazed at her with concern. "Heather, dear, what is it?"

"My mother," Heather whispered and handed her the phone.

"Bridget, help her to a chair," Mrs. Oldham said crisply. "She looks like she's going to faint. I'll see what's going on." She put the phone to her ear and began to talk with Tanner.

Within a few minutes, she hung up. "Bridget, see if you can get a hold of Lester. Tell him we need a ride to Heather's apartment, and then later we'll need to go to the airport. Her flight leaves at one-thirty."

☙

Heather spent both the flight to Denver and then to Salt Lake City praying. With the two hours gained by the time zone difference, Heather arrived in Salt Lake just before six-thirty in the evening. Almost mechanically, she retrieved her hastily packed luggage and rented a car.

Originally, Tanner had planned to pick her up, but after she recovered from the initial shock, Heather had called him and begged him to stay at the hospital so he could let her know what was happening. Mrs. Oldham had loaned Heather her cell phone to receive the calls, but Tanner had talked to her only once more—and that was before her first flight even left—to tell her the baby had come and seemed to be making progress. Her mother, however, had undergone emergency surgery right after the baby had been born and was still unconscious.

Heather arrived at the hospital in Provo at seven-thirty. She hurried inside and was directed to the Intensive Care Unit on the second floor. In the waiting room, she saw a man leaning back in a chair, one foot resting on the knee of his other leg. The supported leg bounced furiously up and down, and Heather knew the man had to be Tanner. She let out a sound and rushed toward him. Immediately, he was on his feet and turning to greet her.

Heather let him draw her into his arms. His familiar smell was comforting, and she longed to stay with her head buried in his chest, avoiding reality. But she was full of questions that demanded answers. She lifted her head. "How is she?"

"Still unconscious since her surgery this morning, but she's stable. And there's a lot of brain activity, so that's a good thing."

The colossal fear that had tightened around Heather's heart lessened just a bit. She had almost expected to hear that her mother was worse. "The baby?"

"Still on oxygen, but other than that she's holding her own."

"Thank heaven!" Heather drew away from him. "I need to see my mother."

"Well, I'm not sure how many they'll let in. Your dad's in there with some of your brothers and sisters—the older ones. The others are with my mom. We can ask the nurse if you can go in. At the very least, they can tell your dad you're here, and you can trade places with one of the others."

"Okay, let's do that." Heather looked past him to see where she might find a nurse to talk to. Her expression faltered as her eyes paused instead on the stunning blonde woman who sat on the chair next to where Tanner had been seated. She recognized her immediately. "Oh, I didn't realize . . . I thought you were alone . . ." Her voice trailed off.

The woman jumped up and crossed the two steps separating them. She held out her hand. "Hi, Heather. I'm Amanda."

Heather shook her hand briefly. "Yes, I remember you from high school. Nice to see you again."

"I'm sorry it has to be under such circumstances." Amanda's sincerity was obvious, as was the sympathy in her green eyes that oddly reminded Heather of Tomás, though that was the only similarity between them.

Heather looked back and forth between Tanner and Amanda, feeling suddenly lost. "I'm sorry if I interrupted your plans or anything by asking Tanner to wait here for me. I wasn't thinking."

"Oh, no," Amanda said. "He was glad to wait. Me, too. Anything to help."

"Thank you," Heather managed faintly. Her gaze returned to Tanner, who appeared uncomfortable.

"Come on," he said. "I'll go with you. They haven't let me see her, but I know how to get in."

"I'll wait here," Amanda said.

Heather followed Tanner, her worry about her mother returning and blotting out the discomfort of encountering his new girlfriend. Seeing her here with him made their relationship all too real.

In only minutes she was allowed to see her mother. The nurses didn't have many patients, and if there were any rules about how many people were allowed inside, they had been temporarily stretched since her mother was not in immediate danger. Heather found her mother encircled about by the older children, almost like in her painting. Yet unlike in her painting, they weren't asking anything of her. Thirteen-year-old Kathryn was stroking her hand, while Kevin and Aaron, eighteen and fifteen respectively, took turns reading from a book. Her father and ten-year-old Alison were rubbing her feet. There was a sense of calmness that contradicted the desperate feeling that had been with Heather since Tanner's call in Boston.

Aaron was the first to notice her. "Hey, it's Heather," he said softly. Kevin stopped reading. Each left their posts and hugged her in a subdued manner. No one raised a voice, and movements were calm and careful.

"I'm glad you came," her father whispered.

Heather's tears began down her face. She felt no older than Alison. "Oh, Daddy, is she going to be all right?"

"Yes. She has to be." But there was uncertainty in his round face.

Heather walked to the head of her mother's bed and stroked the short hair that seemed more gray than blonde in the flourescent lighting. "I'm here, Mother," she said, bending to kiss her mother's cheeks. "I love you. Please get well."

The children and her father quietly resumed their places. For a long time they stood or sat, listening to Kevin's voice reading from the book. Heather didn't hear a word or even register the title of the book. An hour must have gone by before her father gently cleared his throat. "Heather, why don't you take these guys home? They've been here all day—mostly out in the waiting room. I don't even know if they've eaten."

"You could go, Dad," she said, seeing that Alison was nearly asleep in his arms. "You've been here all day, too. I could stay—all night, even."

He shook his head. "No, I can't leave her. But you all should go home and get a few winks. She's not in any immediate danger. I'll call if there's a change."

Heather saw the determination in her father's blue eyes. She didn't blame him, but she wanted to stay, too. "Kevin can drive them."

"I'd feel better if you took them," her father coaxed. "We've been up since last night, and Kevin's tired. Maybe tomorrow you could stay with her for a while so I can go home and shower."

Heather had no choice but to agree. The last thing they needed was Kevin driving off the road on the way home. She gave her mom another kiss before hugging her dad goodnight. On the way out of the room, Alison and Kathryn clung to her sleepily. Heather was grateful for their presence, yet she felt strangely alone. She couldn't help but wonder where Tanner was at that moment and what he was doing.

Chapter Fourteen

After Heather went in to see her mother, Tanner sank again into his seat in the waiting room. Amanda sat next to him. For a long moment neither spoke, and then Amanda said, "Well, I guess we should get going. We'll be late, but that's all right."

"Huh?" Tanner looked at her, momentarily confused.

"I'll understand if you don't want to go anymore." Amanda put her soft hand on his, stilling the drumming of his fingers on the arm rest.

Tanner suddenly remembered tonight was her single ward's family night and that she had invited him to go with her last week. After the lesson, the group planned to watch a video and eat snacks.

Amanda waited for him to say something. "I don't think I should go," he said awkwardly. "They might need me. I don't think they'll stay here all night. They might need a ride home. I hope you understand, Amanda. These are my friends. I spent half my life since I was sixteen at their house. Oh, I can't believe this is even happening." He leaned forward and let his head sink into his hands.

Amanda rested her hand on his back. "It's okay. I do understand. They're lucky to have someone like you."

He lifted his head, shaking it. "I just can't see trying to enjoy myself while they're going through such turmoil."

Amanda arose. "Well, I'd better get going then—unless you'd rather I stayed."

"No, you have to work tomorrow. You go ahead." Tanner stood beside her, taking her hand. "And thanks for coming down here in the first place. I appreciated not waiting alone."

She smiled. "That's okay. You just be careful driving home."

"I will. You, too."

She stood on her tip-toes and placed a brief kiss on his lips. That surprised him because they had been taking things in that regard very slowly. "How about tomorrow?" he felt compelled to ask. "We could have dinner."

"I can't," she said. "I have plans. But how about Wednesday?"

Tanner nodded slowly. "Okay, I'll pick you up at, say, seven?" He wondered if her plans tomorrow night involved her friend, Gerry. He knew she was still dating him, but since he didn't feel ready to make a commitment, he hadn't pushed the matter. Even so, he would be the first to admit that he and Amanda had gone just about as far as they could go on this level of dating. Soon, they would have to decide whether or not they had a future together—which would include dating exclusively. In the past weeks he had felt they were headed in that direction, but tonight his brain couldn't even think along those lines. All that seemed to matter was whether or not Karalee Samis and her baby made it through another night alive.

Amanda smiled and left. Tanner sat again in his chair, settling back in preparation for a long wait. Thoughts of Heather sprang to his mind. For all her consternation, she looked great. Her light brown hair, while always long, had grown longer; and the highlights of summer had darkened, making the hazel color of her eyes stand out more than usual. He wondered if she was dating that Nate guy, or anyone else.

His thoughts drifted and he began to doze. Though he had only heard about Heather's mother that morning, the day had been long and trying.

"Hey, it's Tanner," came a voice.

Tanner jerked awake to see Heather and her siblings emerging from the ICU. Heather caught his gaze, and he saw her gratitude. In that moment he was glad he'd waited. "Yep, it's me," he said, coming to his feet. "I'm harder to get rid of than old gum."

"I like old gum," Alison said.

"You'd better not be putting it under our desk again," Kathryn said, but her voice didn't hold any rancor. Alison shrugged and laid her head sleepily against Heather's side.

"I need to get these guys home," Heather explained. "And I probably should go to your house and get the others as well."

Tanner check his wristwatch. "Don't worry about that. It's nine and Mom's got them in bed by now. She's a stickler for bedtimes. Besides, I bet the little girls are sleeping in the castle room. You don't want to deprive them of that, do you?"

"Guess not." Heather smiled wistfully. "I know how much they love playing in your sisters' old room."

"Hey, someone should use it. My sisters think they're too old."

"I love that room," Alison stirred long enough to say.

Heather didn't seem to be making any progress toward the door, so Tanner moved ahead of her. "Come on, I'll walk you to the car." Heather's brothers came directly behind him, while Heather and her sleepy sisters brought up the rear.

Outside, Heather took the lead. "I rented a car at the airport," she said. "Has just enough seatbelts." She unlocked the door and the children scrambled inside.

"I could drive you," Tanner offered.

She snorted. "Tanner, you look more tired than I feel, if that's possible."

"Well, I've been here for a while." He ran his hand through his hair and grinned. He was relieved that her easy tone was the same one she had always used with him. No matter what had happened between them, they really were still friends. It was worth the long wait and disappointing Amanda just to know that much.

"Thanks, Tanner."

"Hey, I'm not finished yet," he said. "Alison here may be half asleep, but for me it's still rather early. I'll meet you at the house."

Heather's eyes watered. "Thanks," she whispered. "I could use a friend right now."

03

Back at her parents' house, the children were suddenly wide awake. They gathered in the living room, obviously reluctant to go to their own rooms. "Don't you all have school tomorrow?" Heather said half-heartedly.

Kevin nodded. "Yeah, but Dad said we could stay home again. We'd like to be there or close by when Mom wakes up."

"Well, you can't miss too much school," Heather said.

"Don't worry. We'll make it up." Kathryn yawned. "I couldn't possibly think about verbs and algebra and stuff when Mom's still . . ." Tears welled up in her eyes. Heather placed an arm around her and drew her to the couch.

"It'll be okay," Heather murmured, not at all sure if it would be. Did parents always feel so vulnerable when they tried to comfort their children?

"But what if she's not okay?" Alison asked, standing in front of the couch dejectedly. "Who's going to take care of us?"

"Don't think that way!" Aaron practically yelled. He glared up at her from his favorite spot on the carpet next to the entertainment center where their GameCube was stored.

Heather frowned at him as she pulled Alison close. "Aaron, now's not the time for that. It's okay to ask questions if it makes us feel better." She looked at Alison. "We're certainly not giving up hope, though, are we, Alison?"

"No. I've been praying really hard," the little girl said in a small voice.

"Why don't we have a prayer right now?" Heather said. "And then we'll go find some blankets or sleeping bags and sleep right here with each other." Their enthusiastic replies told her she had hit on the right solution—obviously no one wanted to be alone.

They knelt together in a loose circle and each took turns praying as they always did when there was something serious going on at their house. Afterward, as the children ran for their blankets, Heather lifted her gaze to Tanner's. "We'll be okay," she told him.

"I can see that." His brown eyes met hers, and she almost drowned in their depths. She had missed him so much more than she would ever admit.

He came to his feet. "But you forgot to eat. I'm going into the kitchen to heat up one of the casseroles I know the sisters in the ward brought today, and you're all going to have a good meal before you go to bed."

"That was so nice of them." Tears came to her eyes for what seemed like the millionth time. "I was wondering what I was going to make."

"No need. The good sisters and I will take care of it for the next few days. But while I'm in the kitchen, you, Heather, are going to open up the couch bed, because if you're anything like me, you've grown too old to sleep on a hard floor."

She smiled despite her melancholy. "You can say that again."

"Okay. If you're anything like me, you've grown . . ."

"Stop!" She tossed a throw pillow at him. "I didn't mean it! I don't need another reminder that I'm not sixteen anymore. Now get into that kitchen."

"Yes, ma'am."

Heather watched him leave. Being with him was like old times—and yet somehow better. There was an underlying tension she wasn't sure she wanted to examine too closely. Was it because she knew he'd once felt something more than friendship for her? Was that what made being with him better? But why should that tension still exist? He was obviously dating Amanda now; any question of them being together romantically was long gone.

Her smile faded. She didn't dislike Amanda, but she had to admit that she hadn't cared to be around her in high school. In fact, she had been happy when Tanner stopped dating her. Had she been jealous? Perhaps. It seemed ridiculous to contemplate, but now she was feeling similar emotions. "We're just friends," she whispered. "Just friends. That's the way I wanted it."

The children came thundering back. No longer accustomed to their constant chatter, she felt besieged—and they made up only half of the Samis children. No, less than half, now that the new baby was here. She was glad when Tanner called them to eat.

An hour later teeth were brushed, and the children were snuggled into their sleeping bags or blankets. Heather walked Tanner to the door. "If you need me," he said. "I'll just be next door. I'm going to be staying with my parents for a few days so that I'll be around to help. I'll have to be in and out at work, but I'll check in with you a lot."

"I'll be using my mother's cell number, instead of Mrs. Oldham's," Heather said. "It's long distance, and I don't want to take advantage of her generosity."

"What's the number?" He programmed it into his own phone.

"They won't let me use it in the hospital," she added.

"Okay."

They stared at each other for a long time. The door was open, and while the November night air wasn't anywhere as cold as in Boston, Heather shivered.

Tanner took her hand. "Promise me that you'll call if you need anything. I want to help. Promise?"

"Promise." His hand was warm on hers, and Heather felt the warmth travel up to her heart. She almost couldn't let go.

Giving her a half smile, he turned and sprinted down the steps to his car. Heather shut the door slowly, leaning her back against it.

After a few minutes she went into the living room, met by soft snores coming from the children. Too tired to change into her pajamas, Heather retrieved a blanket from the cupboard, turned off the hall light, and settled down on the sofa bed next to Alison. She stared at the dark ceiling, her eyes gradually adjusting to the dimness.

"Heather?"

She turned her head and saw that Alison's eyes were open. "Yes?"

"I tried and tried but I can't sleep. My mind is thinking too much."

"What about?"

Alison snuggled closer and whispered, "If Mommy isn't okay, you'll take care of us, won't you?"

Heather tucked her arm under Alison's head. "Oh, honey, don't worry. Everything's going to work out. And no matter what, Daddy and everybody else is going to be here for you."

"And you?"

"Yes, and me, too."

Satisfied, Alison closed her eyes and went to sleep.

Chapter Fifteen

All night long Heather dreamed about Alison and her question. What would happen if her mother died? Her dad would do his best, but he had to work to support the family. Who could ever take her mother's place in the home? Heather knew she was the only one who could fill in for the smaller children, especially the new baby, and the idea frightened her.

What about my painting? The words kept reverberating in her head. Toward daylight, she knelt down by the bed and prayed for relief. At last she fell into an undisturbed sleep.

When she awoke again it was only seven and the others were still sleeping. Heather changed her rumpled clothing, brushed her teeth, and woke up Kevin. "Look, I'm going to the hospital, okay? You watch the kids, and I'll call to tell you what's going on."

"I want to go, too."

"I know. I'm just going to try to send Dad home for a shower. He can bring you back." She frowned. "Of course, I don't know what to do about the little kids."

"I can call Sister Wolfe and see if she needs them to come home."

"Can you make pancakes for everyone?"

"Of course."

Heather straightened. "Good. They'll need a heavy breakfast to keep them longer between meals. When you come to the hospital with Dad—if that's how it ends up happening—maybe you could try to bring a few sandwiches, or maybe some of that casserole with ice packs. Who knows how long we'll be there."

Kevin sat up. "Okay, I can handle it."

"I know." Heather smiled wistfully, controlling her urge to rumple his hair. "I just wish you didn't have to."

She was almost to the door when her brother's voice stopped her. "Heather?"

"Yes?"

"I'm glad you came home. We really needed you." For an eighteen-year-old, that was a heavy confession.

Heather smiled. "Hey, we're a family. We pull together. We'll be okay." She was rewarded by his sober grin. "I know."

CR

On the way to the hospital, Heather called the gallery in Boston to give them an update. Since her father hadn't called, she expected to find everything the same as the night before. Her father was dozing in the easy chair by her mother's bed when Heather tip-toed into the room. Even in repose he looked worn, and the unshaven stubble on his cheeks added to the impression.

His eyes came open. "Any change?" she asked.

He shook his dark head wearily, looking much older than she remembered. "No. I thought she might have squeezed my hand around midnight, but I'm not sure."

"I can stay with her while you go shower. You could even sleep a bit."

"Maybe later." His voice was noncommittal. "There is one thing you can do."

Heather tore her gaze from her mother's face, which in contrast to her father's looked much younger and less burdened than usual. "What?"

"I haven't been to see the baby. I'm just so afraid of leaving your mom. But all night I've been worried about the baby. One of us should be there to hold her, to tell her how glad we are that she's here. The nurses do well, but they're not family."

"I'll go . . . if they'll let me."

"She's early, but stable, so I think it won't be a problem. I told the nurse to tell them to let you in if you came. She's on the fifth floor."

"Okay, I'll go see her. But then I'm coming back, and you're going home to shower and take a break." She kept her voice firm and was relieved when her father nodded. She paused at the door. "Oh, does she have a name?"

He shook his head. "I always left that up to your mother." He frowned and looked away.

Heather nodded and slipped into the hall. She went to the fifth floor and followed the signs until she came to the NICU, the Newborn Intensive Care Unit. After talking to the nurses, she was taken to a parent lounge where she could see the baby.

147

"She's doing rather well," said a tall, black-haired nurse whose strong, bony features made her look more like an army colonel than a baby nurse. But her gentle voice more than made up for her appearance. "We were wondering when anyone would come to see her. We have her in an incubator to keep her warm—she's very tiny, but we've really turned down the oxygen. She's practically breathing on her own. The only real problem is that we can't get her to eat. We were about to try again, if you want to help."

"Sure." Heather couldn't keep her eyes off the tiny infant the nurse placed in her arms. The baby was so small that it seemed almost impossible for her to be alive at all. "She's so tiny," she murmured.

"She weighs just over four and a half pounds," the nurse said. "That's actually really good. You should see some of the tiniest babies we have. You would hardly believe it. Now, I'll be right back with her breakfast."

"Hi there, little one," Heather cooed, careful not to dislodge the oxygen tube or the wire sensors on the baby's chest. "I'm your big sister, Heather." The baby's eyes came open. "Ah, so you're awake. Good. I hear you haven't been eating. What's that about, huh? You've got to eat so you can be strong. You want to come home, don't you? You have a lot of brothers and sisters who are very anxious to see you, you know. You're going to be spoiled rotten." She continued to talk to the baby, cuddling her with the experience of many years taking care of newborn siblings. As she talked, the baby appeared to listen, watching her with wise and solemn brown eyes.

"Here we are." The black-haired nurse approached carrying a bottle with a minuscule nipple on the end. "I see you've had practice at holding babies. They love being held that close. Have you used a bottle before?"

Heather nodded. "My brothers and sisters were older, though. My mom usually nurses the babies when they're this new."

"Well, it's the same principle as when they're older. Just make sure she doesn't gag. She may not take anything at all. The nursing reflex usually kicks in about the fifth month of pregnancy, but eating is still one of the things preemies have a hard time with. Most times we have to feed them through a tube in their nose. Not fun for any of us." The nurse handed her the bottle and stepped back to watch. Heather was glad the nurse didn't put the bottle in the baby's mouth as she had expected.

Heather touched the baby's lower lip with the bottle. The infant appeared surprised. "What's that?" Heather asked. "Is that what you want to know?

Well, it's food. Let me squeeze a tiny bit on your tongue. There. Does that taste good? I wouldn't know, but I hope so." She eased the nipple into the baby's mouth and moved it around, gently touching it to her tongue and to the sides of the tiny mouth. "Come on, try to suck. Believe me, you want this. It'll make your tummy feel so good. Besides, if you don't you will never hear the end of it. You have ten siblings who have long memories. You'll be getting married and someone will say, 'Yes, look at her now, you'd never know that she refused to eat when she was first born.' Trust me, you don't want that. Come on now, bright eyes. Show me how you do it."

The baby's tongue teased the nipple. Then at last her tiny lips closed in a suck, her eyes opening wide as the smallest gushes of milk trickled over the tongue and down her throat. "See?" Heather told her. "I knew you could do it. Try again."

Slowly and intermittently, the infant sucked. Though it was never more than a few pulls at a time, and the gestures awkward, the amount of liquid in the bottle gradually lowered. An emotion Heather didn't remember experiencing with her other siblings filled her heart. She wasn't sure what it meant, but she knew that no matter what happened she was going to be there for her baby sister until her mother could take over.

The nurse made a pleased sound. "Not exactly pro sucking, but that's a start. We'll have her home in no time. Good job, baby!" The nurse's words reminded Heather that her sister still had no name—and wasn't likely to as long as their mother remained unconscious and fighting for her life. Heather asked the nurse almost reluctantly to return her sister to the incubator so she could report to her father.

Her dad looked up as Heather entered her mother's room. "How's the baby?" he asked.

"She's doing better. She wouldn't eat before, but she did just now. The nurse thinks it's because someone from the family was there."

His round face took on a trace of guilt. "I couldn't leave your mother," he said. "And the nurses couldn't bring her here. Maybe now that she's doing better . . ."

"Go see her, Dad." Heather took two steps toward him. "It's just for a minute."

He studied the unconscious Karalee. "What if . . . I can't leave her!"

"Yes, you can." Heather placed a hand on his shoulder. "Think about what Mom would want. She'd want you to go see the baby and then come back and tell her all about it. Don't you think that would help her heal? To know that we're taking care of her baby?"

Her father's brow furrowed, but he nodded slowly. "Yes, you're right. I will go, just for a minute."

"Oh, and isn't there anything we can call her?" Heather asked as he arose to his feet stiffly, like a man who had been in one position for too long. "Not that we have to put it on her birth certificate or anything. A name just for now. You and Mom must have discussed something."

"Seren."

"What?"

"Your mother mentioned naming her Seren, you know for serendipity— something wonderful and unexpected. Neither of us expected another child, but we were grateful. Your mother thought that name would reflect our joy. I wasn't so sure—it sounded a bit strange to me."

Tears gathered in Heather's eyes, and she turned her face so her father wouldn't see. "Sounds like Mom."

Conrad's voice lowered to a scarce whisper. "Well, for certain this is our last child. They had to take out her uterus yesterday to stop the bleeding. I know she'll be disappointed, but at least we'll never have to almost lose her like this again." He didn't add the words "If she lives," but Heather heard them all the same.

She blinked rapidly. "Go on, Dad. Hurry. Seren's waiting."

Instead, he walked closer to the bed and leaned over his wife. "Sweetheart, I'm going to see our new daughter. When I come back, I'll tell you everything, okay? Heather's going to stay with you while I'm gone. I love you, honey." Conrad kissed her cheek, and then he met Heather's gaze. "Thanks for coming home, Heather. We need you." Without another word, he left the room.

Heather went to the bedside and took her mother's hand, the one without the IV. "She's really beautiful, Mom. And smart, too. I think she knew who I was. I know it's stupid, but for some reason I pictured *Saturday's Warrior.* You know, the heaven scene with the oldest daughter and baby before she was born. I felt . . . I don't know. There was a connection. It makes me understand just a little why you had so many children. Not that I want to do that," she added hastily. "Oh, Mom, try to wake up! Fight if you can. We all need you so much. *I* need you. There are so many things I've been wanting to ask you—about life, about painting. Please, Mom. Kevin said you had a blessing and that it promised you would heal."

Heather stopped talking. For the first time in her life she was utterly conscious of the fact that a blessing didn't always guarantee a desired outcome. Sometimes healing didn't mean in this life. Sometimes it was necessary to let go.

But not now, she thought. *Oh, please, not now.*

For over an hour Heather sat with her mother, the quiet of the room interrupted only by a nurse who routinely came to check on Karalee's progress. Once, Heather tried to read aloud to her mother, but her eyes refused to focus on the words, and she had to content herself with holding her mother's hand.

When her father returned, his countenance was lightened. "She's perfect," Conrad said. "Believe it or not, she actually ate a bit more from me. The nurses think she'll be able to go home in a week or so—if she continues to eat like this. They said maybe tomorrow they could bring her in here to see your mom. And when your mom recovers enough, there's even a place in the NICU where they can be together almost constantly."

"That's great!" Heather relinquished her place by her mother's side. "So are you going home to take a quick shower?"

"No. I'm not leaving—not yet. Maybe tomorrow."

Heather knew there was no changing his mind. "Okay, but I've got to call the kids. They all want to come and see Mom again."

"I think it's good for them to visit—at least the older ones. Your mother likes to have them around. But maybe they shouldn't all come at once. One of the nurses spoke to me this morning about limiting visitors—especially now that a few more patients have arrived."

"Okay. We'll work it out." Heather kissed his cheek, and his arms went around her. "I love you, Dad."

"I love you, too."

Heather bid her mother farewell, hoping that on some level she could hear and understand.

Back at home, she found the four smaller children had returned from the Wolfe's and were eager for information. She recounted her experience with baby Seren and soon had them laughing and talking about the teasing they would give the infant when she was older.

The day passed slowly as they waited for something to happen. Heather sent Kevin to the hospital with eight-year-old Brett, who hadn't yet been to see their mother. They stayed until their father could help with another feeding for baby Seren and then came home. After their return, Heather took Mindy and Evan, who were five and six respectively, for a brief visit. Then Kevin drove Aaron and Alison, who was near tears at having to wait so long. As late afternoon approached, Heather instructed the older boys about re-heating another meal the sisters in the ward had brought, and then headed back to the hospital with Kathryn. Only three-year-old Jane hadn't yet been for a visit. She didn't appear to understand any of what was going on, and since she was perfectly content hanging out with her siblings, Heather decided not to take her to the hospital at all.

After assuring herself that her mother was holding steady, Heather left Kathryn with her father and went to see Seren. The nurses were happy to let her try to give her another bottle. Again, Heather felt a connection with her sister, and she believed the connection was helping Seren find strength. If only her mother could find that same strength from her children and husband.

She was headed back to find Kathryn and take her home when she spied Tanner in the hallway near the NICU. He saw her at the same time. "There you are," he said. "I've been looking for you."

"You have?"

"Yes. I've left you a million messages on your mother's phone, and I've been here twice—at the hospital, I mean."

Heather self-consciously accepted his hug. How odd that she couldn't even be around him anymore without noticing how handsome he was. "Now that you mention it, I forgot to even turn it on. Oops. Sorry."

He laughed. "I don't blame you one bit. I'm sure you've had other things on your mind." They fell into step together. "So the nurses tell me the baby's doing well."

"Hey, isn't that privileged information?" she said, trying to make her voice light.

"Well, when you're as good-looking as I am . . ."

"Oh, you sound just like your father! Remember how we used to tease him about saying that so much?"

Again he laughed. "Ah-ha. There's the smile I wanted to see. You're even more beautiful when you smile."

Heather didn't know how to reply. Though he hadn't shown any new indication of pursuing her romantically, this was not the behavior she was accustomed to from him. She stopped walking. "Thank you," she said softly.

He returned her gaze with wide eyes. She could tell that either his comment or her reply had surprised him. Before she could consider that further, he shook his head sharply. "Oh, I almost forgot. I brought you something." He lifted a black carry-all in his hand.

Heather arched a brow. "What is it?"

"Open it."

She accepted the carry-all and opened it. Inside she saw a sketchbook and pencils.

"I couldn't exactly remember your favorite pencil," he said. "So I got a variety. But I did remember you were partial to this brand of sketch pad. Since you've been spending so much time here, I thought you might as well record your impressions."

Heather hugged him. "Thanks," she murmured into his shoulder. "I didn't even think to bring any supplies. Only today I was wishing I could draw the baby."

"I bet you didn't bring your camera, either," Tanner said. "I put mine in there so you can use it while you're here."

She drew away. "You're a great friend. There aren't many people who know me that well."

"Hey, I promised I'd always be your friend." His words had a seriousness to them, but when she looked up at his face, his eyes didn't quite meet hers.

"And you've been that. It means a lot to me." She began to walk down the hall again.

"So, what's next?" he asked as they stepped into the elevator.

"Well, I can't seem to get my dad to go home to rest at all, so I guess I'll call home and see how the kids are doing. If everything's under control, I'll stay here for a few more hours and then take Kathryn home."

"I can take Kathryn home right now, if you want. That way we can check personally on everyone."

Heather sighed. "That would be great. She's been here too long already. I don't want her to get depressed. Besides, she's the best with the little kids."

"All right, it's settled. You go wait with your mom, and Kathryn and I will check on the kids. Hey, maybe I'll even take them to a movie."

Heather opened her mouth to protest that it was a school night, but changed her mind. "If you do that you'll have to use my mother's van. Kevin knows where the keys are. Jane and Mindy are in car seats and Evan uses a booster. And keep in mind that Jane still wets the bed. She'll need a diaper."

"Car seats, diaper." Tanner grinned. "Doesn't sound too hard."

They had reached the adult ICU on the second floor. Heather paused, placing her hand on his arm. "Thanks so much."

"It's nothing, really," he said earnestly. "I care about your family, Heather. And about you. I don't want you to worry about your siblings—at least not in the evenings when I'm home. I can even take some vacation time, if needed. I have an 'in' with the boss, remember? And at any time I'm just a phone call away."

Heather stared at his dear face. "Thanks," she whispered again.

"You just go get Kathryn." He turned her gently and pushed her toward the door.

CR

Heather left the hospital at ten-thirty that evening. She hadn't been able to convince her father to go home, though he had visited Seren again and fed her. Meanwhile, Heather had filled five sheets of the sketch pad, drawing her mother and her siblings as she had first seen them gathered around the bed yesterday. Another drawing depicted her father holding her mother's hand and another showed him dozing on the nearby chair. She'd also drawn a few pictures of baby Seren.

Sketching released much of the tension in her body, making her feel better. Knowing that Tanner was with her siblings also relieved worry. Many times during the evening, she whispered a silent prayer of thanks for his support.

Her mother also seemed to be improving. The bleeding hadn't returned that day, and she hadn't needed any more transfusions. The doctor seemed confident she would soon awake. "It was a difficult pregnancy and delivery," he reminded them, "but she's a fighter."

So Heather drove home with a more positive outlook than she had felt that morning. When she arrived home, she gazed up at the starry sky and prayed aloud, her breath emerging as a white cloud in the frigid air. "Thank you, Father, for Seren. And thank you for my mother's life."

As she approached the front stairs, the door to the house burst open, spilling Alison and Kathryn onto the porch. Alison rubbed her arms against the cold. "We saw the neatest movie!" she exclaimed. "It was cartoons and soooo funny. We *have* to get the video. And guess what? Tanner promised to take us to another movie tomorrow!" She put her hands on her hips. "You know, I wish you would marry him because he'd make a great brother-in-law."

"Shhhh!" Kathryn said. "He'll hear you!"

"Is he still here?" Heather asked.

Alison took her hand as they went inside. "Yes. He and Brett and Evan are having a battle on the GameCube."

"Brett and Evan? Hasn't Tanner ever heard of bedtime? It's almost eleven!"

"Guess not," Alison said. "But Mindy and Jane fell asleep on the couch bed."

Heather hoped someone had remembered Jane's diaper.

Tanner looked up sheepishly as they entered the family room. "Tell me," he said, "how I can lose a video game to a—how old are you guys?"

"Six," Evan said.

"Eight," Brett said.

"To a six-year-old and an eight-year-old?"

"Maybe because it's past your bedtime?" Heather said pointedly.

"Oops. Okay, guys. Put away that licorice and brush your teeth and get into whatever it is kids sleep in these days."

"I want to sleep in my clothes," Evan said.

Alison shook her head. "Mom won't let you." She frowned. "Or wouldn't, if she was here."

"Hurry and change," Tanner urged. "I'll time you on my watch. Try for record time now. Get set—go!"

The children scattered—even the older teens, who had been watching the video game contest with obvious amusement at Tanner's ineptitude.

Heather checked the sleeping girls, both of whom were still in their play clothes, but at least Jane was wearing a diaper.

"So how'd it go?" Tanner asked from the floor where he sat on someone's sleeping bag.

Heather gave him a genuine smile. "I think she's going to be okay. It's just a matter of time now."

"And the drawing?"

She pulled out her notebook and offered it to him, feeling suddenly shy to let him see her work.

"Wow, I love this one of the baby. I had no idea she was so small—I can't wait to see her. And this one of your father. You have the expression just right." He thumbed through the others, making similar comments.

"You're my best critic," she said.

"Your best fan, you mean." He handed back the sketch book and climbed to his feet. "Well, I guess I'll see you tomorrow. I promised the kids I'd be here at five for dinner and a movie. Hope that's okay."

"As long as you don't have plans."

His brow furrowed. "Oops, now that you mention it, I do remember something I was going to do." He shook his head. "But I can change the day. It's not a big concern."

"Oh, are you sure?"

"It was just Amanda. We were going to dinner. She'll understand."

Heather felt as though she'd been punched in the stomach. *Stupid reaction*, she told herself. "Well, if you're sure."

"Hey, maybe she'll come along."

"Maybe." Heather reached up and twisted a lock of hair. Tanner's eyes went to her hand, but he didn't comment.

"I'll see you tomorrow," he said quietly. "No, I'll see myself out. I know the way. I'll even lock the door. But make sure you remember the deadbolt before you turn in. Oh, and try to call me tomorrow, okay? So I don't have to charm any nurses to give me information. At least check your messages."

"Okay."

He smiled and left the room.

Heather sighed, sinking to the couch bed next to her sleeping sisters. Life sure threw a lot of curves. For an instant she desperately wished she was back in Boston. That being an impossibility, she felt an urge to run into the street and scream at the top of her lungs.

Yet maybe these emotions were just what she needed. Somewhere in the house she had left painting supplies. After the children were in bed, she would look for them.

Chapter Sixteen

Heather was still painting in the kitchen at one in the morning when her dad called on the telephone. Fear gripped her heart at his greeting—until she registered his jubilant tone. "She's awake!" he said after his first hello. "She knows who I am, and she's asked about all of you. And she's already begging the nurses to bring her the baby or take her to the nursery. I really think the worst is behind us."

"Oh, thank heaven!" Heather murmured, casting her eyes toward the ceiling.

"Exactly."

"So does that mean you'll come home tomorrow and shower, Dad?" Heather asked, grinning through her tears of relief. "I mean, trust me, you need a shower—not to mention a shave."

He laughed. "Yes, honey. I will."

"Okay, I'll be there bright and early."

"Uh, better wait till I call."

"All right."

Heather hung up and awoke the older children to tell them the news. After dancing madly around the house, they finally settled down and offered a family prayer of thankfulness. When the children were once again snuggled in their makeshift beds in the living room, Heather considered calling Tanner. Earlier, she wouldn't have hesitated, but their conversation that evening had reminded her that he had a girlfriend, who was possibly going to become his wife. Shouldn't she stop leaning on him so much?

But he deserves to know.

After considering it for five minutes, Heather placed the call to his cell phone.

He answered after three rings. "Hello?" he said sleepily.

"Hey, you told me to call you," she teased.

"Wh—Heather?"

"Yes. Don't you remember? You told me to call you on Wednesday. Well, it's Wednesday."

"Ha-ha. I don't remember anything about two in the morning."

"Oh, is it only two?" she asked innocently.

He laughed. "Okay, so what's up?"

"She's awake." Despite the jovial mood she was trying to portray, Heather's voice choked. "She's going to be okay."

"That's great! That's really great. I'm happy for you, Heather."

"Dad says they'll likely be moving her out of ICU tomorrow so she can be closer to the baby. I'm going to take all the children to see her once they get her settled, then make Dad go home for a shower—he really needs one."

"I bet."

"Okay, that's all. And remember, I fulfilled my duty by calling you today. Don't expect another call."

"All right, all right, I won't. But maybe you'll go to the movies with us now that things are looking brighter. How about it?"

Heather's smile vanished, and she was glad he couldn't see her. Going out to dinner with him and her siblings was one thing, but what if Amanda came along? She most definitely didn't want to see them together.

"I don't know," she said slowly. "Mom and Seren—they may need me. Let's play it by ear, okay?"

"Okay."

She heard him yawn. "Well, go back to sleep, Tanner."

"You, too."

"I will after I finish what I'm doing."

"And that is?"

"Painting."

He hesitated. "Do you often paint in the middle of the night?"

"When the mood hits. You have to grab inspiration when it comes. But it also depends on the light needed for each piece. Outside day scenes are difficult for me at night."

"I see. What are you painting?"

"One of the sketches I did today. The one of my mom in the hospital bed with the children and my dad around her."

"Can I see it?"

"Maybe when it's further along." She doubted she would have enough time to finish it here. Now that her mother was awake, she felt a huge lifting of responsibility, and her thoughts had already returned to Boston.

"Well, goodnight," she said.

"'Night."

Heather painted for another half-hour to get her mother's face just right. Then she cleaned the brushes and put everything away, storing the canvas in her dad's home office to assure that no little hands would touch the wet paint. Sighing, she slipped into the couch bed with the younger girls, relieved that she was too exhausted to think about Tanner and Amanda.

☙

Wednesday morning dawned with the same cloudless glory Heather had prayed under the evening before. Everything seemed bright and happy, though she couldn't stop yawning. It was mid-morning before her father called to tell them it was okay to visit. She piled all the kids into the van. They were exuberant, a feeling she shared.

"You know what this means," she said as she backed out of the driveway. "You all have to go to school tomorrow." Her comment was answered by a chorus of disappointed "Ahhh's" but no one appeared seriously upset.

"You know, I still think we ought to go in and visit in shifts once we're there," she said.

Kevin grinned at her from the front passenger seat. "Not used to the noise, are you?"

"I guess not." She returned his smile. "But it has been good to see you all again."

At the hospital each of the other children visited their mother two at a time while Heather went to see the baby. "Your father was here earlier," said the same black-haired nurse of the morning before. "But it's about time for another bottle. Their little tummies are so small—seems like they don't hold as much as they need to."

Heather watched the tall, bony nurse tenderly and skillfully lift Seren out of the incubator. "Hey, she doesn't have the oxygen tube."

"Nope, she's breathing on her own. We'll keep the heart and breathing monitors on, though. That's what these little wires are coming from her chest. She'll probably go home with a monitor and keep it for a few weeks. But her progress these past few days is amazing. I'm always stunned at how resilient these little people are." The nurse rocked Seren a few times before handing her to Heather.

For the first time, Heather looked at the nurse's name tag. "Thank you for taking care of her, Tonya. I really appreciate it." Heather felt awkward calling a woman she barely knew and who was at least twenty years her senior by name, but Tonya's wide smile set her at ease.

"It's a pleasure. She's a perfect angel."

Heather smiled. "Or is until she gets home and realizes that she has ten siblings to compete against."

"Oh, she's lucky. She'll be that much more spoiled." Tonya backed away. "I'll go get her bottle now."

Heather came from her time with little Seren whistling. No matter where she went in the future, she would always remember this time with her. Frowning suddenly, she realized that if she returned to Boston, Seren wouldn't even know who she was. Her heart hurt to think of her youngest sister growing up without her. *But that's the way life is*, she consoled herself. *At least in big families. Kathryn and Alison will be her real big sisters.*

It didn't escape Heather that if she had married instead of going on a mission, she could have a baby older than Seren already. Of course, she wouldn't want to give up her mission experiences, nor her painting in Boston. She had to remember that.

Heather went thoughtfully into her mother's room. Her father, though haggard and unshaven, appeared much happier. "Okay," Heather announced. "I'm here."

"Heather!" Her mother held out her arms from her slightly propped-up position in bed. Alison moved to make room for Heather to kiss her mother. Her heart filled with thankfulness.

"Okay, Mom, now that you're awake, can you help me convince Dad to go home and shower?"

Her mother looked at him and grinned. "Please do, Conrad. Your hair is sticking up, and you know how that embarrasses me. And on your way take some of these children to school. I'll never be able to make up homework at this rate."

"Tomorrow's soon enough for school," Conrad answered. "But I will take them home so you can get some rest. *And* I'll grab a shower while I'm there." Conrad tried to smooth his dark hair, to no avail.

"Good," Heather and Karalee said together.

After they left, Heather sat down on the edge of her mother's bed. "I've just been to see Seren."

Karalee smiled. "I haven't seen her yet, but they promised I would some-time today."

"She's beautiful. Really small, though." Heather could have kicked herself for adding that. Her mother didn't need any more reminders about the ordeal Seren had gone through. "But she's doing well," she hurried to say. "You were the one who really had us worried."

"I'm sorry."

"It's not your fault."

Her mother sighed. "I know, but mothers are always sorry when things go wrong. It reminds us how fragile our control really is."

"I don't know about that." Heather forced a smile. "You got Dad to name the baby Seren. And you weren't even awake."

"So I did." Amusement filled Karalee's voice. "You know, Heather, only you could see it in that light."

Heather shrugged and moved to the easy chair next to the bed. "Well, it's true."

Her mother looked up at the ceiling. "I wish they'd bring her in. Or let me go to her. I've been worried about her all night."

"I'm sure they will soon. Meanwhile, there's a nurse there now—name's Tonya and she looks like she should be an army sergeant, but she's very gentle. She really loves babies. And the other nurses who work there seem to be just as dedicated. They hold the babies when they cry, rock them, feed them, comfort them."

"That's good to know. Still, I *need* to see her."

"I know." Heather sat back in the chair. For a long moment neither mother nor daughter spoke. Heather found herself thinking about the painting at home in her dad's office.

"Is something bothering you?"

Heather looked up to see her mother watching her. "Why do you ask?"

"You're twisting your hair again. It's amazing that little patch hasn't fallen out."

Heather let her hand drop to her lap, but she didn't reply.

"You look really wonderful," her mother continued. "Your hair's longer. Darker, too. Doesn't look like you've been getting much sun."

"I've been inside mostly—painting."

"Ah. And how's it going?"

"Good. Just like I've been telling you in my e-mails." She hesitated. "But there is something I've been wanting to ask you."

"Yes?"

Heather worked hard to get the right tone—curious but not accusing. "Why did you have another baby?"

A soft smile played around Karalee's lips. "Well, actually, she was a bit of a surprise. But I was very happy when I found out she was coming."

"But you had to put away your paints again." Heather leaned forward. "Doesn't that bother you—always having to put off things that you want to do?"

"Things?" her mother asked. "Or just painting?"

Heather stared at the floor. "Painting, I guess."

"Heather, I want you to understand something right now." Karalee's voice demanded attention, and Heather raised her eyes to meet her mother's. "I had each of you because I wanted to. It was my choice. I could have painted instead, but I wanted to have a lot of children."

Heather believed that part at least. "But did you ever regret it—even just a tiny bit? I saw your school yearbooks and what everyone said about your talent. I saw the paintings you did. It's just . . . Oh, I don't think we should talk about this now. You need to rest."

"No, I want to talk about it. I think it's a long overdue conversation." She held out a hand, and Heather reached for it.

"Honey," Karalee began again, "it's true I loved to paint and that I had a talent for it. But in the beginning I was really afraid. Afraid to fail. What if I painted and nobody ever liked my work? What if my best was never good enough?"

"All artists feel that way. It's something you get used to."

"Maybe. But for me it was overwhelming."

"But to simply not paint . . ." Heather would just as soon not breathe.

Karalee's light brown eyes took on a faraway look. "I remember the desire to paint—the urge to create. Sometimes that intensity scared me as much as possible failure."

"Is that why you quit?"

Karalee shook her head. "Oh, no. That's not it at all. I would have continued regardless of my fear—the desire to paint overrode the fear. But then I met your father, and I fell madly in love. And then you were born."

"And you stopped painting." It was just as Heather had suspected. Her birth had ultimately resulted in depriving her mother of her talent.

"Well, your birth wasn't the only reason. I was also called as the Relief Society president in our ward. I was very busy. I didn't have much time to paint."

Heather had said as much to Tanner six months ago. LDS women so involved themselves in family and church that there was no way they could excel at anything else. Spread so thin, a woman artist could never obtain the greatness of past masters. She blinked back tears.

"You can't have it all," Heather said softly, feeling a profound sadness. Why did it seem women always had to make a choice?

"Heather, you're not listening—either that or you're not understanding." Karalee tried to sit up, but quickly relinquished the effort. She motioned for Heather to come closer. Heather left her chair and sat gingerly on the edge of her mother's bed. "Honey, I found something in motherhood that I never expected. For me, it was *more* fulfilling than my painting. I didn't continue to have babies because I was hiding from my talent, but because I realized my best talent was being a good mother. I'm not saying motherhood would do that for you—I don't believe it would—not completely. But I do know that being a mother would fill parts of you that painting can *never* touch."

"I can't give it up," Heather said, new tears beginning in her already sore eyes.

"Nobody's asking you to." Karalee squeezed her hand. "You can't imagine how proud I am to see your work. You have not only a wonderful talent, but the drive I lacked. Don't judge your future success or happiness by my life. I chose what I was best at, what pulled at me. That's all. I developed one talent over another. Remember, your Father in Heaven gave you your artistic talent. He knows what's in your heart. He can help you achieve your righteous goals."

"The Church teaches women to stay home and raise children," Heather said. "Yet if I do that, I feel I'll lose my edge in painting. On the other hand, if I choose painting, I feel as if I'm . . ." She couldn't finish.

"You feel as if you're denying the faith?"

She nodded.

"I understand why. The commandment to multiply and replenish the earth is still very much in force."

Heather sighed. "Will you ever paint again?"

"Oh, yes. In a few years I'll have plenty of time during the day while everyone's at school. It'll be wonderful to focus some of my attention on painting as my children begin to leave home. But for me it's become a hobby. Something to pass the time when I'm not busy with my real ambitions."

Heather's doubt must have shown in her face because Karalee added, "I know my dreams are not yours, but believe me when I say I'm content. I have not once regretted my choice."

"What if I never married or had children?" Heather asked.

Karalee's brow furrowed. "Then I think you would miss out on one of life's greatest joys. And yes, if you passed up the chance to marry and have a family because of your painting, I would worry greatly over the welfare of your eternal soul. Oh, Heather, you don't have to have eleven children like I did, but to never even have one—that price is too high for any measure of worldly success."

Heather remembered the feeling she had experienced with baby Seren. How would she have felt if Seren had been her own? Would there be room in her life for a child and a husband? And why had her mother classified success at painting as being worldly? At times when Heather painted, she felt closer to heaven than she had ever felt—even on her mission.

"If I had felt strongly that the Lord wanted me to paint," Karalee went on, "I would have painted. I might not have had eleven children, but I would have been doing what the Lord had planned for me to do. But I didn't feel that way. I know a woman who has ten children, and she regularly publishes novels. I know another lady with six children who composes songs so beautiful, you weep to hear them. There are many more examples of women excelling and succeeding in the Church. But they do these things because it's what the Lord wants them to do. That's the bottom line. What does the Lord have in store for you, Heather? What does He want you to do with this talent?"

Heather wasn't sure what her mother meant. She hadn't really considered her talent something the Lord could use on earth, but rather as something that opposed her Church beliefs. She tried to explain this to her mother.

"I see," Karalee said. "That's where the problem lies. Your talent and the Church are not mutually exclusive. You just have to realize that."

"I don't know, Mom. The Church—it asks so much."

"Only everything you have," her mother agreed. "So maybe this is not an issue of whether or not to paint, but an issue of faith, of dedicating your talent to the building up of the Kingdom of God."

Heather looked away. Tanner had also questioned her faith, and no matter how Heather tried to explain her feelings, it always came down to the same conclusion. Could her mother and Tanner somehow be right? She had always considered herself a faithful Mormon, but now it seemed she had again come up lacking.

She was spared further debate when a beaming nurse poked her head in the room. "Guess what?"

Karalee looked up eagerly.

"Your baby's doctor is coming here with your little one as we speak. You get to see your little girl!"

Karalee's brown eyes gleamed. She squeezed Heather's hand with a strength that belied her paleness. "Heather, did you hear?"

"I did, Mom."

In less than five minutes, Seren was finally in her mother's arms. Their eyes locked, and Heather saw that for her mother there was no one else in the room. The love between mother and tiny daughter was unmistakable. Heather, overcome with feelings, automatically reached for Tanner's carry-all. After snapping a few photographs with his camera, she began sketching, ignoring the nurses' interested stares.

Her rough sketch was almost finished when her father appeared in the door, a contented smile on his face at seeing his wife and new baby daughter together. He rushed to her side. "Isn't she perfect?" Karalee said to him.

"Yes." His tone was one of reverence.

Heather put the final strokes on her sketch and then snapped a few photos of her parents together and one with the nurses as well. "I'm going to stretch my legs," she announced. "Where are the kids?"

"I left them home."

"Then I'll go home and watch them. I'll call later."

"Thank you, Heather," Conrad said. "We appreciate your help. Oh, that reminds me." He looked at Karalee. "Andrea called and asked if she could come to help out. I told her Heather and I could manage for now, but that later when Heather goes back to Boston and I go back to work we'd be grateful if she'd come stay for a while."

"That's a great idea," Karalee said. "It'll be good to see her."

Heather left the room, feeling somewhat useless. Andrea was one of her mother's sisters and really the only relative able to come and stay, having only two children who were in their late teens. The rest of Heather's aunts and uncles had large families that included younger children. Help from grandmothers was not an option, either, since her dad's mother had died years ago and her mother's mother was very old and frail. Heather knew she should be happy her mother would have time to rest in bed once she came home from the hospital, taken care of by Aunt Andrea. Then why did she feel so sad? Did some part of her want to stay?

She thought of her art and all she had strived to accomplish. Was she really debating throwing it away? No, not throwing it away. Not that. But her choices didn't seem to be as black and white as she has always believed. Good thing she didn't have a boyfriend or fiancé who was waiting for her answer.

Oddly, that last thought only made her feel worse.

Chapter Seventeen

*T*anner left work early on Wednesday so he could be home in time to fulfill his promise to the Samis children. As he walked out to his Blue Bug, he checked his cell phone, hoping there would be a message from Heather. Instead, there was one from Amanda.

He grimaced. He'd forgotten all about her! This morning he had even written a note to remind himself to call her and invite her to dinner and a movie with the Samis children. Yes, he'd had a busy day at work, cramming in all his appointments and paperwork, but that was no excuse to neglect courtesy to a woman he cared for.

He opened the door to his car as his thoughts went to Heather. Would she go with them? No, if Amanda went, Heather would feel too awkward; he knew that well enough. Even in high school she had refused to go anywhere with Amanda. So what he needed to do was to settle things with Amanda and then worry about how to include Heather. Maybe Amanda could help with that—she was very compassionate.

Eyeing his watch, Tanner decided Amanda was likely still at the school where she was teaching. If he hurried he might just catch her. Unfortunately, Amanda had already left the school so Tanner drove instead to her apartment.

She opened the door to him with surprise. "Tanner! I didn't expect you until seven." She smiled, but the action didn't quite reach her green eyes.

"Well, I wondered how you would feel about changing plans a bit."

Her eyes narrowed. "Come in. Let's talk about it." The words sounded serious, much more serious than a mere dinner and movie for a group of children whose mother was recovering in the hospital.

Amanda settled gracefully on the couch and patted the seat beside her. Tanner sat, his eyes scanning the apartment for signs of her roommates. "We're alone," she said with obvious amusement. "So, what's up?"

"Well, it's the Samis children. I sort of promised to take them to dinner and a movie. Would that be okay with you?"

"I guess," she said slowly.

"I want you to come, too," he added. "I know it wasn't the date we'd planned, but you'll like these kids. And they've been through some difficult days lately."

"How's their mother?"

"She's awake now—they think she'll be fine. But the children are still at loose ends. A movie will help take their minds off everything. We won't be too late. I believe they'll be going back to school tomorrow. So what do you say?"

Amanda looked away from him, and for a moment he studied her perfect profile. Truly, she was a stunning woman. At last she returned her gaze to his face. "Tanner, I've put some things together in the past few days—things I hadn't understood before."

"What do you mean?" He slid to the edge of the couch and turned his body toward her.

"I mean what I saw on Monday night at the hospital."

Tanner stared at her blankly.

"It's you and Heather."

"What? She's just a friend."

Amanda shook her head. "That's not what I saw in your eyes on Monday. At first I didn't know what it was, and I went home very confused. Then I remembered what your cousin said about a woman breaking your heart, and that's when it all clicked. It was Heather, wasn't it?"

Tanner leaned abruptly back on the couch, eyes focusing on Amanda's blank TV set instead of her face. "Yes, it was. But it's not like you think. I realized last Christmas that I had begun to have feelings for her. After she left for Boston, Savvy found out and challenged me to tell her. I went to Boston and did just that, but Heather said she didn't feel the same way. End of story. Then I met you, and the hurt faded to almost nothing." His gaze swung back to meet hers. "I thought you and I really had a connection."

Amanda's lips tightened almost imperceptibly. "I thought so, too. But Tanner, there was always something holding you back. And now I believe that something is your feeling for Heather. You may think you're over her— and maybe you could be sometime in the future—but you're not ready for a relationship with another woman."

"I care about you."

"I know. And I care about you, too. That's what so hard about what I have to tell you." She took a deep breath and plunged on. "A few weeks ago Gerry asked me to marry him. I told him I'd have to think about it. Last night I gave him my answer."

Tanner was speechless. He knew they were still dating, but had no idea Amanda might actually love the man enough to agree to marry him.

"You see, I wasn't sure yet about us. Before you came along, I thought I loved Gerry, but there you were. You brought back all those memories of high school, that wonderful time of discovery and innocence. But after a time, part of me began to wonder if it was the memories that made you so attractive or who you are now."

Tanner looked away from her and focused on his right foot, which was tapping furiously against the soft carpet. "And what did you decide?"

"I didn't decide anything. In fact I didn't know *how* to figure that out. And then I saw you with Heather, and the answer no longer mattered." Her hand reached out to his arm. "Oh, Tanner, I really believe that if things were different, we might be able to make a relationship between us work. I could fight for you and wait until you were ready. But it came to me suddenly last night when I was with Gerry that there's no reason for me to fight or wait. And besides, there's still Heather."

"She doesn't want me," Tanner said, not meeting her gaze.

"Are you so sure? I saw the look in her eyes on Monday, Tanner, and it was the same look that I saw in yours."

His eyes rushed to hers. "No."

"Yes." A smile flirted at the edges of her lips. "But don't feel too bad about not noticing. You wouldn't be the first man not able to see when a woman loved him."

Thoughts tumbled around in Tanner's mind. "It can't be."

"But you would like it, wouldn't you?" Amanda's green eyes demanded the truth.

"I guess I would."

"See?"

Tanner shook his head. "Amanda, I never meant to lead you on. I really, really care about you."

"I know that. I do." She took his hand and squeezed it. "But you and Heather have unfinished business. You love her and you're not ready to give that up yet."

"But you and Gerry—are you sure that's the right thing?"

Amanda smiled and her happiness glowed brightly in her face. "Yes, I am. If you hadn't come along when you did, I might have already understood my real feelings for him."

"I really needed you," he said, voice wavering slightly.

She squeezed his hand again. "I needed you, too. I needed to be sure about Gerry. Now I am."

Tanner felt sad at her words, yet also strangely freed. He arose. "Well, give Gerry my regards, okay? And don't forget to invite me to the wedding."

Amanda led him to the door. "I'll think about it." She gave him a teasing smile. "But don't you give up easily. Sometimes a woman tells a man she doesn't love him because she feels it's best for him."

"Are you saying that's what Heather did?"

She drew away. "I'm saying that you gave up too easily. I saw her expression at the hospital. There's hope."

Tanner leaned over and kissed Amanda's cheek. "Have a good life," he said. "And thanks for everything."

With that he hurried to his car.

❦

Tanner went to his condo for a quick shower and a change of clothes. His heart felt light for a man who had just been rejected for the second time in three months. Whistling as he headed for the door, he stopped and adjusted the new painting on his wall—one that had been delivered only four weeks ago. The agent he'd hired to purchase the painting had to beat out five other bidders, but it had been worth the effort and price to have Heather's anchor painting for his own. Somehow it was like having a part of her with him always.

In Alpine at the Samis house, he was surprised when his stepmother answered the door. "Hey, what are you doing here?" he asked.

"Cleaning and doing the laundry," Mickelle replied. "With Conrad and Heather at the hospital with Karalee, there hasn't been much cleaning or chore-doing going on."

"Heather's not here?"

Mickelle shook her head. "Not now. She came home for a few hours this afternoon, but then she went back to the hospital with the little ones. They wanted to see their mother again."

"Oh." Tanner knew his disappointment showed on his face.

Mickelle chuckled. "So, it's finally happened."

"What?"

She placed her hands on either of his shoulders and stared up at him. "Tanner, I really love Heather. I used to pray that you two would be attracted to each other. You have my blessing." Without another word she turned and walked into the kitchen. Tanner followed, wanting to question her, but was stopped by the sight of the older Samis children busily sweeping the floor, loading the dishwasher, cleaning the counters, and folding clothes.

Mickelle went to the refrigerator and began pulling out items. Tanner watched her scrub down the inside with hot, soapy water. She hummed as she worked. At home Mickelle had a housekeeper to clean her appliances, and sometimes he forgot that she hadn't always been so blessed. Once, in what seemed like another lifetime, she had been married to an abusive man who had barely been able to scrape by each month. Later her husband had committed suicide, and she had met Tanner's dad. Sometimes Tanner felt guilty for the terrible circumstances she and her sons had endured, but which had ultimately led to his family's good fortune.

Becoming aware of his gaze, Mickelle turned and threw him a cleaning rag. "If we're going to get done before Heather and the little kids get home, you'd better help."

Smiling, Tanner rolled up his sleeves and dug in.

❦

Heather wished she could drop the children off and hurry away before she had to face Tanner with Amanda. Heather couldn't fathom her feelings and, in fact, had given up trying. She and Tanner were only friends, but she was jealous. And that was that.

She helped the smaller children out of their car seats and then followed as they ran to the house. "Tanner's here," shouted Evan. "See his car? Too bad it's not big enough for all of us to go in to the movie. I like that color. And it really does look like a bug."

The children ran through the garage and into the kitchen door which was unlocked. Heather followed more slowly. In the kitchen she found her other siblings on the floor with rags—Tanner among them. "Wait!" he called out. "Don't come in. We haven't dried there yet."

Heather laughed at the picture he presented down on his knees drying the wet tile. At least he had changed into jeans and wasn't ruining one of his suits. She pulled out his camera from the briefcase and snapped a photograph. "This is too priceless."

"Hey, stop that!" Tanner finished his drying and came to his feet. "No fair using that for blackmail—remember it's my camera. And it's about time you got here. Any later and that slave driver in there would have us scrubbing the walls." He motioned to the laundry room.

Heather froze. Who was in there? Had Tanner brought Amanda to their house, and had she been responsible for getting everyone to clean? Not only was the idea embarrassing to Heather—having a near stranger cleaning among their private possessions—but she most definitely was not in the mood to see them all lovey dovey together.

Female laughter came from the room, followed shortly by Mickelle. Heather breathed an internal sigh of relief. *Of course, it's not Amanda*, she thought. *I am much too paranoid.*

"Thanks, Sister Wolfe," Heather said. "I wasn't really looking forward to hours of cleaning tonight."

"Cleaning? No way, you're going with us." Tanner threw the rag in his hand at Mickelle. "And it's high time we get going." The kids cheered. "Now where are the keys to that monstrosity you call a van?"

Heather was caught in the wave of children as they scrambled out the door. But she stopped in the garage as the children tumbled ahead—even Kevin and Aaron showed child-like excitement at the prospect of a night out.

"What's wrong?" Tanner turned as he noticed she wasn't moving.

"It's just, well, I think I should stay home." Heather looked miserably at the cement floor. The truth was, she wanted to be with Tanner and her siblings, but only if Amanda wasn't going to be there.

Tanner took a step toward her. "I'd really like you to come."

"What about Amanda?"

Understanding dawned on his handsome face. "Oh, she's not coming. I didn't realize that was what was bothering you."

"It doesn't bother me, exactly," Heather said. "But you know the saying. Two's company, three's a crowd."

He smiled. "Ah, Heather. There's eight of your siblings in the van. That's nowhere near two or three."

"They're kids."

"Well, it doesn't really matter, 'cause Amanda's not coming."

Heather blinked. "But I thought you were going to invite her."

"I did. But she has other plans. In fact, she told me she's getting married."

Heather's eyes flew to his. "What?"

He shrugged. "She's been dating another guy, and apparently she told him yes last night."

"I'm sorry." She reached for his hand, suddenly feeling terrible. Here she had been worried about having to watch them together, and Amanda had broken up with him!

"I'm okay, really. It's for the best—I know that." He tugged on her hand. "Come on, race you to the van."

∞

Heather arrived home exhausted. Taking eight children between the ages of three and eighteen out to dinner and a movie took more courage than she remembered. No wonder her parents tended to separate them and take only a few at a time!

Yet beneath the tiredness was the sense of contentment. Tanner had been friendly, amusing, and courteous all night. He didn't become angry even when Mindy spilled her drink all over his lap. He simply said that the sugar would probably help the floor cleaner come out when he washed the jeans.

Back at home, Tanner came inside and helped her put the younger children to bed. Heather insisted that everyone sleep in their own beds so they would be able to wake up early for school. Complaining ensued, but it was short and mostly good-natured.

After the little ones were in bed and the older children at least in their rooms, Heather made a cup of hot chocolate for herself and Tanner. They sat on stools at the kitchen counter, reliving some of the movie's most exciting scenes.

When the talk died down and the chocolate was gone, Tanner arose. "I guess I'd better get going. I have an early conference call in the morning."

Heather was silent as she walked him to the door. Then she said, "Tanner, I really am sorry about the way I acted earlier. Amanda's a nice girl. I'm sorry it didn't work out between you two."

Tanner reached over and hooked a finger under the chain she wore around her neck. Tugging it from beneath her sweater, he exposed the anchor she had kept out of sight. "See, that's where we differ. Amanda is a nice girl, but I find I'm not sorry at all that it didn't work out."

Heather's hand went up to the anchor, grasping it in her palm. "Why?"

"Well, as Amanda pointed out to me today, I'm still in love with someone else."

Heather stared.

He shrugged, half apologetically. "I tried to forget you, Heather. I really did. Amanda's proof of that. But I guess I just couldn't."

Before she had time to react to that, Tanner turned and sprinted down the steps to his car.

Heather let out the breath she hadn't realized she was holding—a warm, white cloud in the cold night air. Her mind reeled, but the most notable emotion was the rush of happiness surging through her heart.

∞

During the next week Tanner and Heather spent a lot of time together. Neither made a reference to their growing relationship. But it *was* growing. Heather noticed that Tanner was very cautious about bringing up the future. She was glad for his patience, though she wished he'd at least take her in his arms and kiss her once in a while. That might go a long way toward helping her make the decision looming over her.

While Tanner was at work each day, Heather spent the mornings baby-sitting little Jane and painting. In the afternoons when Mindy was home from kindergarten, she took her and Jane to visit their mother and Seren in the hospital.

On Wednesday, a week after she had regained consciousness, Heather's mother was released from the hospital. Seren had also gained enough weight to come home, though she had to keep a monitor on at all times. Under the doctor's advice, the baby wouldn't be allowed visitors outside the family or to leave home for at least two months.

That night Heather's Aunt Andrea arrived with enough luggage to show she planned to be there for some time. Heather sat alone in her dad's office after dinner, staring at the paintings she'd been working on that week, feeling lost.

It's time to go back to Boston, she thought.

But what about Tanner? Leaving him had been hard once before, but doing so now seemed next to impossible. She loved him—there was no doubt left in her heart about that. Perhaps she'd always loved him. And she could see the echoing love in his eyes. It would be so easy to stay, to forget about her art and become Mrs. Tanner Wolfe.

Right. And the next thing would be a baby and a Church calling that left no time for the talent God had given her. Hot tears scorched Heather's eyes. Why couldn't there be two of her? It just wasn't fair that she should have to choose. She suspected from her feelings with Seren that she could never be just a part-time mother. Pawning off her children on a nanny or a housekeeper, as some of her more affluent neighbors did, was simply not an option.

Perhaps it was her parents' example, or perhaps it was the Church's teachings that stressed how important it was for mothers to be in the home, but she believed wholeheartedly that if a woman had children, she certainly had the responsibility to make sure they were raised well. If she had been a man, it would be possible to have a family and develop her art to its full potential because she would have a wife taking care of the homefront. But she wasn't a man so where did that leave her?

"Heather?"

She wiped her eyes and turned to see her father's round face in the doorway. "Hi, Dad."

He came and sat beside her. "What's wrong?"

"I—I was just thinking. It's probably time I should get back to work. I have another six-month grant to start and a lot of paintings to finish."

He frowned. "I know that means a lot to you, but I wish you could stay."

"Me, too." She gulped and stared up at him. "For some reason, it's really hard for me to leave. I love painting, but I miss everyone here so much."

"And Tanner?"

So her parents were not blind to her emotions. She looked away and whispered, "He's the hardest to leave. But I—what if it's a choice I regret?"

"Staying or leaving?"

She didn't answer because she didn't know.

"Have you prayed about it?"

"Yes—sort of." She had prayed about her work and she had prayed about Tanner, but she had never really asked the Lord which course she should pursue. Painting was in her soul—why would she ask about that when she'd always felt it was right? The Lord had given her the talent, after all.

Her father placed a hand on her shoulder. "When your mom was unconscious, did you pray for her?"

"Yes, of course." Heather was puzzled at the question.

"How did you pray? Specifically? Fervently? Or just sort of?"

Now Heather understood. "I prayed with my whole heart."

"And what were you willing to do so that she would be made well?"

"Anything."

"Even give up your painting?"

"Of course—but I didn't say that I would. I didn't think that was something the Lord would require."

"It wasn't. But were you willing? That's the question. No, don't answer. That's between you and the Lord. But somehow I feel you must pray with that same fervency to find your solution."

Heather sighed. Her father had never appeared to her to be a strong leader in the world, yet in their home he had always guided their family with unfaltering wisdom. She wondered how he had gained that assurance. Was it possibly from prayer? Or the fiery pit of experience itself?

"You know," Conrad continued, "Jesus once told a story of a rich young man who wanted to follow him. He asked what he should do. Jesus told him to give away his riches and come with Him. The man went away saddened because he could not do that. Each time I read those verses I wonder why the man didn't remember that his riches had been given to him by the Lord in the first place."

Like my talent, thought Heather. But she didn't say the words aloud. The idea of giving up something so vital to her happiness terrified her. Is that what her father was asking? It seemed she was caught in a dilemma like Eve of old. There had been no way Eve could fulfill the Lord's commandment to multiply and replenish the earth unless she broke the commandment of not partaking of the fruit of the tree of good and evil.

Neither can I, unless I give up painting seriously and do it as a hobby. Sadness filled Heather's soul.

"God gave me this talent," she murmured painfully. "Why wouldn't He want me to paint? In the Parable of the Talents, He made it clear talents should be developed, didn't He?"

"I'm not saying He wants you to quit, but that you should pray and allow Him to guide you to an answer. And remember that God doesn't answer your desires, but what is for your eternal good."

Heather didn't reply because she didn't know what to say. *Oh, Tanner,* she thought, *I love you, but I just don't know what to do.*

Her father gave her shoulder a final pat. "Heather, maybe going back to Boston's a good idea. You need some time away to think. Your mother and I have talked about this, and we really feel that this isn't a choice between Tanner and your painting, but rather a choice between whether or not you have faith to follow the Lord's will—whatever that may be."

Heather wasn't sure he was right, but the words comforted her because that scenario no longer questioned her love for Tanner. *No, only for the Lord,* a voice inside mocked.

Tears filled her eyes again. "Will you give me a father's blessing?" Heather asked. "I think I need one."

Conrad took her hands, pulled her from the chair to a standing position, and put his arms around her. "Yes, honey," he said. "I would like that very much."

CR

Friday afternoon found Heather at the airport with Tanner. They arrived in the short term parking lot early, and neither made a move to open the car doors. He took her hands. "I wish you would stay."

"You could always come with me."

He shook his head, his eyes earnest. "I believe with my whole heart that we're meant to be together, Heather. As I told you once before, I want more than anything to be near you. But this is a decision you have to make. And you have to make it alone. I don't want you to ever look back and feel that our relationship is something I forced on you. You have to decide what your future will hold. If you decide in our favor, we can live anywhere you want. But I'm not going to pressure you by following you to Boston."

"What about you?" She smiled through her tears. "This hardly seems fair."

"What's fair isn't important. I love you. I'll wait. I'm learning to be patient."

He had left the car on because of the cold temperature. The radio was on, too, and now the chorus of a song began: *Wherever you go, whatever you do, I'll be right here waiting for you.* The words were so fitting that Heather wanted to throw herself into his arms and sob.

Tanner pulled her close, and Heather went willingly, lifting her lips to his in their first real kiss since Boston. The tenderness and love she felt for him nearly overwhelmed her. Finally she could do nothing but cling to him and bury her face in his shoulder, fighting sobs. For a long time he simply held her.

"Come on," he said much later. "It's time for you to go."

Her eyes met his, and in them she read an unspoken plea.

She looked away. *I want to stay*, she answered silently, *but I just can't.*

Chapter Eighteen

Since Heather hadn't alerted anyone in Boston about her return, she was forced to take a taxi to her apartment. She felt an odd sense of déjà vu as she climbed from the taxi, remembering the first night she had arrived. Everything was still and peaceful, and the house looked the same. Yet now a dusting of snow covered the ground, and the night air was freezing. She was also alone.

Using her key, she opened the door to the house. She was about to go up the steps, when Mrs. Silva called out. "Who's there?"

"It's me, Heather."

"Heather?" The voice became warmer. "Come in here, dear."

Heather left her luggage in the foyer and followed the voice into the kitchen. There she found the housekeeper sitting on a chair spreading petroleum jelly on her large feet.

"Cracked skin," the housekeeper explained. "Always happens in Portugal, but worse here in winter with the heat inside. My daughter say I should wear socks and shoes in the house, but I hate socks." She finished smearing the jelly. "Hand me that sack, would you?"

"This bag?" Heather picked up a plastic grocery bag on the far end of the table.

"Yes. But remember here it is sack not a bag." With an amused grin Mrs. Silva deftly slipped the plastic sack over her foot and tied a knot with the handles. "There." She stood. "I am so pleased you came home now. Lorin say your mother and baby are well, yes?"

Heather nodded. "They are. And how's your daughter and grandbaby?"

"Fine, just fine. Growing big." Mrs. Silva smiled widely, but then her features became solemn. "But everything here not well. Lorin been very sick. She cry a lot. She try to hide it, but I hear. Something is very wrong."

"Is she home now?"

"Yes. She home a lot now. I don't know what is wrong for sure, but I have my suspicions."

179

"What do you think it is?" Heather remembered vividly the night Lorin had passed out. Had she not been eating or sleeping in the nearly two weeks Heather had been in Utah?

Mrs. Silva folded her arms across her ample chest. "I think you better find out yourself."

"Okay, I will. Thank you." With a puzzled smile at the housekeeper, Heather bid goodnight. She left her luggage in the entryway and went up the stairs to the apartment, finding the door unlocked. As she entered, Lorin looked up from where she sat on the couch, her eyes red and swollen.

"Oh, you're home. I didn't know you were coming." Lorin dabbed at her tears with a tissue and tried to smile.

Heather came to her side, pausing only to set her purse on the coffee table. "What's wrong? Mrs. Silva tells me you've been sick. Have you been to a doctor?"

"Nosy busy-body housekeeper," Lorin grumbled. "I'm fine. I'm just a little depressed is all."

Heather sat back against the couch, studying her friend. Lorin's pale face was devoid of makeup, and her short, bleached hair was overdue for a trip to the hairdresser. She wore a loose set of old sweats stained with paint. This wasn't like the Lorin that Heather knew. Even when she was painting for days in a row, she looked better than this.

"You've lost a lot of weight," Heather commented. "And I've been gone less than two weeks. What's up?"

"Well, you know, without you to bug me I've grown a little lax."

Heather decided to play her game. "Okay. I'm back now. What do you say we call the guys and go out to eat. I'm starved after that long plane ride."

"No!" Lorin's face took on a green tint. "Ohhhh!" With a swift movement, she leapt from the couch and ran for the bathroom. Through the partially open door Heather heard her throwing up.

She was about to make sure Lorin was all right, when the open phone book on the coffee table caught her attention. The yellow pages were open near the front, and Heather could see the words *Abortion Providers*.

Immediately it all fell into place. Lorin wasn't sick, she was pregnant!

Heather stared at the address listings, horrified. On the same page, ironically, were advertisements for adoptions. She tried to tell herself that the phone book could have been open to this page by mistake, or if the worst was confirmed, Lorin might have been considering placing her child for adoption. But the sinking feeling in Heather's stomach warned her of the truth.

Anger and revulsion roared to life in her heart. In that instant, she was back in the hospital urging tiny Seren to eat, praying silently that God would spare her life. She recalled all the work the doctors and nurses had given to make the baby well. She recalled the anguish of her parents and family, and how each of them would have given *anything* to help Seren live. And now here was Lorin looking for a place to perform an abortion! Heather felt like throwing up herself. How dare Lorin so easily take a life of an innocent child?

Ripping out the page, Heather stalked to the bathroom, banging the door fully open with her fist. Lorin stared wearily up at her from her place beside the toilet.

"What's this!" Heather held the yellow page in front of her face.

Lorin began to cry, confirming what Heather already knew. Pity did not enter her heart as she crumpled the page and threw it into the toilet.

"Have you told the father?" Heather asked tightly.

Lorin shook her head and stared miserably at the floor.

"Tomás has a right to know."

Lorin looked up at her, a little color returning to her cheeks. "I'm not *that* stupid. That self-centered pig is *not* the father."

Surprised, Heather sat down on the edge of the tub. "Then who is?"

Lorin let her head drop into her hands. Sobs shook her shoulders, becoming more violent by the second. The compassion that had previously eluded Heather now rushed into her heart. She went down on her knees by her friend and put her arms around her. Lorin clung to her as if Heather were the only thing keeping her alive.

"Shhh, it's okay," Heather murmured, rocking her as she would one of her little sisters or brothers who had skinned a knee. "It's going to be all right."

Lorin pulled away slightly, her face red and streaked with tears. "How can it be all right?"

"I'm not saying it'll be easy, but I'll help. How far along are you?"

"Almost three months—I think. But Heather, I can't raise a child—you know that. I can't give up my work."

"Maybe you and the father could share—"

Lorin's face crumpled again. "He won't. Oh, he might actually marry me in the end, but he wouldn't be a father or a husband. I'd just be his support, his maid while he worked on his paintings. He's obsessed, crazy even. He doesn't love me—I don't think he's capable of loving anything except his own creations." Though she had denied his involvement, Lorin sounded as though she were describing Tomás.

"Regardless, he has a right to know, don't you think? In a way this baby is part of his creation."

"No. I'll just take care of it." Lorin glanced at the yellow page in the toilet.

"You can't!" Heather had no doubt about what "take care of it" meant. Standing, she hauled Lorin to her feet and pulled her into the sitting room. Lorin sank onto the couch, tucking her feet under her and sobbing softly as Heather rummaged through her purse. Finally she found what she had been looking for.

"Look!" she shoved the photographs under Lorin's nose. "That's my new little sister. She's out way too early, but she's alive—a real person. I found out a lot about babies when I was there. Did you know that your baby's heart is already beating? That begins as early as eighteen days after conception! And at three months, your child is well on its way to becoming an independent person. Can you really think about killing it? A baby? Lorin, I know you've said a lot of things against my beliefs, but I don't believe you're capable of murder—it goes against everything your parents ever taught you. You can't do it!" Heather was crying now. "If only you could hold my little sister in your arms, you'd know you couldn't. Please, Lorin, think about what you're planning."

"But I can't have it!" Lorin shouted. "I just can't!"

"Then let me keep the baby!"

Lorin blinked at her, so surprised her crying actually ceased. "You want it? But you won't even marry the man you love because you think it'll interfere with your work. Why would you want my baby?"

The man you love, the man you love. The words echoed in Heather's mind. So Lorin had known even before she had. But that wasn't important now.

"I want your baby because murder is wrong. Don't you see? No, I don't want to raise a child on my own, but I refuse to stand by and let an innocent child suffer. It's not your baby's fault you did something you had no right to do. Now you've got to make sure it has a chance at a good life."

Lorin didn't speak. She just sat, looking at Heather and blinking furiously.

Heather took a deep breath. "Look," she said, sitting next to Lorin on the couch. "I promise I'll be here for you every step of the way. But you have to promise me that you'll wait and think this over. Maybe call your parents—"

"I couldn't! They'd be so—" Lorin stopped talking and stared at her hands which were clenched in her lap.

Lorin's parents lived in St. George, and Heather had only met them once, briefly, at her graduation ceremony last April. But she knew they were stalwart members of the Church who loved their youngest daughter deeply, though they were disappointed by her rejection of their beliefs.

"They'd understand," Heather said softly, placing her hand on her friend's shoulder. "They may not agree with what you've been doing, but they love you. They'll support you and help you through. Don't you think?"

A tear fell from Lorin's face into her clenched hands. "I'd be so ashamed," she whispered.

The words were so different from her heartless "I'll just take care of it" and for the first time Heather felt hope enter her heart. Somewhere deep down Lorin knew that hurting her child was an even more serious sin than conceiving it outside the bonds of marriage.

Heather put her arms around Lorin. "I'll be right here. I'm not going anywhere."

Lorin turned into her embrace. "Okay," she said. "Okay. Then I promise I'll think about it."

Chapter Nineteen

One week later Heather was in her apartment studio working on the paintings she had begun in Utah and had shipped to Boston. She was failing miserably—especially on the painting of her mother in the hospital surrounded by the children and her father as they helped her in some way. Her muse, it seemed, had taken a vacation and had not yet returned. This had happened to her before, though never for more than a day or two at most. And even then she'd been able to do the background with some measure of success. Not so now. Lorin joked that she'd left her muse in Utah with Tanner.

Since Heather's return to Boston, she had done nothing except paint—or try to paint—and take care of Lorin, whose morning sickness only seemed to worsen each day. Heather didn't even fill her shift at the gallery because she was so afraid of leaving Lorin alone. She still didn't trust that Lorin wouldn't "take care" of the baby while she was out of the apartment.

With Lorin's permission, she had written to Lorin's parents explaining everything, and each day she prayed their reaction would be one that would help their daughter find her way home.

Lorin jokingly began to call the baby "Heather's kid" when they were alone, and while that didn't bother Heather, it worried her that Lorin hadn't really considered the child's future. She had still refused to tell Heather who the father was, though Heather had narrowed it down to someone connected to the gallery—possibly an employee, a patron, or even one of the male grantees. Keith had left for his home in Kansas a few days ago, so he wasn't a likely candidate. Of the others, McCarty and Nate, she had seen little.

Heather set down her brush with frustration. The part she had painted today would have to be redone—again. It was simply no good. She was using every technique she had ever learned in school, on her own, and from Tomás, but the emotion escaped her. She had even prayed for help with no result.

She had also prayed about Tanner, but so far she had not received an answer. He was almost always on her mind, and she missed him desperately.

But had she prayed with her whole heart as her father had suggested? She thought she had, though she admitted to herself that she felt a reluctance within her that might be preventing her complete commitment. What if the Lord did require her to reject her talent? Or put it aside?

Not that she was getting very far as it was. Her brush refused to obey her commands.

"I need a break," she said to the empty room. She quickly cleaned her brushes and removed her apron. Maybe she could get Lorin to go on a walk to the studio with her. Mrs. Oldham had left a message yesterday that she wanted to see Heather this afternoon.

As she left the studio, she heard voices—McCarty's and Lorin's. Heather was about to call out to them from the short hallway when she overheard Lorin say bitterly, "I knew you would say that."

"I'm not about to give up my career for *anything*. I never wanted children—you knew that from the beginning."

McCarty? McCarty's the father? Everything fell into place. The many days Lorin had spent time at the guys' apartment had seemed odd to Heather before, but now she understood.

"Hey, I didn't plan this," Lorin countered. "It just happened."

"You should have been more careful."

"Me? What about you? This is your problem, too."

Heather wondered if she should go back into the studio or call out to notify them of her presence. She opened her mouth, but she was silenced by McCarty's voice.

"Well here, this should take care of it." There was a slight rustle of paper against paper. "Neither of us needs this now. You know I care for you, Lorin, but this was not in the plans."

"You want me to get an abortion." Lorin's voice was devoid of emotion.

"Unless you want to give up everything to raise this child, yes."

"There are other options."

"Not for me. I don't want any part of it. I'm sorry, Lorin." McCarty's voice sounded firm and not sorry at all.

"Get out," Lorin ordered.

Heather heard the door slam. Obviously, McCarty wasn't waiting for a second invitation. She walked cautiously into the sitting room. Lorin was slumped on the couch, head in her hands. Green bills littered the floor by the coffee table.

Heather sat down by her friend. "I knew a baby wasn't in his plans," Lorin said, sounding lost and forlorn. "But these past few months I starting thinking . . . I don't know. At least I know now that he never really loved me. But I did love him—I swear I did. Oh, how could I be so blind and so stupid? I would give anything to change what happened, but I can't do that now, can I?"

There was nothing Heather could say to help her. Lorin had made her choice, and these were her consequences. The only thing Heather could do was to help her so that she didn't make an even worse mistake—one she might never recover from. She patted Lorin's back for a long time. When Lorin's tears subsided, she scooped up the money from the floor and put it in the cupboard out of sight. Later she would give it to Lorin, but right now she didn't want to cause her more pain—or to give her any temptation.

After a long while, Lorin met Heather's gaze. "You should go to the gallery. Mrs. Oldham called before McCarty came over. Said she'd be there in an hour. That's almost up."

"I'm not going to leave you."

Lorin gave her a watery smile. "I'll be okay, really. I'm just going to take a long nap. I'm always tired now." She arose and went into their room. Heather followed, unsure what to do.

"Go on," Lorin urged. "Come on, I'm a big girl. I can stay a few hours by myself."

"Well, okay." Heather went into the sitting room, where she dawdled, debating whether or not she really should leave. After cleaning the dirty dishes in the tiny sink and wiping down the microwave, she peeked back into their bedroom. Finding Lorin sound asleep, Heather decided to dash to the gallery long enough to talk to Mrs. Oldham.

On her cold walk through the two-inch layer of snow, she began to worry about what Mrs. Oldham wanted. She hoped her absence at the gallery hadn't been looked on unfavorably. She had given the excuse that Lorin was ill and needed her, but she hadn't dared explain the real reason, though one of them would have to do that soon.

Mrs. Oldham hadn't yet arrived, so Heather went to the gallery studio.

Her painting of the weary mother surrounded by the needy children was covered but still on its easel where she had left it on the day Tanner had called about her mother.

Tanner! Heather's hand went to her lips, almost feeling again his kiss at the airport. A part of her wished she had stayed. Yet what about Lorin? And what about her work? If anything, Heather was more confused than ever.

She had told Tanner in an e-mail about the baby, and it had been him who had recommended writing Lorin's parents instead of calling them. He said they'd need time to adjust and to make a decision without an audience.

Thinking of them, Heather once again sent up a silent prayer for their help. She had promised to take Lorin's child rather than let it die, but where did that leave her? A child needed two parents, not a semi-crazy artist like Heather, who didn't know where she was heading in life. And yet . . . she remembered little Seren—she would make a good mother, wouldn't she?

Sighing, Heather pulled off the protective cloth from her painting. The self-sacrifice of the mother hit her anew, but now she saw something she hadn't noticed before: the woman resembled her! Yes, the figure had her mother's hair, but the face and eyes were unmistakably Heather's own. Was this her destiny? The response to her many prayers this past week? Tears came to Heather's eyes.

"Hello, Heather."

She whirled, blinking hard, but unable to hide the tears. "Hi, Mrs. Oldham," she managed.

"I've missed you, dear." The old lady smiled gently. "Is everything all right?"

"Yes, I . . . it's just this painting." Heather closed her eyes for a minute. "Actually, that's not true. There's a lot going on, but I don't know how to begin to explain."

"It's Lorin, isn't it? That's actually why I called you here. I wanted to know what's going on. Is she seriously ill?"

Heather nervously found the section of hair at the base of her skull and began to wind it around her forefinger. "Well, it is serious."

"I knew there was something wrong."

"She's pregnant," Heather blurted, despite her initial decision to let Lorin announce the news.

Mrs. Oldham gave a tiny sigh. "That's what I feared. I had hoped when

I chose two girls from Utah—especially from Brigham Young University—that we wouldn't have to face such circumstances."

Heather was surprised, though she didn't know why. Months ago Mrs. Oldham had admitted to choosing Heather and Lorin because they were friends; this additional reason made even more sense.

"When we first organized this grant I wanted only women," Mrs. Oldham went on, "but my husband insisted on men as well, just as he insisted on Tomás. I gave in because I knew that while he was ultimately doing this because of me, he needed to go his own way about it. I worried that men and women being thrown together in such a concentrated program might cause some . . . well, romantic problems, but I thought . . ."

"You thought two Mormon girls would be the safest bet." Heather felt terrible. In a way, she and Lorin had been representing the Church—and they hadn't made a very good showing.

Mrs. Oldham's mouth twisted into a slight frown. "Yes, I guess it was rather naive of me."

"Not really." Heather wanted desperately to explain, to redeem not only herself, but all members of her church. "But Lorin, she basically left the Church when she left home. She really hasn't lived any sort of values since then. I mean, she's not a terrible person, I think she's just confused."

"Oh, I'm not blaming only her. McCarty's the real problem. He's going to be just like Tomás—no connection to reality."

Heather almost choked. "How did you know it was McCarty? I only found that out today."

"I came upon an interesting little scene between them a few weeks ago when you were in Utah," Mrs. Oldham admitted. "Nothing terribly big—an exchange of a few brief kisses. At the time, I was relieved because I had suspected she was falling for Tomás."

Heather was amazed at how Mrs. Oldham's suspicions had mirrored her own. "McCarty wants her to have an abortion."

Mrs. Oldham gave a swift intake of breath. "And how does she feel about that?"

"She's really confused—and scared. To tell the truth, right now I think I'm the only one standing between her and that decision. I even told her I'd take the baby. But I've written her parents, and I'd like her to learn more about the long-term emotional consequences so she can realize exactly what's at risk here. I think too many women don't understand what they're choosing when they opt for abortion."

"I can help with that," Mrs. Oldham said, her brow furrowing thoughtfully. "An acquaintance of mine is an advocate for women in similar situations. She can put Lorin in touch with counselors, some of whom are women who have made that choice and have regretted it all their lives."

"That's what I worry most about," Heather admitted, relieved that Mrs. Oldham seemed to be an ally, instead of someone who would encourage Lorin to take what might seem like the easy way out. "I'm afraid she might do something she'll regret forever, something she can't take back. Something worse than she's already done, I mean."

They fell silent. Heather noticed Mrs. Oldham studying her painting. "I still don't know what's wrong with it," Heather said half-heartedly.

Mrs. Oldham's eyes went to hers. "I've been thinking about you and this painting quite a lot in the past weeks. I hope I might be of some help. First let me ask you, does this painting show the truth?"

"Yes. I think so."

"All right then. Tell me, is it the whole truth? Is this always the way you feel? Is it the way your mother feels—that she's wasted her life or sacrificed it for her children?"

"No," Heather said. "She told me she finds fulfillment in the children, despite the effort. More so than she did with painting. She *chose* to be a mother, to have so many children."

"Do you believe her?"

"Yes."

"Then may I suggest this painting represents *a* truth, one you see, but perhaps not the whole truth?" Mrs. Oldham's brown eyes gleamed with intensity. "That could be why you're not satisfied. And it's only fair to tell you that if you paint this way, showing all the agony and sacrifice of motherhood, you will likely achieve much notice. Yet will doing so feed your soul? Only you can answer that. Tomás and artists like him may be happy with part of the truth, but you may find that you need the whole truth."

"The whole truth?"

"Come with me. I'll show you." Mrs. Oldham's frail hand touched her arm. The skin covering the bones was sagging and paper thin. The older woman had definitely lost more weight. Had she been sick while Heather was gone?

Mrs. Oldham went into the gallery, found Lester, and asked him to drive them to her home. Without raising an eyebrow, Lester agreed.

Heather had only been to the Oldham estate once before months ago, and now she stared at the impressive two-story structure, surrounded with spacious lawns clothed in white snow. The house was every bit as large and stately as Tanner's parents' Victorian mansion, though the style was more that of a southern plantation home.

They were greeted at the front door by a smiling, middle-aged housekeeper dressed in a service uniform and wearing her hair in a low bun at the base of her skull. After greeting the woman, Mrs. Oldham led Heather through a large vaulted foyer and into a long sitting room. As they walked, Heather stared around her. The furnishings clearly showed the Oldhams' connection to fine art; their house held enough art of all kinds to stock several small galleries. Paintings Heather had never seen lined the walls of the sitting room. Mrs. Oldham motioned for Heather to examine them.

"These are all yours," Heather said, reading the artist's name in each painting.

"Just those on this wall," Mrs. Oldham replied with a smile. "We have the largest Amelia Degroot Oldham collection in the world."

Most of the paintings showed families, but there were landscapes as well. "They're wonderful," Heather said, catching her breath at the lifelike scenes.

"Now let me show you some others I did earlier in my career." Mrs. Oldham left the room and slowly climbed a long set of stairs. Her face was flushed, and she was breathing heavily when she arrived at the top. She stopped to catch her breath while Heather watched her with concern. Mrs. Olham was in her late sixties, to be sure, but she was acting more like eighty. Was something seriously wrong?

Smiling apologetically, Mrs. Oldham began to move again. She led Heather down a long, wide hallway and into a rectangular room that resembled the sitting room downstairs, only smaller. "This is the room next to the nursery," she told Heather. "When my children were small I'd sometimes come in here to hear myself think, to escape—if you know what I mean."

Heather did. She had used her dad's office for just such a thing during her visit home.

Mrs. Oldham fell silent, and Heather realized she was waiting for a comment on the two oil paintings in the room. Heather shifted her gaze to the first one which portrayed the sideways view of a mother giving birth. All alone, she arched backward in pain, the large mound of her belly straining against the sheet that covered it. Her hair was wet with effort, and sweat beaded on her forehead, becoming a rivulet down her temple and cheek. Her entire facial expression was one of tremendous agony. Veins stood out on both her neck and arms. Her hand, clenched to her swollen side, curled in a thin hook. One leg was in view, the back of which was mottled purple with thick varicose veins. The emotion and the pain in the painting made Heather shiver. It was the ugly, gritty side of birth, with none of the joy or glory.

"I gave birth naturally to all four of my children," Mrs. Oldham explained. "That was back in the days when there really weren't many options. I was often in labor for days." She smiled sadly. "Looking back, I wonder that I had as many children as I did."

"It must have been very painful," Heather said, though she noticed that the mother in the painting did not resemble Mrs. Oldham in the slightest.

"At times I felt so alone—as if even my husband had deserted me."

"And what about God?" Heather didn't mean to ask the question, but rather it came of its own accord.

Mrs. Oldham studied her. "During those times I didn't believe in God at all," she said simply.

Heather didn't know what to say to that, so she kept quiet.

"But though this painting shows my feelings at certain moments, it wasn't the whole truth," Mrs. Oldham continued. "I was not alone. I had a very dear friend with me every minute, the best doctor and nurses money could buy, and my husband never once left my side. This"—she motioned to the painting—"was only part of the truth, the hard part. You don't see the husband rubbing her feet or the tears in the friend's eyes. You don't see how supportive the nurses were." She shook her head. "I sold this painting once, but many years ago bought it back because I realized that it wasn't the whole truth, and I didn't want it to be taken as such."

She turned slightly and motioned to the other painting on the opposite wall. "In this one, I didn't paint the whole truth either."

Heather looked at the second painting. This one portrayed an expectant mother dressed in a business suit, glancing mournfully at her watch as she hurried three children out the door. Her face was a mask of hidden rage, contrasting sharply with the innocent abandon of the children.

"But didn't you ever feel that way?" Heather asked. "Angry and frustrated because it took you two or three times as long to leave the house because of your children?"

Mrs. Oldham arched a brow. "Certainly. More times than I care to admit. But again it wasn't the whole truth."

"Then what is?"

Mrs. Oldham smiled, as though expecting the question. "Come with me into the nursery."

Heather followed her obediently to the room next door. The lower half of the walls were painted a light blue to match the carpet, and a festive border of small children atop rocking horses marked where striped wall paper began, stretching to the ceiling. A white crib, dresser, and changing table stood in their places, as if awaiting the return of a child, though the unaired smell of the room hinted that no child had used the room for many years. As a final touch, an old-fashioned rocking chair sat by the shuttered window, its beauty unmarred by the obvious years of use.

Heather's eyes went to the painting near the rocking chair. In it a young mother sat in that very chair, modestly nursing a small infant, who stared up into the mother's eyes. The love between the two was apparent.

"I felt God at moments like these," Mrs. Oldham said softly.

"But this isn't the whole truth, either," Heather protested, though the painting touched her deeply, reminding her as it did of her mother and Seren.

Mrs. Oldham nodded. "Exactly. This is another moment caught on canvas. Just as a happy ending in a book is a slice of a character's life, this painting is only a small glimpse of the overall story. Tomorrow, things could be difficult again—for both a character in a book and for this mother."

"That's what you meant when you said my painting was a truth. There are several different kinds."

"Yes, or several different views of the same situation."

"Then what's an artist to do? We can't possibly show it all."

Mrs. Oldham touched her arm. "That, my dear, is the dilemma. Come." As they retraced their steps down the long hallway to the stairs, Mrs. Oldham continued, "Heather, I came to the conclusion some time ago that artists have a responsibility, one we should not take lightly. What we choose to portray—and the way we portray it—reflects directly upon who we are and what values we espouse.

"Let me give you an example. A friend of mine—a very talented writer before her death—once wrote a poem. This poem was about her two children and how limited she felt and how enclosed—how imprisoned by their needs. In fact, your painting at the gallery studio reminds me very much of that poem. She was eventually offered a good sum of money for the piece, but ended up not selling it because it did not represent the whole truth."

"Then it should have been in a collection."

"Perhaps." They had reached the stairs and now fell into silence as Mrs. Oldham struggled to descend. Her breath came heavily. Heather offered her arm, and Mrs. Oldham accepted with a weary smile.

They didn't speak again until they had returned to the sitting room on the main floor. Mrs. Oldham's housekeeper was in the room, and she hurried to the older woman's side, helping her sit in an elegantly carved Victorian chair. "Shall I bring tea?" the housekeeper asked.

"Yes, please do. Lemon, if you will."

Heather scarcely noticed the woman leave, as she was already studying the Amelia Degroot paintings she had seen when they'd first arrived. After discussing the others upstairs, she knew exactly what to look for. In each of the paintings in this room, Mrs. Oldham had tried to show the whole truth, instead of only a portion. In a painting of a happy game of tag, one of the children had fallen and was wiping away tears. In another, a mother looked weary as she hefted a child, but her husband had his arms outstretched as though he was about to take the child or aid the mother in some way. In a painting of a funeral, a nest of baby birds peered out of a tree at the cemetery, and an expectant mother was in the crowd, a secret musing on her face as her hand rested on her stomach.

"I see," Heather said wonderingly.

"Oh, it's not always possible to show the whole truth," Mrs. Oldham said from her chair. "And sometimes you must paint only a part of that truth because of a need inside you—like I did with those paintings upstairs. But in the most important things—like family and children—I feel that I must never allow the negative to completely overshadow the good. To do so is being untrue to both myself and society, because without family, society is nothing. Of course, a family is an effort, as you no doubt realize, but they also bring great joys that a person cannot experience in any other way."

Heather tore her eyes from the paintings and stared at Mrs. Oldham. Her mother had said something very similar in the hospital. She walked over and took the chair opposite Mrs. Oldham. "Did you ever regret having children?" she asked.

"No." The answer came without hesitation.

"But don't you think you could have reached higher goals with your art? Sold more paintings, touched more lives?"

"Once I used to think that very thing." Mrs. Oldham paused as the housekeeper returned with a tray of hand-painted china. Steam boiled up from the teapot, and an impressive array of small sandwiches, cakes, cookies, and chocolates filled a large serving platter. The housekeeper poured each of them a cup before leaving the room.

"What happened?" Heather asked, stirring a teaspoon of sugar into the yellowish liquid in her cup. She had grown fond of lemon tea in Italy, as it didn't contain the harmful ingredients that banned most teas from her use.

"I had a baby. Mr. Oldham wanted a child, and I loved him enough to give him that. And from the moment they placed the baby in my arms"— Mrs. Oldham's eyes were far away—"I was never the same. Ever." She focused again on Heather. "Slowly, I realized that sacrifice brings about blessings."

Heather had heard that all her life. Paying tithing brought blessings; going to church brought blessings; fulfilling a calling brought blessings. She had even mocked members of the Church for talking so much about sacrifice, but in the end not really giving up something vital to their existence. Yet hadn't she been guilty of just that? She was willing to be a member, to obey the commandments, as long as she didn't have to give up or in any way sacrifice her art.

And now here was Mrs. Oldham, who to her knowledge didn't attend any church at all, telling her that sacrifice was more than worth the effort.

"I could not have painted any of these with authenticity," Mrs. Oldham continued, waving a hand in the direction of the paintings on the wall, "until I had children. Yes, I could have painted other things that I did know, things

I could observe. But I was always drawn to painting families, and the feeling is simply not the same before you experience it for yourself."

"But Tomás, he's so talented. And he's, well, definitely not a family man."

Mrs. Oldham took a sip of her tea. "Once I was more like Tomás. But he has no life except for painting. Can he be good, even great? Oh, yes. History is rife with fanatics who have dedicated their lives to art—or other endeavors. Their stories are often tragic—dying young, penniless, friendless. Getting high on drugs or alcohol to create their masterpieces—masterpieces that often require a trained professional to interpret."

Mrs. Oldham set down her cup. "Painting can consume you, if you let it, Heather. It will take everything from you and leave you empty and alone in the end. But you see, I found that a family gave me stability. They grounded me so that I could not become insane with my obsession. My family also gave me insight that allowed me to paint the whole truth. Don't you see, Heather? Tomás and those like him will likely achieve great success, but at the cost of their happiness and their sanity. That is not an exchange I was willing to make."

"But don't you think that with that focus a person would be a better overall artist?"

"It depends on what type of artist you want to be."

Heather nibbled on a sandwich as she considered the woman's words. She admired Tomás from an artistic standpoint, but did she want to paint like he did? No, she wanted to paint like Mrs. Oldham. She wanted her work to be real. And what if that never brought her the fame or fortune she had always dreamed of? With dawning understanding, Heather wasn't sure that mattered to her anymore.

"Did you resent the time you spent away from painting to care for your family?" Heather asked, needing to know.

Mrs. Oldham smiled. "Oh, yes, there were many times when I resented it. Many times I had to help children with homework, arrange meals, or attend some child-related function. And it wasn't only the children. I remember one day my husband was going skiing with one of my sons and needed some ski pants. He was busy at the gallery all week and couldn't take the time to purchase any. I had to give up a day of painting to find him the pants. I was resentful that day, but when my son came home, eyes glowing, all the effort became worth it. Later I painted them together—hands red and chapped from the cold, but eyes bright. It was a special piece. My son treasures it to this day."

Tears pricked behind Heather's eyes. "And how did they feel about you painting? Did they know you sometimes resented them?"

Mrs. Oldham frowned. "You're asking if my family ever suffered because of my painting."

"I—I guess so. I think I'd feel terrible if I neglected a child because of my urge to paint."

"Well, I would have to say there was sacrifice on their parts as well. Yet perhaps it was not the kind that damages, but the kind that sparks independence and respect. I always made it a point to tell my children they came first. I know they understood that. So while maybe they had to fend for themselves every now and then for dinner, or had to stay home from an activity because I simply couldn't take them—well, that was evened out by all the many more times I was available to them. I loved being at home with my children and they knew that. It makes all the difference."

"Did you ever worry that you wouldn't paint?" Heather asked, thinking of her mother.

Mrs. Oldham shook her head resolutely. "Never once. It has always been a sort of calling with me. But everything has a price, my dear. You just have decide what price you are willing to pay."

"I must paint," Heather mused aloud, more to herself than to Mrs. Oldham. "You know what it's like? Breathing." If anyone would understand that analogy, surely Mrs. Oldham would.

But Mrs. Oldham wrinkled her brow. "Breathing? Perhaps that's a touch too strong. Surely your family and perhaps your faith in God is like breathing. It might be more apt to say that painting is like eating."

Heather felt shame wash over her as she considered what the older woman was saying. She remembered all too vividly how in her prayers this past week she had been unable to put her painting on the line with her Father in Heaven. Could that be why she couldn't seem to paint a stroke?

"Have you ever not been able to paint?" she asked Mrs. Oldham. "Not just for a day, I mean—we all have bad days—but for an extended period?"

"Well, actually, yes." Mrs. Oldham turned her cup in her hands. "The first four months of a pregnancy—though that was mostly due to sickness. And then for a few weeks after each birth. But it happened also when I was in an emotional turmoil. Not emotional as in happiness or sadness, but rather confusion. Like before my marriage, before coming to a conclusion that God did exist. Those were moments that everything I painted came out stiff. Those I mostly painted over when the fit had passed."

"I feel that way now," Heather admitted. "I don't understand it. In Utah it came so well, and now here—well, I was hoping that it was due to all the worry about Lorin, but maybe God . . ." Heather let the words die, not wanting to say aloud that maybe God was punishing her for her lack of faith. The admission might sour Mrs. Oldham on the Church forever, and Heather's missionary training wouldn't allow her to say the words. But now that she'd thought them, she suspected they were true.

"You told me once that your God wanted you to develop your talents," Mrs. Oldham said into the silence. "But did you ever think that perhaps painting is not the only talent you have?"

Heather shook her head. Such a thing had never entered her thoughts.

"Take this business with Lorin, for instance. It's not everyone who would be such a loyal friend."

"You've given me a lot to think about," Heather said slowly.

Mrs. Oldham sipped her tea. When she spoke again, her words had nothing to do with art. "While you were home, did you see that boy who came to visit you here? I heard all about him from Bridget. She seemed to think he was someone special."

Heather smiled. "He is. We've been best friends since we were sixteen."

"It must be hard to be without him."

"Well, we've been apart a lot these past years as we've pursued our lives."

"But do you love him?"

Heather had to set her cup on the table for fear she would drop it. "I think so." There, she had finally admitted it aloud to someone. "But I haven't been sure about my future."

"He wants you to marry him?"

Heather blushed, feeling awkward under Mrs. Oldham's intent stare. "I know you want me to stay for the grant, and I'm grateful. But I . . . I guess it's time that I stop depending on my own understanding. I think I need to find out what the Lord wants for me—my whole truth, so to speak."

Mrs. Oldham set down her cup and watched Heather for a moment in silence. "You've been honest with me about your personal life," she said. "I appreciate that. Now I want to be honest with you and tell you something very few people are aware of. You've noticed that I've not been at the gallery much in these past few months. That's not only been because of my children visiting. The truth is, I have cancer." Ignoring Heather's gasp, she continued, "It was diagnosed last year, and they gave me only six months to live. That's why Mr. Oldham and I decided to offer the grant. He knew how much I loved having young artists around. He wanted to do something that would encourage me, and I wanted to give him a reason to go on after I was gone. All these years he has been my best supporter and friend, and I've been his. I don't know what he'll do without me."

The tears Heather had been holding back sprang into view. "I'm so sorry," she whispered. Part of her felt guilty at not guessing the truth earlier. Mrs. Oldham had obviously been growing weaker over the past six months.

"I've already outlived the doctor's expectations by three times," Mrs. Oldham said with a faint smile. "But I have to admit, I feel very weary. And now as I face death, it's strange for me to admit that my painting—the passion that has gripped my soul for more than sixty years—is not what matters. Rather it is my relationship with my family. I am so grateful to have them. I will not die alone. I shudder to think where I would be now if I had followed Tomás's path."

Heather's heart burst with love for her friend and mentor. "Is there anything—can I help?"

"No, dear. Or rather, you have helped by just being here. By talking with me, by following your dreams. That helps. I only wish . . . well, I must have faith that God has a plan for us."

"He does," Heather said, leaning forward. "He really does." She paused, garnering her courage. "Mrs. Oldham, I know you said once that you didn't go to church. Has that changed? I mean, if you'd like, I'd really love for you to come to church with me on Sunday."

Mrs. Oldham considered her for a long moment in silence. Then she smiled gently. "I think I'd like that very much. I know you Mormons really value families. I would like to hear about families now."

Heather was amazed at the ease of her acceptance. Had she not been so blind and self-absorbed, perhaps Heather could have already given Mrs. Oldham the comfort of the gospel of Jesus Christ.

"I'll have Lester pick you up," Mrs. Oldham said. "And we'll go together."

They finished their tea, talking about inconsequential things, though Heather noticed that Mrs. Oldham didn't touch anything except her tea. Heather instinctively understood that her disease had robbed her of appetite. Yet her face was serene and her conversation continually positive. Heather wondered at her courage in the face of such trial.

Later, Lester drove Heather back to her apartment. New snow had fallen while she had been with Mrs. Oldham, making driving difficult, but also leaving the world looking pure and undefiled.

After thanking Lester, she practically ran up the stairs, anxious to see Lorin. To her relief, her friend was still sleeping. The urge to paint overcame Heather, but she was leery of the feeling. She didn't know if she could take another day without the inspiration of her muse.

Her muse? Or was that mythical entity really God's inspiration? She was beginning to believe that for her this must be true.

She went into the apartment studio where her paintings from Utah stared at her, looking considerably worse for her week of work on them, though she could point out no certain flaws. Feeling self-conscious, she fell to her knees.

"Dear Father," she began in a whisper, "You gave me this talent, but I know I can't do it without You." More words tumbled from her heart, too rapid for her lips to form. Heather sent out a plea to her Father and also a desire to follow His will. She prayed as if her very life depended on it— which if her parents were right, it did. When she at last arose, a peace that had long escaped her grasp filled her soul. For the moment, she felt capable of facing anything—of doing anything.

Slipping back on her coat, she made her way to the gallery studio, barely noticing the additional inches of freshly fallen snow covering the cobbled sidewalk. She went directly to her painting of the weary mother encircled by the seven needy children. Starting in the corner where the mother's eyes were focused, she drew a golden yellow light, extending it like a bar of iron into the darkness of the mother's prison. To Heather, the light represented the invisible, yet tangible help of a loving Father in Heaven and the promise of an eternal family relationship. Then she changed the mother's expression slightly, adding an unfailing thread of hope to the patient endurance. "There," she said. "That's closer to the truth. We're never alone."

In that moment, Heather found her whole truth; and as promised, the truth set her free.

Chapter Twenty

Heather worked almost nonstop on her paintings from Friday evening until late Saturday night. She finished up the one of Tanner's house that she had been working on before her visit to Utah, as well as the one of her mother in the hospital. The work came easily, as if her hands were guided by some unseen power. Heather had never felt so blessed or so full of energy. She began to understand that God had not been punishing her the previous days by taking away her inspiration, but rather He had allowed her to see what would happen when she trusted solely in her own ability—or the arm of flesh. But with His help, mistakes were minimized, and she accomplished her work in record time.

She had understood this on some level before. In fact, it was partly for this reason that she didn't paint on Sundays—so that she could feel worthy of inspiration. But now it became clear to her how much the Lord was a part of her talent . . . and how much He loved her and wanted to help her succeed.

She also realized that He didn't want her to give up her talent at all, as she'd feared, but simply required that she be *willing* to do so. Heather felt like the widow in the scriptures who had given her last bit of meal and oil to make a cake for the prophet Elijah, and who then had been rewarded with greater abundance of the same. The level of help and inspiration she had received in the past two days amazed her. What marvelous things she could accomplish with the Lord's help! At last she began to truly believe that she could be both an artist and a wife and mother—and serve in the Church as well. If she put the Lord first, everything else would fall into place.

All my life I've been raised in the gospel, and only now do I understand, she thought. Only now had she begun to have faith enough to trust in Him to know what was best for her future. And if, as with Mrs. Oldham, her painting career should come to a quick end? Well, Heather now knew beyond doubt that somehow God would give her equal fulfillment and blessings by some other method. It was as her father had said—God knew what was best for her eternally. Heather's happiness was nearly complete.

❧

On Sunday, she awoke early and dressed for church. She carried a tray of dry toast and chocolate milk to Lorin, hoping to convince her to come along. But Lorin stayed in bed, looking pale and fragile.

"No," she said in a whisper. "I'm not ready for that. I feel too—too unclean. But I would . . . do you think the bishop would come and see me? I think I need some advice."

"Yes, I do." Heather smiled, liking the change she could see in Lorin's countenance. Mrs. Oldham had been as good as her word. On Saturday while Heather was immersed in her painting, several women had come to the apartment to talk with Lorin. Heather hadn't heard what they'd said, but since their visit, Lorin had been much more positive about her future. She no longer referred to the baby as Heather's, and Heather believed she was finally taking responsibility for her actions. The biggest disappointment was that Lorin's parents had not yet responded to Heather's letter.

"Mrs. Oldham's going to church with me," Heather told Lorin. "Or she said she would. She should be here by now."

"She'll be here, don't worry." From her prone position, Lorin nibbled her toast. "I can't believe she's dying. She's such an incredibly talented woman." Tears came to her eyes. "You know, even though I've made a lot of mistakes in the past months, I'm grateful to Mrs. Oldham for her faith in me. I never believed I was very talented, but I know that I'm an artist now. No matter what happens in the future, I will always have that."

Heather nodded. "I know exactly what you mean."

The doorbell rang and Heather ran downstairs to open it. Lester smiled at her. "Sorry we're late," he said. "At the last moment, Mr. Oldham insisted on coming as well."

"Mr. Oldham?" Heather peered past Lester to the silver Cadillac Deville where she could see Mr. Oldham in his customary white suit. "That's a surprise. Well, there's still enough time to get there if we don't hit too many red lights."

Lester gave a little bow. "Let's see if we can oblige."

With Lester's expert driving, they arrived in good time at the church, where Heather introduced the Oldhams to the bishop and to the missionaries. After the service there was a new light in Mrs. Oldham's eyes. She readily accepted the bishop's invitation to return the next week. Mr. Oldham didn't speak, but the gentle gaze he rested on his wife's face clearly showed his support for anything that would ease her suffering.

When they dropped Heather off, Mrs. Oldham walked with her to the door, stepping carefully around a small pile of snow someone had neglected to remove when they shoveled off the walk. "Thank you so much, dear," she said, taking Heather's hands in hers.

Heather frowned, thinking how little she deserved the thanks. With her absorption in her own problems, she had too nearly passed up a chance to share the gospel with this special lady. "I wish I had asked you to come earlier."

Mrs. Oldham chuckled. "Don't waste time on regrets, Heather dear. We learn as we go. As long as we make sure we're learning from our mistakes, we're headed in the right direction. Besides, I don't think I was ready before now. I disapproved of organized religion, you know. Before I met you."

Heather believed the Lord had more to do with preparing Mrs. Oldham than Heather ever had, but she felt it better to stay silent on that matter—at least for now.

"So what have you decided?" Mrs. Oldham asked.

Heather took a breath, not knowing how to announce her decision. "You've given me so much—more than you know."

"But you're leaving us."

Heather nodded. "Much as I've loved being here, I don't belong anymore. I need to go back to Utah—to my family and to others who love me. But I will always paint."

"Of course you will," Mrs. Oldham said with a smile. "You have to eat, after all. Or is painting still breathing for you?"

Heather smiled. "It's taken me a long time, but you're right. Painting is eating, not breathing after all. The breathing—that's the gospel and those we love."

Mrs. Oldham hugged her. "I'll miss you, Heather. You will keep in touch, won't you? For as long as I'm here?"

Tears filled Heather's eyes. "Yes. Of course. But I don't have to leave right away. I haven't even told Mr. Oldham yet. I can stay another few weeks. Or maybe even the whole six months."

"And make your beau wait that much longer?" Mrs. Oldham shook her head. "You leave Mr. Oldham to me, my dear. This is my program, after all.

I do have a list of artists who will be glad to come and take your place. Besides, I remember as if it were yesterday how I felt being separated from Mr. Oldham before we were married. You go on home to Utah. Let me know when, and I'll ask Lester to drive you to the airport."

"Thank you." Heather hugged her again.

"Be sure to leave us any paintings you have finished for the gallery," Mrs. Oldham called as she walked slowly back to the car where Lester waited to open her door. "And send us those you paint in the future. Oldham's will always be happy to carry your work. You are very talented, Heather. Never forget that."

Heather nodded, unable to speak past the tears. She knew this was likely one of the last times she would ever see Mrs. Oldham. But instead of feeling depressed at the thought, Heather was filled with hope for the future. She watched Lester pull away from the curb before going inside the house and up the stairs to her apartment.

However, her peace and serenity immediately shattered when she found Lorin packing her suitcase in the apartment. "What's wrong?" she asked, thoughts racing through her mind. Had McCarty changed his mind and asked Lorin to marry him? Had Lorin decided to check into a clinic? Heather mentally gathered her arguments, praying silently for help.

Lorin stopped her packing, tears glistening in her eyes. "They called. My parents. Just now."

"They did?"

"Yeah, they're at a gas station here in Boston. They wanted to surprise me, but they got lost and had to call for directions. I'm going home with them—they want me to."

"What about the baby?" Heather asked.

Tears slid down Lorin's face. "My parents are going to help me find him or her a good home with both a mom and a dad. You know, Heather, for the first time in my life since leaving home, I'm going to do the right thing. Thanks to you. You've been the best friend a girl could ever have. I know I haven't appreciated you, and that I've given you a hard time about a lot of things, but you were always right. I only wish I'd listened earlier. Then neither this baby or I would have to go through this. I know it's going to be hard—I'm only beginning to understand how hard. But I'm going to do the right thing. I promise."

Heather opened her arms and hugged Lorin. "I'm so glad," she whispered.

Lorin clung to her for a long minute before drawing away. "Help me pack, would you? I want to be ready when they come."

ᛜ

Heather stayed two more days in Boston, wrapping up details. She packed and sent both her and Lorin's unfinished paintings to Utah, with the exception of one that was too wet, which Bridget promised to send later. She also packed her Mother and Children painting, unable to part with it now that she had found her truth.

She picked up dry cleaning, closed her local bank account, and bought a plane ticket home. Tanner had written her an e-mail, but Heather was too excited to write back. His birthday was coming up this week at the tail end of November; she would surprise him herself.

Finally, she bid goodbye to Mrs. Silva, the Oldhams, the gallery employees, and McCarty and Nate, the only two grantees left of the original group. Tomás was off on one of his crazy binges, so Heather wrote him a note, thanking him for his instruction. She smiled as she wrote, thinking of the most important lesson he had helped teach her without meaning to—of how important a family was.

"I owe a lot to you and Mrs. Oldham," she said to the absent Tomás as she left the gallery for the last time. "But of you both, it's you I feel most sorry for."

She boarded the plane, and only then did nervousness seep in. She had finally made her decision, and she knew it was the right one. But a moment of great importance was pending—now that she had found her whole truth, would things really work out between her and Tanner?

ᛜ

After Heather had left for Boston again, Tanner had resumed his old routine. Only this time there was no Amanda to help him pass his free time. He found himself battling both depression and anger. Why couldn't Heather see that they were meant to be together? Ten times a day he bemoaned the fact that he hadn't begged her to stay.

Sometimes he felt an irrational jealously toward her painting, though he believed it was her lack of trust in the Lord that held them back, not her passion for her work. He continually debated with himself if he had indeed

204

made the right decision to stay in Utah. Should he move to Boston and prove to Heather that he was willing to give up everything for her? Yet deep down he believed that it had to be her choice. Still, not following her was the hardest thing he had ever done.

On Wednesday, he came home late from work, resigned to face another lonely evening in his condo. Hands full with documents and his briefcase, he kicked his door shut with more force than intended. The action didn't help his tension. Sighing, he placed his burdens on the coffee table, sat down on the couch, and flipped on the news.

On the coffee table was a short stack of birthday cards that friends had sent to him in anticipation of his twenty-fourth birthday, which he would celebrate tomorrow. Many of the well-wishers were married friends his own age. He knew logically that he wasn't old—members of the Church seemed to marry younger than the rest of the world—and yet he felt old when he read their cards and saw photographs of their small but growing families.

Loneliness ate at him. For the first time, he wondered how long he could endure this separation. There was always the chance that Heather might never return—no matter how much she loved him.

But I felt we were right together, he thought. *I felt it. And I know that she very nearly did stay, that she wanted to stay. She'll come home. I just have to be patient—and pray.* But the patience he had claimed was wearing thin, and while prayer was comforting, there were only so many times a day his ego would allow him to pray for Heather's return.

The doorbell rang. Sighing, he climbed heavily to his feet. He hoped it wasn't Savvy, who had been threatening to come over and make him go out with her and her roommates. He would rather be alone tonight. Maybe he'd call Heather and see why she hadn't answered his last e-mail. Any excuse to hear her voice.

The door swung open and Tanner's jaw dropped. "Heather," he said. She looked more beautiful and radiant than he remembered. With effort, he prevented himself from crushing her to him in a hug.

She smiled tentatively. "Happy birthday, Tanner."

He couldn't think of a reply. Her return was in fact the only gift he had craved for his birthday.

"I think I found what I was looking for," she added softly.

"And what was that?" His hand clenched the door.

"My faith. I forgot that the Lord will make us equal to the tasks He asks us to do. His help makes up for everything we lack. I think maybe I can be a wife and an artist . . . and a mother, too." Her voice wobbled during the last sentence.

"I always knew that."

"I thought to be great I had to choose."

He let go of the door. "You do. And I think you made the right choice."

They closed the space between them with a step, meeting in the middle. His lips found hers for a long moment, and then he simply held her. "I love you, Heather," he whispered in her hair. "And I promise to make you happy."

"We'll make each other happy," she said. "I finally know where I belong."

Epilogue

eather and Tanner's wedding was set for the third week in February, a month after Heather celebrated her twenty-fourth birthday. Mrs. Oldham was too ill to attend the reception—she was now bedridden and fading fast—but the week before the ceremony she phoned in best wishes and sent Heather two paintings as a gift. One was the solitary woman in labor and the second was the woman in the rocking chair nursing her baby. There was also a note enclosed:

Dear Heather,

No one else will ever appreciate these as I know you will. May they always be a reminder to find the whole truth. I am so grateful for the time I had to know such a remarkable young woman. I am still investigating your church, and I confess that its teachings fill me with joy and hope. Thank you, dear. I wish you a fulfilling life, like the one I've had. I have no doubt you will become both a great wife and mother—and artist. But remember, don't paint so much that you forget the need to breathe. Let God help you become equal to your tasks. You are never alone.

Love from your eternal friend,
Amelia Degroot Oldham

In the new apartment she would share with Tanner, Heather hung Mrs. Oldham's paintings on either side of her Mother and Children painting. Together they would help her remember.

About the Author

Rachel Ann Nunes (pronounced *noon-esh*) learned to read when she was four, and by age twelve knew she was going to be a writer. Now as a stay-at-home mother of six, it isn't easy to find time to write, but she will trade washing dishes or weeding the garden for an hour at the computer any day! Her only rule about writing is to never eat chocolate at the computer. "Since I love chocolate and writing," she jokes, "my family might never see me again."

Rachel enjoys camping, spending time with her family, reading, and visiting far off places. She stayed in France for six months when her father was teaching French at BYU, and later served an LDS mission to Portugal.

This is Rachel's seventeenth published novel. She also has a picture book entitled *Daughter of a King*. All of her books have been best-sellers in the LDS market.

Rachel lives with her husband, TJ, and their children in Utah. She enjoys hearing from her readers.

You can write to her at P.O. Box 353, American Fork, UT 84003-0353 or rachel@rachelannnunes.com. Also, feel free to visit her website at www.rachelannnunes.com.